HAREM SECRETS

Alum Bati

Cover from a painting by Yelena Dontsova.

Order this book online at www.trafford.com/07-2587
or email orders@trafford.com

Most Trafford titles are also available at major online book retailers.

Note for Librarians: A cataloguing record for this book is available from Library
and Archives Canada at www.collectionscanada.ca/amicus/index-e.html

Printed in Victoria, BC, Canada.

ISBN: 978-1-4251-5750-0

*We at Trafford believe that it is the responsibility of us all, as both individuals
and corporations, to make choices that are environmentally and socially sound.
You, in turn, are supporting this responsible conduct each time you purchase a
Trafford book, or make use of our publishing services. To find out how you are
helping, please visit www.trafford.com/responsiblepublishing.html*

*Our mission is to efficiently provide the world's finest, most comprehensive
book publishing service, enabling every author to experience success.
To find out how to publish your book, your way, and have it available
worldwide, visit us online at www.trafford.com/10510*

 www.trafford.com

North America & international
toll-free: 1 888 232 4444 (USA & Canada)
phone: 250 383 6864 ♦ fax: 250 383 6804 ♦ email: info@trafford.com

The United Kingdom & Europe
phone: +44 (0)1865 722 113 ♦ local rate: 0845 230 9601
facsimile: +44 (0)1865 722 868 ♦ email: info.uk@trafford.com

10 9 8 7 6 5 4 3 2

For Alia

*Without whose encouragement this book may
never have been written*

PRINCIPAL CHARACTERS

Adam Pasha	Chief Justice of the Ottoman Empire. Officially known as the Kadiasker, or Military Judge. The 'askeri', in the Ottoman sense, is the ruling class. It includes the military and bureaucrats. The vast majority of the Sultan's ministers are European and Christian in origin. Adam is the senior of two Chief Justices. He is the Sultan's slave. To be a slave of the Sultan is an honour which many actively seek. 'Pasha' is a title given to ministers.
(Shaykh) Hajji Yusuf Ali	President of the Covered Bazaar's Administrative Council. The respectful title of Hajji shows he has performed the Pilgrimage to Mecca. Shaykh is an honorific often applied to learned men.
Andreas	A Greek shipowner and merchant.
Daud Aga	Deputy to the Chief Eunuch, Selim Aga.
Farooq	Adam Pasha's Standard Bearer (*bayraktar*). Two horsetails dangle from the standard, signifying his elevated rank.
Gritti	Alvise Gritti. Rich merchant and the illegitimate son of the Doge of Venice.
Hafsa Sultan	The mother of Sultan Suleyman and daughter of the Khan of the Giray Tatars of Crimea. She rules the Imperial Harem.
Ibrahim Pasha	Grand Vizier – the Sultan's Chief Minister. After the Sultan, the most powerful, and richest, man in the Empire. A freed slave of the Sultan.

Karim	Chief Inspector of Markets responsible for the Covered Bazaar.
Khurrem	A concubine. Mother of two princes (and a princess). Possibly, Polish (Ruthenian) in origin. She has captured the heart of the Sultan to the exclusion of all others, including Mahidevran.
Mahidevran	Khurrem's rival. She has lost the favour of the Sultan but has the advantage that she was the first to bear him a son, Mustafa.
Mikhail Effendi	One of the Sultan's leading physicians. 'Effendi' is a title given to senior bureaucrats. He comes from Greek-speaking Coron. The only Greek physician in the Sultan's service.
Murat	The narrator. Adam Pasha's valet and chief steward. Adam's slave, confidante and friend.
(Prince) Mustafa	Eldest son of the Sultan and Mahidevran. Whilst there is no law of primogeniture, Mustafa is well-liked and regarded as Suleyman's successor.
Nilufer	Chief lady-in-waiting to Shireen. Beautiful but in poor health.
Sarah	Jewel broker. Serves the ladies of the Imperial Harem.
Selim Aga	Chief Eunuch. Head of Security in the Imperial Harem.
Shireen	Cousin of Francis I of France. A captive slave who has risen to the position of Chief Treasurer of the Imperial Harem.

(Sultan) Suleyman	Reigned 1520-66 over the Ottoman Empire which stretches over most of eastern Europe, the Near and Middle East and part of North Africa. Dubbed in the West as "The Magnificent" but to be better known to his subjects as "The Lawgiver".
Yaqoob	Adam Pasha's Chief Equerry.
Zaman	Cavalryman in the service of Adam Pasha.

GLOSSARY OF TERMS

Aga	A title given to senior officials and high-ranking army officers.
Akche	Small silver coin. The basis of Ottoman currency.
Alim/Ulema	A religious scholar/ the whole body of religious scholars.
Azan	Muslim call to prayer delivered from the minarets of mosques.
Bayraktar	Standard-bearer. Rank at the highest levels is signified by the number of horsetails hanging from the standard. Adam Pasha's standard has two horse-tails.
Beylerbey/ Beylerbeylik	Provincial governor/ Provincial governorship.
Buzkashi	A Central Asian game involving the picking up and dropping off of the carcass of an animal.
Chovkan	A polo-like game played on horseback.
Dervish	Followers of Muslim Sufi, or mystic, orders, some more orthodox than others.
Dhimmi	Protected peoples 'of the Book' i.e. primarily, Christians and Jews who, subject to the payment of poll taxes were entitled to live in accordance with their own communal and religious laws.
Dhul-Kada	The name of a month in the Muslim lunar calendar. In 1530 AD, this roughly coincided with July in the solar calendar.
Divan	The Imperial Council, the highest court of law and executive body in the Empire.
Fatwa	A legal opinion whose importance is determined by the seniority and prestige of the religious scholar issuing it
Franks	The usual term for Venetians and a general term for Christians outside the Empire.

Hamam	Steam bath.
Harem(lik)	In the Western imagination, a hotbed of licentious living but in reality no more than the inner domain of any household where only the male head of the household and his close family (together with female servants) are permitted.
Janissary	Elite member of the Sultan's bodyguard and feared throughout Europe. In the early sixteenth century, almost invariably Christian and European in origin.
Jariyé	A female Harem slave
Jinn	An invisible race of beings. Genie.
Kadi	Judge, magistrate
Kadiasker	'Kadi' (judge) + 'asker' (soldier) i.e. 'Army Judge' or, more precisely, judge for the 'askeri' or ruling class. A senior judicial position, akin to Chief Justice, usually held by religious scholars. Two Kadiaskers sit in the Sultan's 'Cabinet' (Divan), one responsible for the East ('Anatolia') and one for the West ('Rumelia' or 'Rhum' (Rome)). In addition to hearing petitions, a Kadiasker sometimes acts as an advocate – a sort of Advocate-General.
Madrasa	Theological college.
Odabashi	Barrack-room officer i.e. platoon commander.
Ottoman	A term applied to the ruling class in the widest sense (it included slaves of the Sultan). The language spoken by most members of this class is 'Ottoman', a language based on a Turkish grammar but with strong Persian and Arabic influences.
Pasha	Title normally given to the Sultan's ministers.

Rhum	The western (i.e. European) territories of the Empire. The word is derived from 'Rome'. The Empire is divided into two basic parts, Rhum (the western lands, Rumelia) and Anadolu, the eastern territories (or Anatolia). There are two Kadiaskers, the senior one responsible for Rumelia and the other for Anatolia.
Serasker	Commander-in-Chief of the army.
Shariah	The body of Islamic law comprised of the Koran and the deeds and sayings of the Prophet Muhammad.
Sipahi	A cavalryman. These were of two types – a form of feudal cavalryman, who in exchange for military service, was given land to cultivate and maintain; and soldiers who constituted part of the imperial bodyguard i.e. the Household Cavalry.
Tar	A stringed instrument
Ulema	see 'Alim'.
Yaya/yaya-bashi	A company of Janissaries/ company commander.

Note on weights, measures, dates and names

The Ottomans tended not to interfere with weights and measures in customary use in the various territories under their control. As a result, there is no standardised usage and sometimes the same term denoting a weight or measure varies considerably from one territory to another. For the sake of consistency and intelligibility, the metric system has been used throughout.

Dates are given in the Historical Footnote as Christian era dates but otherwise are in accordance with the Muslim calendar.

No special system has been used for transliterating names, although efforts have been made to give the version in English that most closely resembles its pronunciation. In a few instances, where real characters appear or are mentioned but who bear the same name in Ottoman, the names have been transliterated slightly differently in order to make the characters more easily identifiable. Unfamiliar terms explained in the glossary are italicised the first time they appear in the text. Other italicised terms are explained in the text itself.

Historical Footnote

In 1520, Suleyman a shy, intelligent youth, ascended the Ottoman throne. In western Europe he came to be known as 'The Magnificent' but to his people he would later come to be known as 'The Lawgiver'. Both were apt descriptions of the ruler of a great power, the Ottoman Empire. What in the nineteenth century was to be called 'The Sick Man of Europe' was, in the sixteenth century, in the very best of health.

Sultan Suleyman immediately embarked upon a succession of victorious campaigns, extending his empire's frontiers, both east and west, as he consolidated his sprawling domains. In 1521, Belgrade was toppled and Rhodes fell a year later. The gallant Hungarian nobility was annihilated in 1526 and even Vienna felt its vulnerability, besieged as it was in 1529. The Mediterranean became an Ottoman lake. Suleyman's Grand Admiral Khaireddin, feared along the whole south European coastline as the 'Barbarosa', turned a nascent navy into a power to be reckoned with. And he proved the power by claiming Tunis as his prize in 1533.

Suleyman was amongst the great Renaissance rulers. The decorative arts flourished and the imperial economy thrived. His expansionist reign coincided with those of Francis I of

France, Charles V, King of Spain and Holy Roman Emperor, and Henry VIII of England. But Europe was embroiled in the horrors of the religious wars of the Reformation and the unending crusade against Islam. And the premier Islamic ruler was Suleyman.

Yet, political calculation, though often expressed in the rhetoric of religion, was as important as religious allegiance in the shifting alliances amongst the monarchs and princes of Europe. France, constantly fearing encirclement by its co-religionists in Spain and Northern Europe, sought to break the circle by entering into an alliance with Suleyman. A union much advocated by the Grand Vizier Ibrahim Pasha, the brilliant Barbarosa was given orders to cooperate with the French and a formal treaty was concluded in 1536. Ibrahim Pasha, however, was barely able to celebrate his success, executed as he was in the same year. Exactly why the Sultan chose to eliminate his closest friend and adviser has been a matter of speculation ever since. But Ibrahim's execution did illustrate a sixteenth century fact of life – no matter how secure and powerful anyone seemed to be, no one was beyond the reach of the executioner.

Venice, which dominated Levantine trade, must have viewed the French alliance with trepidation. It brought nearer the day when the Illustrious Signory would lose its trading pre-eminence. France was allowed to install a permanent ambassador in Constantinople which, until the time of the treaty, had been a right granted only to the Venetians. Indeed, Venetian envy was such that it was not long before the Ottomans were dragged into war with their vassal, the Venetian state.

But in the spring of 1530, it was not war with Venice which was exercising Suleyman's mind ...

HAREM SECRETS

I   THE DEAD OF NIGHT

Spring that year in Istanbul should have been a time of happiness. The plum, cherry and apple blossom, budding in quick succession, were sure signs of new life awakening. But that it was a year to remember had little to do with the joy which sunshine and warmth should naturally bring.

***

Galloping hard to the rise, gun-smoke and mist swirling in the air, "There!" cried Adam Pasha, pointing to shadows in the early morning mist. "Look! On the right. There they are! Grab them before they reach the woods!"

We turned our horses, dug in our heels and raced after my master. I saw the pasha's standard, carrying his insignia of two horsetails, speed past me, those mud-stained horsetails swinging in the gloom like spectres on the wind.

The battlefield was thick with the stench and sounds of war – the acrid smell of gunpowder, the whoosh, thud and bang of cannon shot masking the howls of agony. But the sight of battle was worse: death was everywhere as blood congealed in the dirt, bloodied soldiers stumbled helplessly over the muddied grass and corpses rotted before our eyes. Riderless nags thrashed about, snorting and neighing, gnashing their teeth and bucking aimlessly in terror. And desperate men clutched at their half-severed limbs as horses, with sword gashes a metre long, sprawled in stagnating ponds of water.

Our mounts struggled over the sodden ground, kicking up clods of mud high into the air. What, in the name of Heaven, were we doing here? My master, after all, was a

1

Kadiasker, a judge. In the name of Allah, he was no soldier – and I was no old campaigner's orderly! We were not even fighting the enemy – we were chasing our own, our very own Janissaries, our finest infantry: forget the cannon fodder, these were our best.

"We've got them!" came the cry. The deserters had nowhere to go but heavenward.

***

"Why are we always at war? Let me tell you", said Adam Pasha in didactic mood. "For any sovereign a war has only three merits: it humiliates his enemies; it keeps his own troops busy so they don't humiliate him; and it overawes his subjects so they don't take to backing those troops and hacking him to bits. Now, a failed war has no merits at all and, so, we're always victorious." Thus, my master neatly summed-up the politics of war.

"It was a shambles! A total shambles!" he said, with emotion locked in his voice and in his eyes. This was, I thought, no time to argue with my pasha. "And, I don't understand how Ibrahim Pasha can still be patting himself on the back for 'our glorious thrashing of the infidel'."

"Well," I suggested, "if he didn't, no one else would."

"You know, Murat, I personally sentenced thirty-three soldiers to death for looting and desertion. What sort of victory was that? True, we took Buda quick enough but we can't afford to hold up our advance with any delay – a few days can cost us the campaign. I don't doubt that our Grand Vizier is a great general but another victory like this one and I wouldn't want to guess at the consequences."

"Next time, Pasha," I said comfortingly. "The next time we won't make the same mistakes."

"There won't be a next time, Murat. We can't do it. We

2

can't take Vienna. It's too far away – by the time we've mobilised our forces and have marched them all the way across he plains and valleys of *Rhum*, winter is just around the corner. If we're lucky, the rains will be late so we can bring up our heavy guns to batter down the walls but who can afford to chance the whole empire on a gamble like that? And if we dig in for a prolonged siege we risk losing our entire army, picked off one by one by marauding bands of irregulars. But if we don't dig in and try for a quick kill, recklessness will finish off most of the army and the cold will do for the rest."

***

There was a shrill cry of panic ringing around the Imperial Harem. "Selim Aga! Selim Aga! Come quick! It is Lady Shireen ... Something terrible has happened!" Daud, deputy to the Chief Eunuch, was hurrying as fast as his short legs would allow him.

In the late hours of the night the Imperial Harem was a quiet and peaceful place. That tranquillity had been pierced by a woman's shriek and the sound of eunuchs running along the cobblestones, their shouted commands echoing along the cold stone of the Harem's narrow corridors.

"Daud Aga! Be still!" commanded Selim, the Harem's Head of Security. "I'll not tolerate such behaviour inside the Palace – we're not in a Greek tavern. Now, what's all the fuss about?"

Daud drew in a deep breath, sucking in a part of the white cotton veil that was looped around his head and across his face. "Aga, Lady Shireen ... She's dead. Nilufer, her chief *jariyé*, has tried to wake her but ..."

Selim Aga was the silent type. His immediate reaction was a tilt of the head and a simple wrinkle of the brow. He

3

was no stranger to death in the Harem, whether from old age, fever or fracture. Yet Shireen had been one of the most talented and beautiful of Harem girls. And barely twenty-four years old. Though not in the best of health, nothing had indicated her malaise could be fatal. And she had so much to live for: as Treasurer of the Harem, within its confines she had possessed both power and prestige.

"Have you sent for a physician?" asked Selim. Daud shook his bowed head. "Do it!" ordered Selim. Daud moved away briskly and Selim called together two of his eunuchs. To one, a dopey-looking specimen, he gave instructions to empty Shireen's quarters of her handmaidens, to seal her apartments and to post a guard. The other, more alert and agile, he sent to the Queen Mother, ruler of the Harem, with word that Shireen was dead.

Selim himself wasted no time in leaving the Old Palace, in the centre of Istanbul, for the New Palace, located at the confluence of the Bosphorus and the Sea of Marmara. There, he knew, he would find the Sultan.

As Selim left, it was still dark – half an hour or more till the call for the dawn prayer – but already the Harem was a hive of activity. Flickering candles multiplied as sleepy girls were stirred from their mattresses by the sounds of scurrying feet and squeaky eunuch voices.

Gossip was no stranger to the Harem. But it surprised even the worldly Selim to hear the whispered abuse being heaped upon Shireen by ladies who so recently had purred at her in their most flattering voices. Shireen was perverted, Shireen had had lovers, Shireen was a suicide. "Shireen..., Shireen..., Shireen ...," her name echoed through the Harem with open contempt. The Lady Treasurer, only hours earlier flattered and fawned on by all, was now denounced as a schemer, a sexual degenerate, an unscrupulous adventuress greedy for power and wealth.

The tittle-tattle of the Harem was one thing but what would the Queen Mother say when the truth tumbled out? After all, she had showered Shireen with gifts and favours and to what purpose? More important still was the question everyone was silently asking: what would *he* say – the only man who really mattered, our Sultan, Suleyman? For, as sure as the coming of the Day of Judgement, Shireen had been destined for his bed.

***

Victory or no victory, at least we were back in Constantinople, or Istanbul, call it what you will. We had been away far too long, first with the Vienna campaign followed by a short sojourn in Damascus to help the new magistrate, my master's successor when, on the eve of war, he was elevated to the *Divan* as Kadiasker.

Still, we were back in Constantinople and, after the hardships of a long campaign, I for one was looking forward to the sweet promise of adventure that only Constantinople can offer – in boatloads. That is not to say that we, my master and I, had not partaken of our fair share of thrills in Damascus. But pleasant city though it is, it was no place for my master. He was bored and his attachment to Gulshan, a Damascene prostitute with presence, could have spelled the end of his career – at least, it might have done had it not been for some devoted slave (me) going to extraordinary lengths to protect his reputation. He came close to scandalising the town and the mullahs, especially the mullahs, but a few bags of silver in the hands of the most grasping of them saw off the threat. That, regrettably, had to be coupled with fewer visits to Gulshan, which made me less than popular in the brothel quarter. But the Magistrate of Damascus, as Adam Pasha had been, or Chief Justice, as he now was, just cannot be seen idling his time with a lady of the night, even one so enchanting as Gulshan. Not that Adam Pasha cared very much what people thought but sometimes it is the caring steward whose hard work permits the master's little indiscretions. And, I don't mind saying so myself, I did a pretty good job of damping down the gossip.

The Sultan was so impressed with my pasha's hard work and organisational skills (as a magistrate) that he made him a Kadiasker or 'army judge'. Now, there's a job-title that needs revision, barely touching, as it does, on the significance of the role, a heady mixture of chief justice, counsel to the ruling elite and advocate general all rolled into one.

It is a considerable achievement for any man to be appointed Kadiasker, thereby gaining a place in the Imperial Divan, but, when you consider the pasha's humble origins, from orphaned farm boy to government minister before he had reached the age of thirty-five, that takes a formidable degree of ability – and a fair dose of luck.

Constantinople did not whisper the same call to adventure to my master that it bellowed out to me. For one thing, he had taken a stomach-full of adventure on the battlefield. For another, there was my pasha's new house, his childhood dream-come-true, which was still edging its way to completion. Construction had begun long ago but the onslaught on Vienna had brought work to an abrupt halt as most of the artisans and labourers joined the imperial army on its long muddy trudge along the valleys and fields of Rhum.

The fighting all done, we now had to bear a daily routine of banging and crashing, profaning and bashing, the raucous cries of carpenters and masons, the jarring noise of sawing wood and cracking stone, and the cacophonous braying of the asses – there was a joke Allah had played on humanity, even imprinting perverse grins on their faces to mock the human race.

And now that the pasha was one of the grandees of the empire, the dwelling as originally planned, sited in close proximity to the Grand Vizier his patron, naturally needed a few tasteful additions and careful alterations. A decorative tweak here, a wistful flourish there was the intent but the well-built builder was never shy about proffering some extravagant suggestion for improvement: "A man of Adam Pasha's stature just has to have the very finest!" he would say in answer to my sceptical queries over cost. Fortunately, with all those marble columns and half-demolished pavilions lying around the ancient Hippodrome, our builder could indulge his whims without it wholly overwhelming our budget.

Still, a few weeks more and the new residence would be complete. That, at least, was what our emboldened builder had us believe. From one week to the next!

For all the contractor's 'minor revisions', the residence retained a simplicity of design. Organised around two courtyards, the pasha chose to sleep in a large room that linked the *selamlik*, or public quarters, with the private harem. He intended to move into the harem when it was complete and hung on to romantic notions of watching the fountain burble amidst a clutch of lemon trees centred in the inner courtyard.

My master was not an ostentatious man. Even with the suggested improvements, mine and the builder's, the two-storied house was a modest affair for a man of the

Kadiasker's rank. But unmarried and no prospective spouse in sight, he had no one to pamper and no need to maintain a grand household.

In Damascus, my master, bored with the tedium of work, had succumbed to the charms of Gulshan. Not inconsiderable charms either but what else was my master to do? Either you find a wife or you find a brothel. Personally, I thought the slave market a much better place to look for a companion and it was certainly more fun than that old ploy of swapping tired poems with your heart-throb on the wings of an equally tired (and often wayward) carrier-pigeon – so common an event was it that I was never sure whether the pigeon settling on our roof was actually intended for us.

"Get yourself a wife," was the simple-minded advice of my master's friends at court, always ready to lecture him on the importance and value of marriage. More likely than not, they were quick to conclude their homilies with some casual comments about the charms and qualities of their eligible young (and not so young) daughters. Even the Queen Mother thought it her duty to get involved. She could hardly have set eyes on Adam Pasha but, ever since his elevation to the Divan, he had become "my judge" and finding him a wife had evidently become her sole mission in life. At least, that is how the eunuchs in the Old Palace put it and I had every reason to believe them. After all, this was no new interest of the Illustrious Mother: barely four years earlier my master had been engaged to one of the Sultan's more accomplished Harem girls – Leila, I think was her name. Sadly, she had died in a ferocious attack of plague. I had never seen the girl, of course, but then neither had my pasha. I doubt if he had even known very much about her. So it can hardly have been love that caused him to mourn as deeply as he did. Perhaps, having prepared himself for the state of marriage, the loss of his bride-to-be dragged him into morose reflections on the brevity of temporal life. The grieving over, the whole idea of marriage became a distant memory (as it should always have been).

My master, though, was contrary as ever. On recall to Istanbul, he eschewed female company and stubbornly refused to follow my advice and take a concubine. That was not hypocrisy. The pasha was passionate for justice and, back in the capital, could find little time for passions of other kinds. Whatever he might have had me believe, the majesty of his new office was weighing heavily on his shoulders. And so, the isolated privacy of a harem held little appeal for him. Instead, it housed a few doddery female slaves, some washerwomen, and a seamstress or two. A Nubian eunuch saw to their security, not that that collection of womanhood was in much danger of unsolicited attention. As for the rest of the household, there was the usual sprinkling of mindless servants, and tough disciplinarian eunuchs looking after the welfare of the dozen or so page boys training for senior service in the pasha's household. And, quartered in an annex to the complex, there was also the pasha's personal troop of cavalry.

Now, my pasha had some odd habits, talking to trees being amongst them, but for the most part they were innocuous enough. I repeat, for the most part. One early summer's day, I was about to attend on the pasha when I saw it and even I could not believe my eyes.

"Pasha," I said, the hint of indignation rising in my voice, "it's just not seemly for a man in your position".

My master turned to me with that infuriatingly sheepish grin which told me that he knew exactly what I was going to

9

say … and that he intended to take no notice of it.

"What isn't seemly, Murat?"

"A man of your importance tramping about the kitchens. The empire's most senior judge …"

"The empire's second most senior judge," said my master, correcting me with a lawyer's pedantry and a grin straining to break into a laugh. I knew it was hopeless but certain standards had to be maintained and it was my duty to point it out.

"And they are my kitchens, after all," added my master. "Why shouldn't I 'tramp' about them?"

"You get in the way of the cooks and the scullery staff. They get edgy – think you're checking up on them."

"Nonsense. I simply happen to like cooking. It was one of the few pleasures of childhood – helping the priest's mother make supper." Adam Pasha's nostrils seemed to quiver at the thought. "My bread was legendary."

"No doubt it was, Pasha. But that was a long time ago. Best keep quiet about it now. What would people say today if they knew …?"

"They would say I was a good judge of bread," cackled Adam Pasha, tongue firmly in cheek. He, at least, thought the conversation was comical.

I had almost given up the struggle but then he added, "They would think, Murat, I, too, was human; that I was of the common people."

"But that is just my point, Pasha. You may have been an orphan raised by a Greek priest and once-upon-a-time you may have counted yourself one of the common folk. But you are no longer a simple peasant from a Thracian hamlet. You are not even a common judge – after the Mufti of Istanbul, you are the Empire's highest religious authority. And the

Mufti is not in the Sultan's Cabinet – you are. People have an image of a Chief Justice: all learning with a long, grey beard; a man of deep thoughts buried in his dusty books and scrolls. But look at you. You have a short black beard shot with a few streaks of grey. Add to that this childlike yearning for tossing about lumps of dough and … Well, you just don't fit the image."

"I am very glad to hear it!"

That complex mixture of judge, religious authority and secular adviser that made up a Chief Justice's role was well-tailored to my master's enigmatic personality. Looks belied his bookish tastes. An avid collector, his library unusually included printed books, not least of which was a copy of the Gutenberg Bible. He had read the ancient philosophers, jurists and historians and could write in Persian, Greek and Arabic as well as Ottoman. He was a fair poet, a bit too sentimental for my liking, but his calligraphy showed real boldness and a flair for design. All that learning was wasted in the kitchens and I was not going to give up without a fight.

"Well, Pasha, I don't see why you feel the need to be counted as one of the common folk. Why can't you be like other members of the Divan?"

"Would you rather I was a politicking courtier?"

"No, Pasha but you don't need to try so hard to be different. And, what's more, you might think about my position. The Grand Vizier's servants are always poking fun at me. Your behaviour simply makes me a laughing stock."

What was the point? I knew I was wasting my breath and I could see Adam Pasha was tiring of the conversation quick enough to switch the subject.

"Which reminds me, Murat. This wretched beard of mine

needs a trim. Personally, I would rather not have one. It itches and doesn't suit me – it's all over the place and makes me look as if I have one foot in the grave." Adam Pasha tried to curl the short hairs of his irregular beard around his long, slim fingers. Not classically handsome, he had an aristocratic mien out of keeping with his humble origins and the beard did not help project the noble appearance he aspired to.

My master lapsed into deep thought and I began to wonder whether I had made an impression after all. He hated to admit that I might have a point but, well, there was the question of appearances.

***

It was, in part, the Kadiasker's role to relieve the Divan of the pressure of work, whether as a court of appeal or one of first instance. Five days a week, the early morning was spent with me running through the agenda for the day. Nibbling on fresh sheep's cheese and hot fragrant bread, baked with fine flour at the royal bakeries (and mercifully without assistance from my pasha), I read out the case summaries appended to each petition. The Divan was not due to meet that day but, all the same, there was a heavy caseload demanding urgent attention. Some petitions were directed to the Kadiasker and others delegated to him by the Divan but it was pot-luck which were the more interesting or weighty.

"Take a look at this one, Murat," my master said, flicking breadcrumbs off his raggedy beard. "It's a petition from an orphaned Jewish girl. She must have a smart lawyer at her side, advising her to petition the Divan like this. And, so," he mused, clicking his fingers, "she neatly sidesteps the rougher justice of the Rabbinical courts. She expects a kinder hearing from us and we will make sure she gets it."

It was then that I heard the clatter of horses' hooves on

the cobblestones in the courtyard below and I rushed to meet our visitors. My master craned his neck out of the window to see what all the commotion was about. He strained to understand the garbled sound of an apprehensive voice. It was my voice. He heard footsteps, my footsteps, scrambling up the stairs. Whatever anxiety I felt I could not permit it to overcome proper etiquette and so I stopped and caught my breath before I entered the sweet-scented room in customary fashion, touching my forehead and lips with the fingers of my right hand and bowing my head a little.

"My Pasha," I said, working hard to steady my voice, "our Sultan has summoned you. And he has sent a troop of the palace guard as an escort."

Now, say what you will but no man, however eminent, can hear such a command without a tremor of trepidation and, hard as one might try to hide it, a shiver of sheer terror.

Why did the Sultan demand to see my master so urgently? In the last twelve months or so, since his elevation to the Divan, my pasha had not even seen the Sultan at its meetings let alone been so summarily summoned. Our Sultan had succumbed to a sovereign's tendency to remoteness and mystery, no longer personally attending the Divan's deliberations but keeping a discreet eye on Council proceedings from a small room perched above the Divan. So what could be so vital that it could not wait for my master to deliver his regular reports to our Sultan? Why all the melodrama?

"Murat, have my horse saddled," my pasha said a little uncertainly, "and lay out my kaftan. My best kaftan." The first command I had already seen to and, from a scented cedar trunk, I now took out my pasha's finest full-length coat. It was a heavy crimson silk one, edged with ermine,

13

presented to him as a gift upon his appointment as Kadiasker by no less a person than the Grand Vizier himself. This Adam Pasha put on over his embroidered red tunic and baggy blue trousers. I set a grand turban on his head, not an easy matter given my pasha's unease.

As my master stepped into the courtyard, he caught sight of the *aga* of the red banner. The officer bowed gracefully, as correct, cool and silent as only an imperial officer can be. Stepping on a stool, my master mounted his chestnut-coloured mare and, with a flick of the reins, our small party trotted smartly out of the courtyard.

We turned into the Hippodrome where the Roman circuses of old used to be held. On the far side stood the sprawling palatial mansion of Ibrahim Pasha, the Grand Vizier. We trotted past the Janissary apprentices sweeping the paved thoroughfares around the dusty, vandalised ruins of Constantinople, though my pasha barely noticed them. He was a worried man and, as we covered the few hundred metres to the perimeter walls of the New Palace, he reflected on his fate. Not unnaturally, in asking why the Sultan might possibly want to see him, the more sanguine reasons bounced into his mind first: perhaps the Sultan wanted his advice on some important judicial appointment. That had to be it. But, hard as he tried, the inevitable fears continued to prod and poke about in his mind, like great rocks settled in mid-river, sending a stream of thought this way and that. What could be so urgent that he needed to be summoned - under escort? Did His Highness want a legal opinion on some delicate point of law? It was only reasonable that he should turn to his Chief Justice. But, then, why not consult the Mufti of Istanbul? And why send a regimental commander and four fully-armed *sipahis* to fetch him when a palace chamberlain would have done well enough? He mumbled, he muttered and he agonised but his mind always returned to the same two intrusive thoughts, alternating in rapid succession: his master had summoned him and his master was not pleased.

The Sultan was my pasha's master in more ways than one. The Kadiasker was the Sultan's slave in law, as I was a slave of my master, and his life could be ended at the whim of his master. Kadiasker or not, he had no life of his own and, like naphtha from Baku, this thought was now floating at the very top of his mind. And the oil was ablaze.

To be sure, my pasha had his detractors at court. Not everyone found him a sympathetic character. He had his flaws but who does not? In truth, some of his fellow courtiers could not countenance the Kadiasker's near incorruptibility. Is it not simpler to control the acts and thoughts of one who can be easily corrupted? No one had yet found a way to corrupt my master and that made the venal wary, the greedy ingrate and the power-hungry pernicious. It was only a matter of time before some suspicious swindler or over-mighty power-broker deemed my pasha a threat too close for comfort.

And, as these thoughts somersaulted in his mind, my pasha's palms began to sweat. The reins slipped uncontrollably through his hands. He tightened his grip and his body tensed. His mount, sensing distress, tossed back her head and jogged nervously forward. For Adam Pasha, the cool early morning breeze did not help. The morning had turned hot, uncomfortably, unbearably, hot. Why had the Sultan summoned him? And why the armed escort?

II GALATA

Across the waters of the Estuary that the Franks enigmatically call the Golden Horn, and clearly visible from the New Palace, lies the Christian district of Galata. The skyline dominated by the cone-capped watchtower, Genovesan Galata was largely left in tact by Sultan Mehmed, the Conqueror of Constantinople. That was as reward for an oath not to aid the Roman resistance and it was now once again a thriving commercial centre, albeit no thanks to the skulking Genoese who had betrayed the magnanimity of the Conqueror.

By the water's edge, life was bustling, the fishermen stitching their nets, caulking their boats and selling their catches of the day straight off the boats at the jetties. The air was full of the smell of fresh fish, at least for the most part it was fresh though here and there lay the odd stinking fish head, the remnant of some stray cat's supper.

The fishermen, vying with each other to attract the attention of thrifty shoppers, sang out loudly in their long drawn out phrases, "Fresh fish! Fr...esh fish! Come buy! Lowest prices!"

Amid the fishers' yells and the fishy smells, one person, a grand old Ottoman gentleman, stood out from the crowd. In his person there was nothing distinctive. He was not tall or short, not thin or stout. That he was well-to-do was plain from his attire, wearing as he did a sleeveless and fur-trimmed emerald-green silk kaftan over his mud-green tunic. To be sure, a wealthy Ottoman strolling along the quayside in Galata was a little out of the ordinary – Ottomans are not strollers and certainly not by the fish docks. But this man, with his thick white beard, followed at a respectful distance by two veiled wives, was a common sight in Galata. He was the administrator of a pious foundation established for the comfort and succour of seafarers. He was also the owner of a large number of ferries that plied between the opposite shores of the Estuary of Constantinople. What made him particularly notable was that he was a *sayyid*, a descendant of the Prophet of Islam. At least that is what his distinctive headgear announced – a green and white turban, not bulbous or out-sized like some but a small modest affair. He was not quite a saint but his birth had assured him a revered status. He was a man to whom even a minister of my pasha's stature and importance would defer. And Christians, too, would readily give way, though whether that was out of respect or just good sense it was better not to pry.

It was, therefore, an act of startling stupidity when a Venetian sailor launched himself upon the taller of the two veiled women. The sailor, a captain returning to his ship in a half-drunken stupor, had just staggered out of a Galata tavern. He sniggered like a jackal as he planted a kiss on the frightened woman's bosom. Onlookers, and the sayyid too, stood dumbfounded. The frightened woman shrieked. Then the half-witted Venetian let out a great stinking belch and struck off the sayyid's turban. That was an insult too far. The crowd, by now quite sizeable, began to sizzle. "Grab him!" someone yelled. "Grab him!" echoed the others.

The tall Italian, suddenly regaining his senses, realised the quayside was no place for him. He bolted, heading up a long, steep street, narrowing as it approached the cylindrical watch tower. Brushing past a couple of spectators, he dodged the out-stretched hands clutching wildly at his flowing shirt and leather jerkin. But he needed his long legs, pursued as he was by a baying blood-hungry mob bent on playing *buzkashi* with his head.

The sailor heard the howls and cries behind him. Glancing over his shoulder, he lengthened his stride. The alcoholic haze evaporated and he ran like a man possessed. He ran as if his demon captors were after him. But the demonic gaolers held him in their sights and the rattle of the dungeon keys rang in his head. His heart pounded against his chest as his feet pounded the cobblestones. Rivulets of sweat streamed off his brow. He stripped off his damp leather jerkin and threw it behind him. His legs were growing heavy. He struggled to move forward, as if his feet were mired in a peat bog.

His pursuers, a rag-bag of beggars, vagabonds and, given any other day, respectable merchants and traders, were closing on him. He could smell their blood-lust. And their numbers were swelling fast. First a few, then a dozen, then a score. And soon it was three score who were chasing him. Few knew what the Venetian had done. Some bellowed, "Thief!" others "Murderer!" The actual offence hardly seemed to matter. It was sufficient that he was guilty of some heinous crime – why else would there be such a hue and cry? But few really cared about the crime – it was the thrill and excitement of the hunt that lured most of them in.

The captain slipped, he staggered, he stumbled. A hand clutched at his collar and, gasping for breath, he snatched himself free and darted forward again. A renewed burst of energy surged through him. The sedentary merchants and traders were no match for his long legs and stamina. The distance again widened between him and his pursuers. And as he ran up the steep cobbled hill, he picked up another outcast for a companion – a small mongrel dog. The grey mutt yapped at the pursuers, ran forward to join his new friend and then stopped to wait for the howling mob before recommencing his cycle of defiance.

The sailor, tiring on the jarring cobblestones and the gradient of the hill, was driven on by desperation alone. But, in front of him was a group gathered in a circle - a score or more of people jeering and gesticulating wildly. He was trapped. With no turning back and no way forward, he stopped abruptly, took several deep breaths and prepared for the worst.

But the crowd had no interest in him. They were cheering and cursing as they wagered on two bloodied fighting cockerels. Unwittingly, they blocked the captain's exit. Some of the gamblers, distracted by the cries of the mob, turned round to face the sailor. As the circle opened up before him, he saw his chance. He leapt into the ring, the two startled birds hopping back with a frenzied flapping of wings.

The gamblers were spitting angst. As they cursed the sailor, two large Greeks took hold of him and tossed him out of the circle. But by now the howling mob had arrived. It descended on the confused gamblers with a fury. A bony fist was raised, a swinging punch was thrown, a white turban fell and its burly owner crashed dazed to the ground.

Amid the scuffling and confusion, the sailor and his mongrel companion made their escape. He breathed more freely as he again put distance between himself and the mob. Once around a gentle bend, out of sight of the receding mob, he slackened his pace. He leaned against a wall and sank down on his haunches, sweat dribbling down his nose. He made the Catholic sign of the cross in gratitude for his deliverance and the mongrel sat down beside him, with a smug look of success on his face.

As the sailor took in several deep breaths, a squad of four soldiers, led by their sergeant, pounced on him. They had witnessed the chase from the watchtower, not without a certain sporting gratification, and had been sent by their *odabashi* to restore order.

"Ya' must 'av done somethin' pretty serious to 'av sparked that ov'," the sergeant said almost jovially.

The sailor replied in Italian that he did not understand. He hoped that his inability to communicate might be enough to gain his release. His heart sank when he found the sergeant spoke fluent Italian of the Genoese variety. Though taken as a prisoner at sea twenty years previously, the sergeant was quick to recognise a fellow Italian speaker. And he knew the Venetian vernacular when he heard it.

"I'm innocent! I haven't done anything wrong!" pleaded the sailor.

"No? Well, well, well! Wot 'av we 'ere. An innocent Venetian!" The sergeant grabbed the sailor by the scruff of the neck and turned to his men.

"Take a good look, me boys. This," snarled the sergeant, "is the first – and last – innocent Venetian you'll ev'a see." The sergeant shook the sailor violently and then pulled him in close till they stood nose to nose. Both men wore scowls, though it was hard to tell whether that was because of the homebred rivalries or in recoil from each other's foul breath.

"So, 'Innocence', my dear, why the hue and cry? What're ya' running fer if y'er so innocent?" He threw the sailor back into the arms of two soldiers who gripped him tightly.

"Sir, this dog, this … this flea-bag, bit a fisherman. It's been following me about and they thought it was my dog. So I get blamed. Just my luck!" the sailor lied, waving his hand dismissively in the direction of the dog. The story had the ring of truth. The sergeant was inclined to believe him; but the Venetian did not know when to keep his mouth shut. He added, "I swear, Sir, I'm innocent."

"Quiet! Search 'im!" the sergeant commanded. Two of the squad held the frightened Venetian whilst the other two roughly ran their hands over him. Consumed by fear, the sailor's grey eyes gave him away. He shuffled against the wall, a sign of defiance, which caused one soldier to grip the sailor's wrist and to bend his arm painfully behind his back.

They stripped off the remaining tatters of the Venetian's white sweat-filled shirt and discovered two leather pouches hung inside his brown green-striped breeches. The sergeant held the purses, one in each hand, as if he were weighing them. He held them by their leather ties and dangled them in front of the sailor's large nose. Their contents jangled.

"Now, what do we 'av 'ere?" asked the sergeant. "What's in these, eh?"

"Money." There was no point lying about the obvious and the captain needed precious time to think.

The sergeant opened one of the pouches, after placing the other inside his tunic. He poured some of the contents onto his outstretched palm and one Venetian gold sequin followed another. The purse must have contained thirty or more such coins. "Yeh," said the sergeant as he contemplated the riches resting in his hand. "Money. There must be at least fifty gold coins here and even more silver ones. If I'd known you were carryin' these I'd 'av doubled the odds on ya' being torn apart by the mob. Where'd ya' get 'em from? Steal 'em did ya'? Is that why they were chasin' ya'?"

"No, Sir," the captain replied respectfully. "I'm the Master of the Leonora. It's only a small galley. Nothing to get

21

excited about. I have to buy the ship's provisions."

"And y'er on your way back to the ship, I s'pose?" asked the sergeant, faced with another plausible answer.

"Yes, Sir."

"Why were ya' still carryin' this, then, …" the sergeant asked, spinning a gold coin in the air and catching it in front of the sailor's sweat-pulsating nose. "If yu'd already bought your provisions?"

The sailor paused for thought, a pause that convinced the sergeant of his guilt. "Lyin' Venetian turd. Take 'im away!" ordered the moustachioed veteran of three European campaigns. "Our oda-bashi will get the truth out of ya'."

"Let me go!" the captain cried as he tried to wrench himself free. "You have no right to hold me! I demand you take me to the ambassador of the Illustrious Signory. I'm a Venetian citizen and only the Venetian representative in Constantinople has authority over me!" The sailor had dumped the respectful tone, which had got him nowhere, but replacing it with arrogance got him even less.

At first, the sergeant was taken aback by this boldness. He could do without a diplomatic incident, but he had a soldier's duty to perform. And he hated Venetians. "Shut up, ya' infidel slime!" he said, as he struck the sailor across the face with the rear of his hand, causing the Venetian to throw his head backwards and hit the wall. "Demand?" asked the sergeant with evident disgust, "Who're ya' to demand anythin'?" Momentarily stunned, he was pulled and dragged towards the Galata Tower. He tried to struggle free but a few well-directed blows from the sergeant showed him the futility of the attempt. And that was just the beginning.

III THE REQUEST

As we passed through the imposing two-storied Imperial Gate, my whole body shivered with excitement. Glancing up, I could see the years of construction, '863 to 872', boldly chiselled into the stone above the portal. Adam Pasha, however, was directing his gaze somewhat lower, at the gate's mitred niches where from time-to-time were displayed the heads of officials who had fallen foul of the Sultan. My pasha, staring at those empty niches, was already imagining the tingle of the executioner's sharp-bladed axe slicing across the back of his neck.

The gatekeepers waved us through in total silence. They offered no challenge or comment, whether straightening to attention at the gate or peering inquisitively from their wheeled wagon quarters parked nearby. We had entered the public courtyard of the New Palace.

This first courtyard, lain over ancient olive groves, contained a rambling collection of buildings – armouries, administrative offices, an infirmary and storehouses. People were returning from their early morning prayers and the aroma of freshly baked bread wafted through the air. As it reached my pasha's nostrils, a smile flashed across his face. If he were in danger of losing his liberty (he was trying desperately hard to think of nothing worse) his escort, he reasoned, would surely have been more menacing. Yet what could the Sultan want with him?

Approaching the *Baab as-Salaam*, the Gate of Peace, which gave entry to the second courtyard, my master looked out of the corner of his eye at a squat broad-shouldered man

23

washing his hands in the executioner's fountain. Was this the executioner? Was he readying himself for another day's work? And who would he welcome as his victim?

The second courtyard was where the Divan, Public Records Office and the Grand Vizier's administrative office were located but, before we had gone through the portal, a young member of the Sultan's Privy Chamber approached the aga of the red banner. The youth, blonde curly locks dangling from under his headdress, muttered a few words to the aga whilst Adam Pasha dismounted. The cavalry officer turned to my master and directed him not into the Second Courtyard, as he had expected, but to a small gate to the right which opened onto our Sultan's private garden and menagerie. My pasha took in a deep breath and approached the gate unchallenged and alone.

The silence was broken by the throaty roar of a lion. As if in response to the hungry cry, my pasha let out a low groan. He took a few nervous steps forward and beyond a bush on the right he saw the Sultan, not too tall but with a long neck and a thin face. He gave the impression of a lost romantic, sniffing a blood-red rose. He was looking wistfully across the calm waters of the Bosphorus when his eye caught sight of a thickening plume of smoke rising above the Galata Tower. Our Sultan, a hand shading his eyes from the glare of the sun, seemed to be searching for the source of the smoke.

Adam Pasha stopped at a respectful distance, head bowed and hands clasped in front of him. The Sultan turned, fingering the sable trim of his plain grey-silk kaftan. He coughed nervously. It was hard to tell who was the more apprehensive – the Kadiasker or the King of Kings. The Sultan, with a creased brow and a haggard look, bore all the signs of a tired and worried man.

Clearing his throat gently, the Sultan's grim expression was broken by a smile. His slim, aquiline nose smiled along with his lips and the rigours of rule fled from his face.

"Welcome, Adam Pasha. Peace be upon you." The Sultan turned again briefly to face the shore. "What do you make of that?" he asked, pointing to the billowing smoke, now darker and more threatening than before. But he did not wait for an answer.

"That's a nice kaftan," our Sultan said disarmingly. My master had to restrain himself from showing it off and merely answered, "Yes, my Sultan," assuming the Sultan had not summoned him to discuss the finer points of fashion.

"Adam Pasha," continued our Sultan, "you're a trusted adviser and so when some matter, any matter, requires total discretion I naturally look to you for advice. And what I'm about to tell you requires that level of discretion. If I tell you that my throne and perhaps even the destiny of this blessed empire could depend on how you acquit yourself, you'll think me melodramatic if not a little mad." My master dropped his head further but said nothing as the Sultan continued, "But I am neither. The empire's future – my future – now rests wholly in your hands."

In speaking, our Sultan was looking beyond my master, almost as if he were not there. His tone, indeed melodramatic, and the method of summons, no less so, had left my pasha confused and uncertain. How could he, a simple judge and not one of the Sultan's inner circle of advisers, have the future of the empire resting in his hands?

"My Lord", my pasha uttered hesitantly, "if the matter is of such grave importance I will strain every sinew to do my utmost to assist your faithful servant, the Grand Vizier. I will do my duty to my Sultan."

25

"Kadiasker, I expect no less. However, on this occasion I don't think we will need Ibrahim Pasha's advice and you'll not mention our conversation to him. Is that quite clear? Rumours and suspicion are spreading like maggots in a putrid wound and, if we do not stop them quickly, the well-being of the State is put at risk. Discretion – what we need now is total discretion."

"My Lord ...," stammered my master in complete bewilderment, but the Sultan commanded silence with a sweep of his hand.

The Sultan again ran his strong fingers, in evident embarrassment, over the fur trim of his kaftan. He said that he understood my master's confusion but his voice was crackling with emotion as he spoke. He explained that a lady in his Harem had died that night. Pausing to take in a deep breath, he continued hurriedly, as if wanting to end the session as quickly as possible. He said that Shireen, a very beautiful girl, had been taken as a captive on board a papal galley about five years previously. French by birth and of noble stock, she had been acquired by the Queen Mother and thus had entered the Sultan's service. And now she was dead.

"When," continued the Sultan, "a French embassy made a request for the release of French prisoners and slaves, I offered to send her back to her own country. Imagine my surprise, then, when she refused to go. She said she had adopted Islam as her faith and Constantinople as her home. What will the French say now? Will they accuse us of murder?"

"My Sultan, time and diplomacy will smooth over such concerns," replied my master.

"Pasha, that is the least of it. Listen carefully to me and

do avoid the temptation of jumping to wild conclusions. I liked the girl but the gossip I am hearing – that she was intended as my consort – is beyond belief. Why would I need a new consort? I am devoted to my beloved Khurrem – have no doubt of that." He looked up to the heavens as if beseeching Allah for inspiration.

"Shireen," the Sultan continued, "was a remarkable woman and there is no shame in admitting that. But how could she ever match the vitality and sweet humour of Khurrem Sultan? No one can do that!"

My master was still bemused and shuffled uncomfortably.

"Kadiasker, can't you grasp the seriousness and the delicacy, of what I'm telling you? Where is the philosopher, that pensive youth, who I once watched wallowing in his thoughts to the point of drowning in them? Where is that man who was able to see a single pin amongst a thousand pins? Have I overestimated your abilities?" The Sultan had plainly hoped to be spared the pain of having to relate the entire catalogue of embarrassing details but that is what had to be done.

"Then, Pasha, I will be more explicit but what I have to say is for your ears only. Do you understand me?" The question was, of course, rhetorical. "Khurrem Sultan was jealous of Shireen, though I had never given her cause for that. Khurrem never expressed her jealousy to me but jealous she most certainly was. And Her Highness has a fiery Frankish temper," said the Sultan. "I can vouch for that!" he added quietly.

"Ugly rumours are already spreading, rumours that Khurrem was responsible for the death of this hapless girl. I pray to Allah that it is not true but of one thing, Pasha, I am certain." He lowered his eyes and quietly disclosed his conviction that Shireen had not died of natural causes.

The Kadiasker knew that his Sultan had paused to let him speak but more than ever he was conscious now that he was the slave in the presence of his master. He was no less sure of his course now than he had been before and he hesitated, fumbling for the right words.

"Say something, Pasha! I've asked you here for your help and advice. You must help me find the truth. If, Allah have mercy, Khurrem is behind this, even I may not be able to save her".

"But, my Sultan," interjected my master at last, "you are all-powerful, surely ..." He paused abruptly. He, the jurist, had recognised the difficulty the Sultan was in.

"Yes, Pasha, at last the day has dawned and you see my predicament. The penalty for murder is death. There are those within and without the Palace who will plot – who at this very moment are plotting – against Khurrem. They will use any means, any tricks, any devices, to destroy her but I will sniff out these plots," he said, as he gently tapped his nose, "and I will snuff out the plotters." This, he demonstrated even more graphically with a twisting motion of his hands as if wringing the neck of a chicken. "But, you know that if my Khurrem were in any way implicated or complicit in murder, those plotters will call for her head. I," he said, tapping his chest with his fist, "I, as the Commander of the Faithful, cannot overtly ignore the law – my law and Allah's law. Can I show clemency? Perhaps I can grant that, but, if she were found guilty, at best I would have to exile her and I, my soul if not my body, would go into exile with her. The suspicion of murder must not taint Her Highness.

"So, Adam Pasha, now that you know everything, what

do you advise your Sultan to do?"

My master's own dilemma seemed to him to be almost as great as that of the Sultan's. He knew none of the actors in this drama. He was not even sure what the Sultan was asking him to do. Did the Sultan wish him to investigate a possible murder? Or was he asking him to cover one up? My master struggled with his conscience, torn between his duty to his Sultan and his passion for justice.

"My Sultan, my advice ... my advice is as you have already resolved, namely to carry out a full investigation and to bring the murderer to justice, if murder it was. Only then can Khurrem Sultan be fully exonerated."

"Yes, Pasha," our Sultan said with a resigned air, "that is what I had decided." There was a hint in his voice that some other response from my master would have been more welcome but now all he wanted was to bring the interview to a close.

Adam Pasha, aware that he had to speak now or never, quickly posed a question before he could be dismissed. "My Sultan, may I learn who knows of this affair?"

"Rumours have started, Pasha, but only a few know the details." The Sultan counted off on his fingers the names as he spoke, "Mikhail Effendi is one – you may know him, he was the physician responsible for Shireen and her jariyés; then there is Selim Aga, the Chief Eunuch, and his deputy Daud; the Illustrious Queen Mother, of course; Khurrem Sultan; and, naturally, the Lady Shireen's attendants and handmaidens – perhaps half a score of people."

The thought skipping through my pasha's mind was that he seemed to be the only one in Istanbul not to know what had happened. "My Sultan, I am not skilled in these matters and I have many other duties which Your Highness has placed on my humble shoulders. My advice is still to involve Ibrahim Pasha and perhaps Istanbul's Chief of Police ..."

"Don't try my patience, Adam Pasha! This is a matter far too delicate to be left to a numbskull like the Chief of Police and I've other reasons for not involving the Grand Vizier. You must commence your investigations immediately and your deputy can assume your non-Divan duties. I want this matter dealt with quickly and without fuss or excitement. Is that clear?"

"Yes, my Lord". My pasha bowed in submission.

"Adam Pasha," said our Sultan, again the tempered friend rather than the soulless sovereign and master, "you have many fitting qualities of which two are abundantly evident. Your inquiring mind and honesty will vouchsafe a thorough investigation not tainted by corruption and I know that the advice you give me will be impartial. I'm not blind to the palace intrigues going on all about me but I know I can trust you."

"I am but your humble slave," said Adam Pasha. "Your will is mine. I will endeavour with all that little ability I may have to faithfully execute the trust you have placed in me. But ..." My master paused. He was not given to the fawning ways of some courtiers but he was mindful that he could not overstep the boundary of decorum by presuming too much. He carefully, secretively, wiped dry his sweaty palms on his tasteful crimson kaftan. "But if I am to carry out a meaningful enquiry then I must have access to everyone. I must be able to question anyone."

"Naturally. Granted," answered the Sultan without hesitation, much to my Pasha's surprise.

But the Kadiasker was not convinced that the Sultan had considered the full implications of his bold request. So, he sought to establish the limits to the investigation. "I may need to ask Your Majesty questions of a delicate or sensitive nature. Perhaps involving secrets to which I myself am not privy."

"You need not be concerned with that. I've no desire to keep anything from you. But," the Sultan added hurriedly, "I shall decide which pieces of information will assist you in your investigation and which will not."

My master pressed on, throwing caution to the wind. "I may need access to the Imperial Harem."

"Very well. When you want access, I'll carefully consider the merits of your request."

"And I may need to question Khurrem Sultan."

Our Sultan frowned impatiently. "Enough! Adam Pasha, there are great affairs of State that I must attend to. Make your arrangements and return after midday prayers with a plan of action and your list of needs. Go now."

The Sultan turned his back on the Kadiasker and, stroking his clean-shaven chin, once again looked pensively across the Estuary. This time, however, the view of the Genoese tower in the Galata district had been all but obliterated by a thick pall of smoke and leaping flames. Hell's gates had opened on the opposite shore and the city was burning with fury.

IV THE MIDDAY AUDIENCE

The Venetian captain had been taken into custody but about a hundred metres away, around a corner, the gamblers and the garrulous mob had turned a minor scuffle into a small-scale battle. More and more people filled the narrow alleys. Shutters were flung open as on-lookers caught a glimpse of the thrilling spectacle – all for free.

"*Allahu Akbar*! *Allahu Akbar*!" cried out a wild-looking mullah with a bushy beard and beetle black eyes. Suddenly, the fighting stopped and the yells of the querulous crowd dimmed. An expectant hush descended on the mob. As if a miracle had occurred, the blood lust evaporated. The mullah repeated his chant of "God is Great!" The spectators joined in and the mob, not to be outdone, added its shrill tuneless voice in unison.

The mullah raised his fist and seized his chance for momentary fame. "An infidel has defiled a descendant of our Holy Prophet!" he cried. "Will you let him escape his reward in the fires of Hell? Will you stand here and fight among yourselves while this abomination goes unpunished? Find him! He must suffer! Stone him!"

These words stirred the crowd to a murmuring crescendo of anticipation. It burst out into "*Allahu Akbar*", cried as one, even though, in all probability, not even half the crowd shared the religion of the mullah.

The lead was briefly taken up by a middle-aged and middle-spread Jewish merchant, his faith identifiable by his distinctive yellow headdress. Having taken no part in the fracas, he now called out, "Kill the infidel! Kill the infidel!"

his voice reverberating with venom and harbouring a hatred reserved for the torturers of his father and the looters of his inheritance: those miserable Catholics of Spain. He, for one, did not – would not – distinguish between Venetian and Spaniard. And the Orthodox and Armenians of Galata, having nursed and fed a resentment of Catholic Venice for its sack of Constantinople three centuries previously, were no less vocal than the mullah and the Jewish merchant.

The crowd needed no further urging. It surged forward up the hill towards the Tower. The sailor was nowhere to be seen and there was now a dangerous mob looking to vent its anger. Following the path of the mullah and the merchant in their vengeful pursuit, the crowd grew and the narrow alleys sprang to life.

The mob was turning restless. It was a roaming menace. One group of vagrants, bent on looting and mayhem, veered off the main street along a claustrophobic narrowing alley overhung by the upper storeys of smoke-charred wooden houses. The male inhabitants, who had foolishly ventured out onto the street, were forced to run in front of the charging, pulsating, mass.

The throng was heading for the brothel quarter and the mullah was losing his flock to Satan. Leaderless and loose, in the confined alleys of the brothel quarter it was only a matter of time before the mob ran riot.

The pretty and not-so pretty girls, peeking out coyly from their shambling upper floor windows, took fright at the sight of the milling crowd, baying and shouting and banging at their doors. The embarrassed male clientele, discomfited and terrified, hastily struggled into their breeches, grabbed their shirts and hid themselves under Frankish-style beds, behind scanty furniture, or anywhere they could. The girls

33

pulled tight and barred the rough wooden shutters of their windows and the pimps and madams stood guard at the doors.

But the precautions of the pimps and the prostitutes put no one at ease. A door was kicked down, a girl was seized, a golden-haired woman roughly stroked and cruelly teased. Her face filled with fear amid the jeering and the leering of rude men laughing at her tears and the whimpering nature of her pleas. Stripped of her skirt and shed of her blouse she was spun like a top across the floor of the house. The pimp cowered in a corner not daring to help her but urged on her taunters who mauled her and felt her as she screamed and screamed.

Only one bold man, a tall seafarer and a regular customer at the Armenian brothel, stepped forward to defend the girl. This muscular captain of a large Genoese galley, brusquely brushed aside two of the girl's molesters and adroitly threw a third to the ground. But, kicked hard from behind, he stumbled forward and was caught by two large men, a Greek and a Turk, each of a strength equal to his own. The captain searched feebly for his dagger but his arms were held in a strong grip. He was punched and kicked and punched and beaten and kicked and punched until he slumped to the floor barely conscious. He lay there, groaning feebly and oozing blood.

The fight was the signal to the mob to let rip. Turning to wanton destruction, fists flew, bodies were bruised, heads were cracked and teeth were loosed.

A detachment of twelve halberdiers of distinction, led by a flamboyant subaltern who had been promoted for heroism before the walls of Vienna, arrived on the scene. The soldiers took up their positions at the entrance to the brothel quarter and marched at the double three abreast down the narrow street towards the Armenian madam's house.

The sight of the soldiers had, at first, a hauntingly subduing effect. The fist-fights stopped and the brothels emptied out. The officer's extravagant, flowing gestures of direction to his men transfixed the mob. But that was only until two looters spilled onto the street, staggering under the weight of their spoils – pots, pans, the odd candlestick, bric-a-brac but little of any real value.

"Forward men!" ordered the subaltern. "Get the leaders first."

Some of the mob stepped up menacingly and the halberdiers briefly hesitated. The troublemakers, sensing victory and cheering erratically to keep up their spirits, edged closer to the soldiers as the confident officer moved to the head of his body of men.

"Steady, men! Hold your ground!" he ordered with the panache of the Magyar nobleman that he was. They levelled their halberds at the crowd.

"There's too many of them, Sir," cried one of the soldiers.

"Quiet in the ranks!" barked an experienced veteran.

"We're well armed," added the officer, "and in this narrow street we can hold our own." He drew his sword and pointed it at the leader of the mob.

A loose cobblestone was picked up and hurled at the officer, knocking his plumed hat from his head. Unmoved, he held his position. Then another stone struck him full in the face. He was hurt but refused to show it. Instead, in an act of bravado, blood streaming from his cracked left cheek, he stooped gracefully to pick up his hat. As he bent down, the emboldened crowd surged forward.

"Fall back! Fall back!" the officer ordered, as he slashed

with his sword at one of the ringleaders. The attacker's head was almost severed and the mob again seemed to loose heart. But, unaware that behind them had appeared a section of the crowd led by a drunken foul-mouthed vagrant, the soldiers were trapped.

Within minutes it was all over. Crushed between the two groups, the bodies of the butchered halberdiers were piled up at the entrance of the street and set alight, the flames being fed by doors and shutters ripped from the surrounding houses.

The mob ran riot. Every house in the quarter was looted. No one was safe, no house was spared. A small candle overturned and a lethal fire was started. Flames spread unchecked from wooden house to wooden house, from hovel to hovel. Panic spread as fast as the scorching flames. The cries and shrieks of little girls and toothless women could be heard from one end of the quarter to the other. And still some of the yelling mob ran along the narrow streets of the district, stealing whatever came to hand and destroying whatever they could not carry. Like the raging fire, the violent and demented mob was out of control. A dark-haired woman screamed as she fell beneath the feet of the rampaging mob and people fleeing the flames. Those caught in the upper storeys of the narrow houses were throwing themselves out of the windows onto the panicked crowd below and the brothel district was reverberating with the tramp of running feet, the yells of women and the howls of hooligans.

Acrid smoke mixed with the cackles of the deranged mob and the crackle of burning timber. People were choking and frantically seeking an escape route. But the mad mob simply grew bolder. It was intent on mindless destruction. It thrived on violence. Violence was its lifeblood. And the district of Galata was in danger of ceasing to exist altogether.

***

My master briefed his junior colleagues. So much was easy. More difficult was how to explain to the lofty Grand Vizier the anticipated absences from the Divan. Feigning illness was not entirely practical: my master could not conduct a murder investigation from his sickbed and, if he were to attend at the Palace, his presence would obviously be noticed. Even now, my pasha's colleagues were wondering why he, not an abnormally secretive man, was suddenly so reticent about his changed programme. A more plausible story was needed and that was left for me to work out. For now, more pressing problems faced my master.

For the second time in the space of a few hours, Adam Pasha was about to confront his sovereign but there was a pervasive sense of unreality about the whole affair. There were so many unanswered questions. Why could Ibrahim Pasha not be informed? Was the mighty Grand Vizier himself a suspect? Was my pasha even expected to discover the truth? He would not be allowed to interview Khurrem Sultan, so much he had guessed. Without that the investigation was bound to fail. And what credit was my master to gain from all this? Suleyman was renowned as an honest and pious man and yet he could be ruthless when the security of the State was at risk. If the Kadiasker succeeded in discovering the truth, would the Sultan thank him for his efforts? In carrying out the investigation, my pasha was going to make a lot of enemies and if he failed, his career was surely finished. Was he expected to fail? Was he but a naïve, dispensable scapegoat?

The questions were unsettling but at least, as my master

set off once more for the palace, this time there was no Imperial escort.

Friendly and relaxed as Adam Pasha normally was with us, he said nothing at the time about his morning audience either to me or to our *bayraktar*, the imposing Farooq, who accompanied us to the palace. In fact, my master said very little at all as we made our way to the Gate of Peace, the entrance to the semi-public second courtyard of the New Palace. Having dismounted, he alone crossed the courtyard by the most direct of its radiating paths, to the Sultan's audience chamber. From the gate of the third courtyard, he was escorted to the door of the throne room by one of the senior eunuchs, all the time wondering why there were no sentries on duty or page-boys in attendance. Only a lone, handsome chamberlain stood patiently outside the solid inlaid cedar doors of the throne room, in case a messenger was needed.

The Sultan, as if expecting an important diplomatic delegation, sat on a low bejewelled throne with an extravagant fan of peacock feathers sprouting from its back and topped by a golden-fringed canopy. The trappings were regal but he looked lonely and withdrawn, barely hiding the stresses of recent days.

At first, our troubled Sultan seemed not to notice his Chief Justice's presence. He raised his eyes and stared for a few brief moments at Adam Pasha standing in the half-shadows by the door, head respectfully bowed and elegant hands clasped in front of him.

The Sultan spoke softly. "Well, Adam Pasha, do you understand your duties?" And exactly which duties were those, thought Adam Pasha quietly, the duties to his Sultan or the duties of his office? "What shall I do?" continued our

Sultan. My master was caught off guard – the Sultan was not normally given to asking his slaves so directly for advice and yet, within the space of a few hours, he had twice asked his Kadiasker to proffer it.

"My Sultan, first I must see where the girl was found and then I must speak to the person who found her body."

The Sultan had expected as much but none the less was impelled to say, "Pasha, you want access to my Harem? You know that apart from myself, few men are permitted access. There are the eunuchs, of course, and the halberdiers to carry in the wood. The child princes and the royal physicians and …," he said as a smile flickered across his face, "to satisfy a caprice, Khurrem Sultan's dwarf". He looked sternly at Adam Pasha, adding, "I realise that you, too, must have access and so you will have it but I'll not dwell on the consequences of abusing this privilege. Whatever you see and do there you'll keep to yourself." My pasha bowed his head in acknowledgement.

"Your new duties begin immediately," continued the Sultan. "Do you know Mikhail Effendi?"

Adam Pasha silently nodded his head slightly. Mikhail was a leading court physician whose healing skills were known well enough and he and my master had met fleetingly on a few occasions. Fortunately for me, though, the Sultan himself now fulfilled my most urgent task.

"Kadiasker, I've asked Mikhail Effendi to assist you. First, you will need some reason for not attending the Divan and for paying visits to the Old Palace. Mikhail Effendi will vouch that you are suffering from a mysterious illness and, as there is an infirmary in the precincts of the palace, your regular presence there will not be questioned. At least not for a while. More importantly, the doctor examined the lady's corpse and certified the death so he has intimate knowledge which could help you in the investigation. I have instructed him to deal with the burial procedures as quickly as possible so you have no time to lose. Do you have any questions?"

"For the moment, my Sultan, only one. Who was it who found the body?"

"Nilufer, one of Shireen's retainers. I'll send instructions to Selim Aga to allow you access to the Harem for the duration of your investigation and he will accompany you on all your visits there." The Sultan paused before continuing, "Pasha, despite our precautions, your new appointment as investigator is likely to cause much dangerous gossip. The only way we can stop it is to complete the investigation as swiftly as possible. And, now, if you have no more questions, you may go."

Adam Pasha was backing out of the door when the Sultan, fixing his eyes on him, softly but purposefully added, "If you can prove that Shireen died from natural causes, we shall all rest at ease."

***

Needless to say, I was spending my time as usefully as I could – chatting to the cooks caught loitering in the palace gardens in-between meals, soldiers on and off duty, and anyone else who was willing to talk to me. Suffice to say, what I heard did not encourage my appetite.

"What's the gossip?" I asked a friendly, youthful gardener who seemed to be wandering about aimlessly.

"Can you keep a secret?" he replied in a hoarse whisper unbecoming his age.

"Yes, of course," I lied, emulating the raspy tone.

"A plot's been discovered against our Sultan and Ibrahim Pasha's implicated. The word is that all his protégés are

40

under investigation. Heads will roll," he added, rolling his eyes dramatically. "Mark my words, heads will roll."

It was a tale I did not want to hear. My pasha was one of those protégés.

***

Mikhail's entrance had gone almost unnoticed by a still troubled Adam Pasha. The doctor was a short, stout man and appeared even shorter than he was, having his head almost perpetually bowed as if the tendons at the back of his neck had been cut. He was not a Muslim but a Greek freeman from Coron in the Morea, which a few decades earlier had been a Venetian possession. He had entered royal service as a physician some fifteen years ago and succeeded to his current elevated position when his predecessor, a learned Jew, died choking on a fish bone. Mikhail was the only Greek physician in the royal establishment but his appointment was no sinecure, holding as he did several diplomas from the universities of Padua and Bologna where he had studied the works of Galen and Ibn Sina. And, if that were not enough, he was also a renowned and much sought after phrenologist. Despite my master's less than enthusiastic view of that science, I confess I was most impressed when I consulted Mikhail myself a month or so later.

The Sultan respected Mikhail's advice not only in medicinal matters but also in affairs of state. Mikhail knew the Venetians like few others and he was regularly employed as an interpreter and go-between during visiting diplomatic missions from the Illustrious Signory. Encouraged by the Grand Vizier, he also kept close relations with the resident Venetian ambassador, reporting regularly to the Sultan (and independently to Ibrahim Pasha) the intelligence he gleaned.

Mikhail listened attentively as our Sultan described my

41

master's new role. He accepted, in his humble fashion, his role as the Kadiasker's escort. He did so without expression – or at least Adam Pasha noticed none on what little he could see of Mikhail's face.

My master had an uncanny knack for judging a man's character from the most fleeting of meetings. But his contacts with Mikhail Effendi to date had been far too casual even for Adam Pasha to have yet formed an opinion. But, at least my master knew better than to judge Mikhail by the cruel jokes of courtiers, dwelling as they did on his stocky build, his decapitated demeanour, and the manner in which his turban seemed to sit on his shoulders. Mikhail, for his part, took such jibes in remarkably good-humour. A figure of fun he may have been but he was no fool.

***

Up on the hill at Galata, the fire still raged. Outside the immediate trouble spot, another crowd had gathered. Some tried to help to subdue the flames but there was little they could do whilst the frenzied passion of the mob ran its course.

Meanwhile, two companies of smartly turned-out Janissaries had been despatched to bring the riot and the flames under control – and to avenge their murdered comrades. They forcibly dispersed the shuffling crowd of spectators blocking the narrow streets immediately outside the blazing brothel district. Then, one company of Janissaries, naval grappling irons in hand, set to demolishing the ramshackle wooden houses bordering the district in an attempt to create a fire-break to stop the leaping flames from spreading. The second company of soldiers sealed off the district and positioned archers and arquebusiers at the narrow entrances to the area.

Those frightened inhabitants who could escape had already fled and the scorching heat and choking smoke had grown too much even for the rioters to bear. They scrambled desperately to leave. With each falling timber and terrified screech, the collective panic was raised to new heights. The rioters found their exits blocked and at the first sight of them the soldiers opened fire without warning or hesitation. Musket balls and arrows cut into them, round after round. And, as their dead and injured dropped, the exits were further sealed and so was their fate. Those not killed in the hail of arrows and musket fire, fell screaming into the enveloping flames.

The fire was allowed to burn itself out. Mercifully, it did not spread: the prayers of Galata's inhabitants had been heard. True, the Armenian pimps and the Italian prostitutes had to seek temporary abode elsewhere. And the passions of sex-starved sailors and the wealth expectations of the profit-loving Greek-speaking tavern owners would have to wait to be satisfied but the riot and the flames had been contained. In these troubled times, that was good news.

And as my master was about to discover, good news was a scarce commodity.

***

Once outside the audience chamber, the doctor was all unrestrained eagerness. "Well, Pasha, do you suspect foul play?"

"No, Effendi," replied my master, a little taken aback by the doctor's exuberance. "I don't suspect any thing or any one. Our Sultan has his suspicions – that's clear otherwise he wouldn't have involved me – but, what the exact nature of those suspicions is, he hasn't confided in me. We could speculate, of course, but what would that achieve? Better first

43

to discover the facts and then draw the appropriate conclusions, don't you think?"

"Naturally, Pasha, but do not think it is just idle curiosity that makes me ask." My master's interest whetted, his mind cleared for action. "You see," continued the doctor, "the Lady Shireen was a healthy young woman. She could not have been more than twenty-five or twenty-six. There was no warning, no sign of illness. It was all too sudden."

"Perhaps, Effendi, she had been ill but was treated by one of the other physicians without your knowledge," posited my master.

"No, I would have heard. All court doctors make reports to the Chief Physician and we discuss our cases amongst ourselves. I cannot see any obvious explanation for Shireen's death, at least not a natural one. Anyhow," Mikhail added, "you will want to see the corpse before we bury the poor girl, which will be after evening prayers tonight. There is something I want to show you."

***

"Witch!" cried Mahidevran, the tall, doe-eyed mother of Mustafa, the eldest of our Sultan's three sons. "What have you done to my Sultan? Leave him alone. He's mine! He only thinks of me!" She was deluding herself, of course, but what else but their delusions do the women of the Harem have to comfort them?

"Mahida," replied Khurrem, the Sultan's favourite, calmly using the diminutive in a way sure to further enrage her rival, "the Sultan belongs to no one except his Maker. We are his. No one controls him and he has made his choice. Accept it and the will of Allah."

"Who do you think you are!" fumed Mahidevran. "You're nothing but a bought woman. I'm the mother of

44

Prince Mustafa and when he's Sultan, you'll be fish bait."

"Mahida, do you really think Mustafa will ever become Sultan? Oh, how naïve you are! You can kill all the ladies of the Harem and still you will never become the Mother Sultan." Khurrem smiled softly which merely served to throw her rival into a violent rage. She grabbed at Khurrem's rusty-coloured tresses and wrenched at them violently. Khurrem shrieked and tried to kick Mahidevran away but her rival was bigger and stronger and twisted Khurrem to the ground. Both were now rolling on the floor, viciously biting and scratching, hissing and screaming: this was a fight to the finish.

It was fortunate for Khurrem that two strong white eunuchs rushed in to tear them apart. Even so, amid the flailing arms and legs, it was an effort worthy of Chinghiz Khan to separate them and one of the unlucky eunuchs bore the blue and yellow bruises for days after.

***

Shireen's body lay within the Harem of the Old Palace and the palace stood adjacent to Mehmed the Conqueror's Covered Bazaar, about three kilometres or so from the Palace on the Bosphorus.

The Old Palace was built on the site of a Roman monastery and much of it was constructed from masonry and roofing lead taken from the ruins of Roman monuments and buildings. Though coming complete with extensive wooded hunting grounds, it lacked the pleasant sea views of the newer palace and was now largely given over to the Sultan's Harem and quarters for the boy princes.

The layout of the palace was much like its twin: we passed through a more public first courtyard and dismounted before entering the second. As was usual, I went

45

no further, which was fine by me because it gave me the chance to catch up on the gossip of the day.

The entrance to the Harem lay at the far end of the quadrangle. Suleyman's messengers must have moved swiftly to bring news of our approach as my master and Mikhail were met personally by Selim Aga, Chief Eunuch and head of Harem security.

Selim greeted his visitors in traditional Ottoman fashion, slightly bowing his head and touching his forehead and lips with the fingers of his right hand. He was a white Circassian with a twisted lip and misshapen nose, of average height but with a strong physique and quick, intelligent eyes. He was not beautiful but he had the refined and easy manners of a true Ottoman.

"So, Selim Aga," said my master, "you clearly know of our mission."

"Yes, Pasha, I got word a few minutes ago to be your escort to the Harem. I am ordered to give you access to all parts except the quarters of Khurrem Sultan, the Lady Mahidevran and the Illustrious Mother. I know that you have come about the sorry business last night and I am completely at your service."

"I thank you for your cooperation, Selim Aga," replied my master. "Let us first examine the lady's corpse whilst we have time. After that, we can see where the body was found."

Passing unchallenged by the halberdiers on sentry duty at the perimeter gates, Selim Aga led my pasha and Mikhail along the labyrinthine passages of the Harem.

The Harem was a city within a city. It contained mosques; schools; kitchens; an infirmary; and apartments for eunuchs, princes, Hafsa Sultan (the Queen Mother) Khurrem

Sultan and her chief rival, Mahidevran, as well as for the other leading ladies of the Harem. All this was under the overall control of Hafsa Sultan, aided in its administration by the senior women of the Harem and the eunuchs.

For all his experience at Court, a thrill raced through my master as he passed through these forbidden corridors. He was, as the Sultan had plainly told him, privileged to be allowed access. That was an event so rare that it was rumoured that one foreign visitor had paid Mikhail a considerable sum of money to relate details of Harem life (a tale which, no doubt, he had sprinkled liberally with salacious gossip). No one knew whether that story was true or not but what my pasha did know was that he was now passing through a part of the palace that few men, however noble, were permitted to enter.

***

Khurrem stood head-bowed before Hafsa Sultan, an elegantly dressed lady with deep-ochre henna-coloured hair. She had the soft round features of the Crimean Tatars and looked no more than forty but her stern stare and frowned forehead was enough to subdue any lady of the Harem.

"Who put those scratches on your face? Was it Mahidevran?" the Mother Sultan asked Khurrem.

Khurrem answered calmly and coolly. "I fell. It is of no matter, Illustrious Mother."

"Lady, do not think me foolish. My eunuchs tell me everything. Don't you think I have trouble enough?" said Hafsa brusquely. "The Kadiasker … the Kadiasker is in the Harem! I don't know what my son can be thinking of. It's against all tradition." She glared at Khurrem, asking pointedly, "Is this your doing?"

"No, Mother Sultan. Definitely not," replied a penitent-looking Khurrem, "but our fortune-favoured Sultan knows his business. And I know my duty."

"Take care, lady, that your duty does not conflict with mine," was Hafsa's warning, adding, in a sudden change of tone and subject, "The Kadiasker needs a good wife to look after him. Any ideas?"

***

My pasha's barely concealed delight, marvelling at the decorative wall tiles freshly in from the potteries at Iznik, almost had him skipping down the corridors. He eagerly took mental notes of the delicate floral patterns and lively colour, hoping to obtain similar examples for his new house. Still, he wisely concluded that the superlative plasterwork, the product of the finest Italian craftsmen, was far too ornate and less suited to his more modest domestic needs (or his taste). As he passed through one solid cedar door to another, he was also struck by something else: how not all the rooms were so lavishly decorated – many were small, dark, airless and austerely bare.

The route to the infirmary could hardly be termed direct as the small group wound around, sometimes almost in circles, all designed to avoid sight of a single Harem girl. Though my master could hear the suppressed shrieks and giggles of playful girls kicking around a cloth ball in an unseen courtyard, that was the only sign of life within the Harem on their circuitous walk to the infirmary.

Entering the infirmary, there was in front of them a small heavy door to the mortuary. Selim Aga pulled it open and Adam Pasha led the way in, deeply conscious that time was precious. He, above all others, knew that, if Islamic *sharia* law were to be obeyed, burial could not be delayed much longer. And the Sultan was anxious for quick results. Whatever my master needed to do, had to be done quickly.

The mortuary was cramped and bare, save for a marble slab in the centre. On this lay Shireen's body wrapped in a white shroud, embalmed and prepared for burial, with her auburn hair resting in two strands on her breast.

The air was heavy with the smell of camphor and the chamber dark, devoid of natural light save for a few rays filtering in from some high latticed windows. The floor had been freshly washed but the scrubbing had done nothing for the oppressive atmosphere, which was augmented by a single fat candle that flickered in one corner, throwing ghoulish shadows onto the half-tiled wall opposite.

Mikhail approached the body and drew back the soft brown hair that hid part of the dead girl's white-powdered face. "Look, Adam Pasha," he said, pointing to Shireen's lips, "Tell me what you see." My master saw nothing. There were no obvious signs of violence or anything else that seemed out of place. Mikhail dragged the heavy candlestick closer to the face to give a better light and it was then that Adam Pasha noticed some slight bruising around the girl's mouth. He gently felt Shireen's cheeks and delicately parted her mouth to reveal some small cuts behind the lower lip. He cleared away the dusting of powder around the beckoning fleshiness of the lips to reveal a grey, haunting face.

"I see what you mean," he said, forcing the candlestick nearer and peering ever more closely, his face almost touching hers. Candle wax dripped onto Shireen's bloodless lips, as if sealing them forever. The doctor carefully unfolded the rest of the sheet from Shireen's body, taking care not to expose the more private parts. The remaining inspection was perfunctory and revealed nothing of interest.

"When was the body found?" my master asked of Selim

Aga in a hushed voice, as if Shireen might overhear.

"A little less than an hour before daybreak."

"But she died perhaps six hours before she was found," interjected Mikhail. "Six hours and more before I was called to see the body."

"So, perhaps a couple of hours after the late evening prayer, would you say?" asked my master.

"Yes," replied Selim, "about that."

"That would be after most people had gone to sleep. Aga, do you know if the Lady had had any late night visitors?"

"No, Pasha, but her maidservants may know. I will make some enquiries."

"Good," said my master. "Well, I think we are done here. Let's move on to the Lady's quarters."

As the group walked through one of the open courtyards, Adam Pasha could resist temptation no longer. "Effendi, what do you think happened last night?"

"Ah! Kadiasker," replied Mikhail with a hidden smile. "So you _are_ interested in theories. Rumours, too, I dare say! Abu Hanifa will be turning in his grave!" Mikhail's pointed reference was to one of our great jurists now long-gone who would certainly not have approved of any reliance on rumour.

"Yes," replied my master, trying hard to resist an unseemly smile. "I do not appear to have much choice, do I? At least, you can place the rumours in some meaningful context. The examination of the corpse did not reveal much, apart from those slight bruises and cuts. What do you make of them?"

"Pasha, there is gossip, I will put it no higher than that, that the lady had a love affair but not with a man," said Mikhail, pausing for effect. "It was with another Harem girl.

Can you believe it! Those could be love-bites. If so, perhaps she was killed by her lover. If she were a sinner, Allah has taken his retribution."

"Yes, indeed," replied my master solemnly.

"And then, there is another possibility," added Mikhail, not wishing to waste an opportunity for relating tittle-tattle. "Let us imagine her sins were discovered. If so, she may have decided to take her own life."

"Both explanations are plausible," said my master, with obvious scepticism, "but, as you say, it's only gossip."

Selim Aga walking ahead of the investigators, made no effort to join in the rampant speculation. But, with every careful pace, he deliberately and precisely tapped his silver-tipped staff of office on the sonorous stone floor – a warning to every Harem-girl of the stranger's approach. The whole Harem by now knew of my master's mission.

As the group approached the entrance to Shireen's quarters, the squat eunuch standing guard stepped aside and the three officials passed through the door, breaking the imperial seal that kept prying strangers out.

The small, enclosed courtyard, which they entered, was elegantly tiled but otherwise bare, save for a decorative central fountain and a small ablution fountain built into a niche in one wall.

There were four rooms leading off the entrance hall. To the left were two small chambers, set back from the step that divided them from the courtyard. They had neither wooden doors nor windows, candles providing some faint illumination by night whilst by day a certain amount of subdued light filtered in through a modest window in the wall outside. These were servants-quarters, until that day occupied by four jariyés, slave girls in the service of Shireen.

51

Matting and faded carpets were strewn on the floor. Large cupboards built into the wall stored the girls' few belongings and their rolled-up bedding during the day.

Opposite the entrance to Shireen's quarters was a third room, marginally larger than the other two combined. This one had a door and backed onto an external courtyard, giving it the benefit of three windows which threw a mellow light through decorative metal grilles. Adam Pasha tugged at the ironwork: the grilles were firmly in place. This room, too, was sparsely furnished but less so than the others. Rich carpets covered the ground, a small table stood in one corner and a round brazier occupied the centre. By day, the room was used for entertaining other women of the Harem. At night, it served as the sleeping quarters of Nilufer, Shireen's principal jariyé, a sort of chief lady-in-waiting.

The fourth chamber lay to the right of the entrance of the suite of rooms. This room, with its fine Turkish and Persian rugs thrown haphazardly on the floor, was where Shireen had slept and died.

At one end of the chamber, was a small raised section, separated from the body of the room by a waist-high latticed screen, which ran half-way along the platform. This was the prayer area, where Shireen performed her religious devotions and last obeisance. At the opposite end of the room was another, bigger, dais that formed the sleeping area. It was here, stretched out as if asleep, that Shireen's body was found.

In the centre of the room was a broad-brimmed brazier. By the wall, on a low table and covered by a pretty embroidered cloth, was a birdcage. A door at one end of the room led back into the reception room.

Adam Pasha closed the connecting door and paced out

the sleeping chamber silently and with deliberation. He was, for all that, far from certain why he was doing it. This was a policeman's job, he told himself as his eyes swept to and fro across the room. He was a scholarly judge whose skills lay in citing legal precedents and Koranic verses or, left to his own devices, in baking bread, but his talents definitely did not stretch to investigating mysterious deaths. He felt out of his depth, a complete novice at a game the rules of which he had no knowledge and one that he did not want to play.

My master measured the room in one direction and then the other. He came to a stop by the delicately worked brazier in the middle of the room and looked around, hoping some clue would jump out at him. Turning to Selim standing in the doorway, he asked, "Who has been in here since Shireen's body was found?"

"Only two porters – to carry away the body. I have followed His Highness' strict instructions to leave everything untouched and the quarters sealed until further orders. Daud Aga, my deputy, has personally seen to that."

"Can you be sure, Aga, that no one has entered?" continued Adam Pasha.

"After the room was sealed, yes, I can. Before that, the lady's servants would have had access but the lapse of time between the quarters being emptied and a sentry being posted was perhaps no more than fifteen or twenty minutes."

"Good," said my master, though he hardly seemed to be listening. He walked over to the brazier and looked into it. He drew his finely wrought ceremonial dagger from the sheath tucked into his waistband and stirred the ashes. He was disappointed not to find any clues there. Not that he had expected to find any but he felt the disappointment all the same. He walked over to the birdcage and wiped his dagger clean with a corner of the birdcage cover. This he then purposefully lifted, almost as if he were performing some magic trick. Now, here was something at last.

"Effendi, come take a look at this," he called over to his companion who, overcome by boredom, had sat down on the sleeping platform and would have nodded off to sleep but for the call. "Selim Aga, you, too. What do you make of it?" Excitedly, my master pointed to the bottom of the cage.

"A dead bird," replied Mikhail with a yawn and a hint of sarcasm.

"Yes, Effendi. As you so correctly say, a dead bird. A parrot to be precise. But don't you think it strange that it died on the same day as her ladyship?"

"But it did not die on the same day," interjected Selim Aga. "It died the day before, but her ladyship would not get rid of it. She was very fond of the bird and was clearly upset by its death."

"How so?" inquired my pasha.

"She was very sad. She stayed cooped up in this room for hours and refused to see anyone or eat anything. She only left her quarters once, to make her report to His Highness which, as Treasurer of the Harem, she was obliged to do at least once a week."

"Of course," mumbled Adam Pasha, "she was the Treasurer." He repeated the words over to himself. "Naturally, in addition to influence she must have amassed some wealth, jewels and the like? Where are her jewels now?"

"Most of them were kept in the Harem Treasury but, no doubt, she kept some pieces here," replied Selim Aga. "But, Pasha, if you are going to suggest that Shireen was killed during some robbery, please instantly dismiss any such thought. It's impossible within the Harem. Where would a thief go? How would a thief escape? How could such a theft be conducted under the gaze of so many, shall I say … inquisitive women? And who would be mad enough to incur the wrath of His Highness for some baubles, however valuable they might be? No, Pasha, you are not married. You do not understand the Harem. It could not happen here."

"Yes, I am sure you are right. But, nonetheless, where are her 'baubles'?"

Selim stepped over to a cupboard and opened the doors, silently praying that the jewels would be where they ought to be. And so, thankfully, they were. He pulled out a small wooden chest and opened it.

"You must forgive me, Selim Aga," apologised Adam Pasha. "It's my suspicious lawyer's mind." The delicately inlaid box was brimful of rich and brightly coloured jewels. Evidently, no theft had been committed.

But Selim Aga turned pale.

"No, Pasha, I was wrong!" he said. "There was a pendant necklace set with a particularly large and fine pearl. Her ladyship liked to wear it but we didn't find any jewellery on her body and it's not in the casket."

My master was both startled and delighted. Here, at last, might be a clue. "Selim Aga," he asked, "Who would have known about the contents of the box?"

"Nilufer, her ladyship's principal maid would certainly have known. I shall have her sent for and questioned immediately."

"Very well," concluded Adam Pasha with renewed vigour. "Please see to it."

***

"So," said Mikhail, scratching his right ear, "it looks as if the

55

girl was killed for this jewel. No doubt by some jealous, grasping woman. It may sound heartless but we can count our blessings if that is the case. It provides us with a simple solution. We will win credit for clearing Khurrem Sultan's name and then we can both get back to our real work."

"Indeed. That could be it," said my master.

Selim returned, pretending not to have heard this frank exchange of views.

"Pasha," said the eunuch, "Nilufer is not available. She is preparing the Illustrious Mother's bath. Perhaps you could return at a more convenient time."

Adam Pasha tried to hide his disappointment. Moving over to the sleeping platform, he sat down where Shireen had lain hours earlier. As he rested a hand upon a silken crimson cushion, the cushion began to slip sideways. His hand touched something, something metallic, something cold, something strange. Curious, very curious …

V THE DOG AND THE PARROT

Adam Pasha returned to the Harem the following day.

"Selim Aga?" he asked the broad-shouldered Circassian, once more his escort. "Why would Shireen hide her ceremonial dagger under her pillow? That's not normal, is it?"

"No, Pasha. It is not normal but she was no common harem girl."

"So, what sort of girl was she? I've barely started my investigation and I'm already hearing sordid tales of lovers, male or female, take your pick. Do you believe any of it? Or is it just grubby gossip?"

"Pasha," replied Selim, "the Harem contains many beautiful women who ordinarily don't even sniff a chance of male companionship until they are married off to this or that palace official. Would having lovers be so unusual – or so unnatural? But you asked me what I believe. I have heard the rumours," he said, adding, with the hint of a smile, "even before Mikhail Effendi mentioned them. But until a few weeks ago, it would have been unthinkable. So, no, I don't believe them. It is gossip. Malicious gossip is all it is."

Arriving at the door to Shireen's quarters, Selim dismissed the eunuch on guard and, entering the enclosed courtyard, they sat for a moment on the dry edge of the still marble fountain.

"The Lady," continued Selim, "was a most handsome woman and very accomplished. She was intelligent and remarkably well-informed about the affairs of the world outside these walls," he said as he made a grand sweeping gesture with his arms. "She was much in demand within the Harem for her knowledge of the infidel courts and their fashions but her popularity soon spawned jealousy. That jealousy grew in step with her power. Arriving here only five years ago, aged nineteen, her rapid rise to Treasurer was unprecedented. It's natural that some asked "why?" whilst others, coveting the position themselves, resented her rise."

"She was a passenger on a galley when she was captured, was she not?" asked Adam Pasha.

"Yes, and there began her fateful journey to the Harem," replied Selim.

"Was that before Pavia?"

"Pavia?" It seemed an odd question to Selim Aga.

"I heard she was a cousin to the King of France. He did not fare too well against the Spanish at Pavia."

"Oh, I see. You mean the Battle of Pavia. Shireen was captured after Pavia". He paused, waiting for Adam Pasha to lead him.

"Please continue, Selim Aga. I apologise for interrupting you. After the lady became Harem Treasurer, what then?"

"There is not much more to tell. As Treasurer, she could dispense favours and she acquired power which most Harem girls can only dream of. And yet there was something strange about her sudden rise. But perhaps ...."

Selim, looking and feeling uncomfortable, broke off abruptly. His natural instincts cautioned him against indiscretion.

"Please...," implored my master. "What do you mean?"

"Well, Pasha, positions of eminence in the Harem administration are normally held by women who are, to put it delicately, past their prime and unlikely to catch the eye of His Highness. Yet Shireen was young and attractive. As

Harem Treasurer, she had custody of the Sultan's jewels and rich wardrobe as well as the economy of the Harem. That brought her into regular contact with both the Sultan and the Illustrious Mother in order to make her official reports. She was, what's more, politically astute and took full advantage of her meetings with the two most powerful people in Istanbul.

"In the hours that she waited to be summoned by our Sultan, she would have her hair brushed endlessly. She always looked like a princess but, for an audience with the Sultan, she was at her very best – not a hair out of place, not a crease in her pink silk gown, not a blemish on her face. She was as near to perfection as a man could desire. With long brown tresses cascading over her shoulders, a finely-curved figure, her high-cheeked face full of life and the laugh lines creasing around her thin-lipped mouth, a man would have to be blind not to be charmed by her."

"But the Harem is full of pretty girls," interjected Adam Pasha. "There surely must have been more to her rapid rise than good looks alone?"

Selim lowered his rather shrill voice almost to a whisper. "There are two possibilities and either, I think, could be true. One is that she was used by Hafsa Sultan, the Illustrious Mother, to counter the growing influence of Khurrem, our Sultan's consort." Selim paused and then added as an aside, "You may know, he has taken no one else to his bed for some time." He paused again, as if searching for some appropriate word or phrase. "And, if the plan was to break Khurrem's hold, it was succeeding – until two nights ago. As Treasurer, Shireen had both power and influence. But, in the constant struggle for His Highness' favour she needed all the power and influence she could muster and no one could give her more of either than Hafsa Sultan. So, they needed each other. But ...." Now Selim once more broke off his narration. He looked towards the door, stood up from the edge of the fountain and paced around nervously.

"Adam Pasha," he said, looking my master directly in the eye. "Your honesty is not in doubt. But in a position like mine one requires discretion. Are you also discreet? I have been ordered to help you to the best of my abilities and I am happy to do so – I must do so – but will you swear to me that everything I tell you will be kept in the strictest confidence? You know the delicacy of my position."

"You have nothing to fear, Selim Aga, your confidences are safe with me. But tell me about Khurrem."

"I am not sure what to say. She is more pretty than beautiful but above all extremely elegant. Elegant in everything she does or says. She's a Ruthenian with great cunning and intelligence ... and great charm."

"Charm? I've heard of her scheming and plotting but not of her 'charm'," said my pasha, adding with a sigh, "I regret I don't spend enough time in court circles to catch all the gossip."

"Oh, yes, Pasha, the Smiling One has charm, considerable charm. She also has wit and great vitality. She has used her cunning to manoeuvre herself into the position of His Highness' favourite. In so doing, she has displaced Mahidevran, the mother of his first son, Prince Mustafa. That was no easy task. Our Sultan was very fond of Mahidevran – indeed, he still is. She has served him well. To have broken this bond of loyalty and love took much more than guile. To be sure, Khurrem has fine qualities befitting of a queen.

"Yet, I cannot deny that there is no love lost between the two rivals. Did you hear of yesterday's wretched squabble?"

This was another bit of gossip that had eluded my pasha.

"No, of course not," continued Selim Aga. "They were actually thrashing about on the floor, tearing and scratching at each other. It was unbelievable. Khurrem got the worst of it physically but won the real victory – she has gained His Highness' sympathy and, if it were ever in doubt, her position is now beyond the reach of any rival."

Selim Aga paused to reflect, realising that Adam Pasha could have only the vaguest knowledge of life in the Harem. "You see, Adam Pasha, life here is hard. True, the women wear silks threaded with gold and velvets hung with pearl buttons. They carry rich jewels in their hair and bathe in fine perfumes. But if you have borne the Sultan a male child and are not the first favourite, you are fighting for life: not for your own life but for that of your son. You are a lawyer and you know that since the Conqueror's time the prince who succeeds as Sultan will have his brothers put to death. And each woman in the Harem knows it, too. It's the maternal instinct that drives them in their conspiracies to usurp the position of an established favourite. A mother who is not the favourite knows that her son's life will end with our Sultan's.

"Even without such a desperate incentive to fight for power, life in the Harem for most girls lacks any real purpose unless the favour of His Highness can be won. For one thing, there's a financial incentive – you become a favourite, your stipend increases; you give birth to a child, another pay rise; and, give birth to a male child – well, you are in Heaven, for a while at least. That in itself is enough to breed dangerous rivalries.

"Look here, Adam Pasha, there are about 250 women in the Old Palace Harem. Perhaps about 200 are simple jariyés, domestic slaves with few prospects. Take away the senior women and that leaves about a dozen girls with the potential to scale the ladder to the Sultan's bed. But you know our Sultan as well as anyone. He only has eyes for Khurrem. Whilst the other girls think they might have a chance of success, they will keep their intriguing within limits. But, once that chance evaporates, pure envy and jealousy takes over. And, so, Khurrem beware …

"But," continued Selim Aga, "it would be unwise to underestimate Khurrem or to see her simply as a grasping schemer. She is not. She can be vengeful, to be sure, but she is unusually level-headed and even-tempered. It is hard not to like her. And she can be a good friend. Remember that our Sultan had two concubines when he was governor of Manisa. One was Mahidevran; the other was the childless Gulfem. Gulfem now lives with the ladies in Khurrem's service and the two of them are friends."

My master heard out the Aga. He liked the eunuch and he knew that, concealed by the high-pitched voice, was a man of feeling. But time was not on his side and he had to return to the facts of the case.

"So, Aga," he said. "You believe that Hafsa Sultan was setting up Shireen as a rival to Khurrem?"

"That is one possibility. The Mother Sultan rules the Harem. She can make a girl's fortune or destroy it. And the growing influence of Khurrem is an evolving threat to her power. I can't believe Khurrem would ever directly attempt to oppose Hafsa Sultan but she knows that the Illustrious Mother, not to mention the Grand Vizier, favours Mahidevran's son for the succession. And, so, the Illustrious Mother may have tried to find a rival to the Smiling One, someone with similar qualities, who might break the strong bond between the Sultan and Khurrem. That someone could have been Shireen. That may not have been enough to regain His Highness' favour for Mahidevran but it would at least have ensured her son, Prince Mustafa, would succeed our Sultan."

"Are these mere suspicions, Selim Aga", asked Adam Pasha, "or is there any real evidence to support them?"

"Some. Hafsa Sultan showed a particular interest in Shireen almost since the first day she was brought to the Harem. The girl had a pleasing manner. Just like Khurrem, she was always smiling and happy. The fact that she was now a captive did not seem to bother her. Hafsa Sultan saw personally to her training and, being of noble birth, Shireen already possessed some of those accomplishments expected of a senior woman in the Harem. But the Sultan will not love anyone but Khurrem. How, then, could Her Majesty bring Shireen to her son's notice? Here Hafsa Sultan showed her own consummate political cunning by making Shireen the Harem Treasurer."

"Well," said Adam Pasha, "I must be so naive – I had no idea of the web of intrigue spreading through the Harem."

Both men now briefly fell silent. My master lifted himself slowly from the edge of the still fountain, smoothing out the creases in his grey-green kaftan. "But, Aga, you said you had a second theory."

"I did, Pasha, didn't I? The cynics say that the Queen Mother's interest in Shireen was simply designed to keep a close eye on her. They say that one rival to Mahidevran was already one too many."

"Really?" asked my master, genuinely surprised.

"Yes. And you know why? Because of her lifestyle – nothing about it made sense. For one thing, Shireen had few jariyés. A woman in her position could normally expect an entourage of a couple more. Perhaps the small number of jariyés can be put down to the rapidity of her rise to the top. But, then again, there is the fountain."

"Fountain?"

"Yes, fountain. This courtyard has a fountain in it – we have been sitting on it. That is a privilege normally conferred only on the Mother Sultan. And then there is the daily stipend: that is rumoured to be in the region of 300 *akches*, perhaps half as much again as one might expect. Shireen's position was full of contradictions. Why?"

"Why indeed, Selim Aga?"

"Clearly, someone with influence was supporting her but someone else was also trying to stem her rise. Whether it was the Queen Mother or Khurrem Sultan, and who was doing what, I cannot say. And, for all that, everything is conjecture.

"I am truly sorry but it sums up the Harem. Still, I hope that some of this has proved useful. Do remember that even those of us who live within the confines of the Harem do not have intimate first-hand knowledge of the hopes and desires of its female inhabitants."

"Well, Aga, I'm grateful for your candid insights and I hope we will continue to deal frankly together."

"Pasha," replied the eunuch, "I shall do whatever I can to help."

The two men walked towards Shireen's private chamber. Once inside, my pasha went straight to the birdcage.

"Selim Aga," he asked. "Was the bird very old?"

"I do not know, Pasha. One of the lady's former servants may be able to answer that. Not more than a year, I should have thought. Why do you ask?"

"Is it sheer coincidence that this parrot dies the day before Shireen? I am intrigued."

"Not such a mystery, I think. The Lady Shireen had a cat – a present from His Highness, which she always kept by her side. She was very fond of it but, I fear, a little careless. As you see, the cage door is open. I am sure the cat is the culprit."

Adam Pasha, lifting the blue birdcage cover, bent down to inspect both the cage and the rotting parrot more closely. Straightening up again, he said, "This bird was not killed by a cat. No ruffled feathers, you see. No signs of a fight. So, unless the parrot died of fright, I think the cat is exonerated."

"Well, natural causes, then. I remember a few years ago a couple of parrots, of such beauty and colour, were given to the Sultan as gifts but both took sick and died within six months of captivity."

"Possibly, possibly," muttered my master. "Where is this cat, anyway? I've seen no cat."

"I do not know, Pasha. There was no sign of it when her ladyship's body was found. But it always slept curled up at the foot of her bed – that was common knowledge in the Harem."

"Did she have any visitors on the fateful night?"

"I have not heard so but her former servants should know, especially Nilufer, her ladyship's chief jariyé. They have all been transferred to the service of other ladies and Nilufer herself is now in Hafsa Sultan's service."

"Interesting," muttered Adam Pasha. Stooping, he was once again examining the birdcage. From the floor of the cage, he picked out some crumbled sticky, sweet halva. He wrapped it carefully in a yellow silk handkerchief and placed it inside his tunic. On the table, next to the cage, lay a bowlful of light honey-coloured halva sitting in small green silk square. This he also tied up and tucked away in his tunic.

Then he paced out the room once more, sat down on the sleeping platform and cut a plan of the suite of rooms on a wax tablet he had brought with him. Now and then he cursed as his draughting skill proved inadequate and he was forced to smooth over the soft wax surface and start again. The plan complete, he and Selim Aga walked out into the fountain court.

"Just one more question," said Adam Pasha, as they stood by one of the courtyard windows. "Could someone have entered these quarters without being seen?"

"Not impossible," replied Selim. "But probably only late at night." Just then, a skinny eunuch shuffled into the courtyard and whispered something to Selim. The Aga waved him away and, turning to the pasha, said, "It looks as if Nilufer is busy today also. I am sorry that your visit has been wasted. You will have to return another day."

"Thank you, Selim Aga. The visit was far from wasted. I am finished here at least. There is no need to reseal these rooms. You can release your sentry if you wish. And clear away the parrot."

As the two stepped out from the cool shadows of the Treasurer's quarters into the bright warm sunshine of the open courtyard, my master heard the purr of a cat. He turned his head to catch sight of a cream and dark-brown Siamese cat sitting on a narrow stone staircase.

"Where do these stairs lead to?" asked my master.

"To Hafsa Sultan's and Prince Mustafa's quarters on one side and to Khurrem Sultan's on the other," replied Selim.

Adam Pasha approached the cat cautiously, as if it were a beautiful woman. "Now where have you been my pretty one?" he asked as he stroked it. The cat purred again and licked his hand. "You know what happened to your mistress, don't you?" The cat lifted a paw and placed it gently on my master's arm. On an impulse, he picked it up and, led by Selim Aga, walked away, gripping the wax tablet in one hand and pussycat, balanced on his shoulder, firmly steadied by the other.

Why, Adam Pasha wondered as he exited the Harem, was the Queen Mother preventing him from seeing Nilufer?

***

So, Adam Pasha had a new pet. He sat for hours stroking and talking to the silly animal. Well, the cat may have found a new home and a new master but it did not have a new servant. If my master wanted to pamper it, that was his prerogative but I did not have to. I do not like cats; never have done – just like women, they purr sweetly when they want something, have no substance under all that fur and look their prettiest just before they scratch. And this one could scratch. It was cunning though – it never scratched anyone in front of the Kadiasker.

To its disgust (but not entirely to mine) the animal was tipped out of the pasha's lap onto the floor as my master pulled the two halva-filled handkerchiefs from his kaftan. He laid both on a small writing table, carefully untying the knots and gently unfolding the yellow and green silk squares. He took a handful of honeyed halva from the green silk and brought it to his nose. He sniffed, once, twice. He took a tiny quantity and placed it on the tip of his tongue and then inside his lower lip. What he was expecting, I do not know, but nothing happened. He carried out the same procedure with the halva from the yellow silk with the same result.

"It's no good, Murat", said the pasha. "The halva is far too sweet and flavoured with almonds. I can't tell anything by tasting such tiny quantities." He thought for a second and then cried, "Fetch me a stray dog!"

Now, cats my master seemed to have developed a liking for but never had he let a dog slip into the house. It is not that he did not like dogs but houses are, so I had always thought, for people. That principle was about to be thrown, so to speak, to the dogs. Whether my master now planned to keep an entire menagerie, I did not know and I did not care. In fact, I saw the dog as a potential ally against that cat, whose notions of grandeur exceeded those of Alexander of Macedon himself.

But catching a stray dog is no easy matter. I could think of better ways of spending an afternoon, at the baths perhaps or with Elizabeth at the brothel (what I said earlier about women should not be taken to apply to Elizabeth). Where were the dogs, though? Eventually, I found some – big ones, little ones, yappy ones, and smelly ones, all gnawing, pawing, leaping and defecating over the residue of Byzantium's bygone monuments. I was no match for the big ones and chasing the little ones had me squirming in the dust. I must have looked like a madman because two people threw coins at me in charity. I would gladly have died for my pasha but I swore that, if ever he needed to find another dog, I would get someone else to do it.

It took me almost two hours to get hold of one. I was, though, quite pleased with my handiwork. My pasha, too, would be pleased, I thought. It was a yellow mangy specimen with big, sad, brown eyes (just like Elizabeth's when I am about to leave her).

"Here I am, my Pasha", I spluttered as I half-carried and half-dragged in the pathetic fleabag and set the whimpering animal in front of my master. I brushed down my clothes as best I could with my hands but I felt too tired and sweaty to pick off all the blonde hairs that littered my red kaftan. At least the cat made a hasty retreat, so praise Allah for small mercies.

"Such looks, Murat. So disdainful," chuckled my master. He was amused, I was not.

"I am sorry I took so long, my Pasha, but stray dogs have suddenly become a scarce commodity. Is dog-meat halal? If you ask me, that butcher who supplies us with mutton has found a new source of meat. This scruffy excuse for a dog was the best I could catch."

"He'll do very well, Murat. I don't want to eat him, just feed him a little. Now bring him over to me."

I grabbed the whining animal by the scruff of the neck and dragged him over to my pasha. Needless to say, I was shocked by the whole affair but tried hard to hide it. I failed.

"You needn't look at me like that," said my pasha, "I'm not mad. And handle the dog gently."

Adam Pasha patted the beast softly on the head, muttering "Poor little mutt," as he picked up a chunk of halva from the square of green silk. The mongrel at first sniffed suspiciously at the morsel. He nibbled it, and then happily lapped it up, his tongue searching out every last crumb. Wagging his tail in joy, he looked up expectantly at my pasha. My master leant forward with a piece of halva from the yellow handkerchief. But, before the dog had a chance to taste the second morsel, it was seized with convulsions. It vomited violently, curled up into a ball and then sprang open like coiled wire, writhing in horrible agony. It twisted round its head and died with a final yelp. Poison - the halva was poisoned.

VI NILUFER'S TALE

Adam Pasha knelt down and stroked the dead dog's head, tears welling-up in his eyes. He called out for one of the servants to carry away the contorted carcass and to clear up the mess.

It had been eight years since Adam Pasha had bought me in the slave market and in all that time I had seen nothing so extraordinary. Forget the pasha's efforts in the kitchens, now he had taken to poisoning dogs. Was the world going mad, or was I (and should I be more careful about eating the pasha's bread)? The pasha said nothing about it. Whatever clues the death of the dog had raised in his mind, he was not confiding in me. That, too, had never happened before. But, as every good slave knows, patience brings its own rewards.

***

"Adam Pasha! Adam Pasha!" hollered Mikhail from the courtyard, sitting uneasily astride his grey mare. He was patting her neck gently with one hand and waving at my pasha's window with the other. Now, the doctor was an odd-looker at the best of times and he was not a gainly horseman. Trying to wave as he leant forward in his saddle hardly made him more impressive and it almost caused him to slide off his mount. In fact, as a Christian, he should not have been riding at all but everyone in the Sultan's service in Istanbul seemed to do so, Muslim, Christian, and Jew alike. In the eastern provinces such arrogance would have raised more than a few eyebrows but, in cosmopolitan Istanbul, nobody seemed to care two figs.

The pasha walked out onto the verandah that stretched

along the upper storey of the house. "Greetings, Effendi. To what do we owe this pleasure?"

"We must ride to the palace! Quickly! We have no time to lose."

***

"Do you still want to see Nilufer?" the doctor asked, struggling with the reins as his horse violently shook her head to dislodge an irritating fly.

"Of course, Effendi. Can you doubt it?"

"Well, I heard this morning that Hafsa Sultan is plotting to have the poor girl married off to some courtier or other. If you do not see her now, it may be too late. I took the liberty of telling Selim Aga that you would be coming to see her today. The Aga said he would try to arrange a meeting. I do hope I did the right thing."

"Effendi, you're a marvel."

"Unfortunately," continued Mikhail, "I cannot join you myself. There is no illness in the Harem and I have no other reason to be there. Everything, however, is arranged with Selim Aga so you should have no problem of access. Still, there is one thing I would like to ask of you."

"Of course, Effendi. Anything."

"I am curious, Pasha. I have no right to ask but I would like to know how your meeting with Nilufer goes. Call it idle curiosity, though I may be able to shed some light on what she tells you. But if that would cause you difficulties ..."

"Not at all, Effendi. It's the least I can do." Adam Pasha welcomed the help and, knowing of the doctor's interest in gathering (and selling) gossip, was only too pleased to oblige. "Effendi," he added, "with your knowledge of the court and the Harem, we'll make a good team. Without your help, I doubt I'll get very far."

71

"Pasha, I am delighted to be of help. But now I must get back to the pharmacy."

"One question," said Adam Pasha as Mikhail's horse was turning away. "Can you tell me anything about Nilufer? I know nothing about her."

"You will find it hard to keep your eyes off her," replied the doctor with a smirk.

"Why? Has she got warts or something?"

"Girls of the Imperial Harem do not have warts," said Mikhail. "Nilufer is a very beautiful girl – that's obvious even through her veil. She's of a high-born family, taken captive by Khairadeen, our Governor in Algiers, who presented her to His Highness as a gift. May Allah grant the Red Beard many more such victories." Mikhail's occasional references to Allah may have sounded strange on the lips of a Christian, even one in the service of the Sultan, but each syllable dripped with sincerity. "She's an intelligent girl," continued the doctor, "and only twenty-two or twenty-three. A truly worthy prize."

"How do you know so much about her?"

"Pasha, she's a beautiful girl but not in the best of health. I suspect she would have been a potential consort for our Sultan if her health had been better."

"What does she suffer from, Effendi?"

"Difficult to say. I have tried various treatments, none of which have had much success. I am a palace physician, not the palace magician. I am hardly allowed to make a proper or thorough examination of a Harem girl. I can't work miracles."

"Was she long in Shireen's service?"

"Not so long. About a year or so. She was one of Khurrem Sultan's retainers before that but her growing ill-health persuaded Khurrem to transfer her to lighter duties with Shireen – in exchange, no doubt, for detailed reports on her new mistress. And now, Pasha, I really must go."

***

From behind the thick Harem walls came the sound of gentle laughter as Khurrem, our Sultan's favourite, waddled across the floor of her reception room in a cruel imitation of a young girl trying, and failing, to learn the art of courtly dance. Her friends giggled as the loping of a pregnant camel turned effortlessly into the light touch of a graceful gazelle. Khurrem, the elegant mother of two princes royal, to gasps of admiration and warm applause, sensuously curved her delicate petite body, twisting and swinging her arms like rippling waves. The dance came to an abrupt end when the Chief Linen Mistress entered the room. The older woman bowed her head, her henna-dyed hair showing under her cap. She waited silently, apprehensively, but Khurrem was in a gay mood. She skipped jauntily around the Linen Mistress, coming to a stop squarely in front of her.

"The matter is forgotten," said Khurrem dismissively with a spirited smile, the laugh lines creasing around her thin lips and ending in little dimples. With a sweep of her arm and a toss of her long, rusty brown hair, she moved lightly between the Linen Mistress and the door. "You may go," said the Sultan's favourite. As the Linen Mistress moved to the door, Khurrem turned round smartly, treading on the woman's toes. But it was the Linen Mistress who, stifling a cry, apologised and hobbled out of the room. She knew from the day that Khurrem had become a royal favourite that Khurrem would reap her revenge, revenge for those bygone days when the Linen Mistress had admonished her for allowing her high spirits to interfere with her lessons. It was only the power of the Queen Mother that prevented the old woman's life being a complete misery. Khurrem was fair and even-tempered but Khurrem did not forget. And Khurrem did not forgive.

Soon, however, it was Khurrem's turn to be summoned – by the Queen Mother.

***

Selim Aga led Adam Pasha to an empty room. It was small and sparsely furnished, light filtering in from two high openings. Rows of velvet cushions lined the wall and a tasteful Ushak carpet added a dash of colour and comfort.

"Please wait here, Adam Pasha," instructed Selim. "Nilufer will be brought to you. It would be most improper for you to be left alone with her but I recognise the need for privacy so I have asked permission to dispense with the usual guard and to stand watch myself."

As he waited, my pasha looked around him. He was trying hard to imagine what life in a harem was like. As a bachelor, a state of affairs that I had worked hard to maintain, he had no real idea. The harems of his friends were closed to him and, not being born a Muslim, he had not been raised in one.

Life, I imagine my pasha thinking, must be pretty dull in the Imperial Harem, a small city full only of women fantasising about trifles and trinkets. For the most intelligent and gifted, there were administrative roles and for the lesser minds the trinkets and baubles would probably suffice. But that still left a large number of women who were not allowed to have ambitions, loves, or lives beyond the Harem walls – at least not until the Queen Mother approved a marriage outside the Harem. The tall and beautiful Mahidevran, the Moon Favoured, was a loving and devoted mother but one who had tempered her ambitions, at least until Khurrem came along. That threat from the Smiling One she would not, could not, let pass without challenge. But the favour of the moon was no match for the good humour and companionship of the smiles of her rival.

Khurrem and Mahidevran were so different. Khurrem was confident, determined, quick-witted, worldly and sure-footed (and not just in the toe-treading arena). And then there was that captivating smile. (One smile from Elizabeth could melt the heart of a *jinn* and I imagine Khurrem's was rather like that.) Mahidevran was physically more attractive but no match for Khurrem in intellect. By all accounts, she had no desire to get involved in affairs of State but her mother's instincts told her that, if she did not out-manoeuvre Khurrem, her beloved boy would not survive his father's death.

Selim Aga's return interrupted my pasha's musings. He ushered in Nilufer. Now here was a beauty: veil or no veil, this was a woman of exceptional loveliness.

She lowered herself gracefully onto a cushion in a corner where the sunlight played on her hair and face. Adam Pasha sat on another cushion at some distance away and Selim Aga stood guard outside, with the door prudently left ajar.

Nilufer was veiled but her refined and delicate features were evident through the two loosely tied pieces of gauze. Her full-length pink silk gown, tantalisingly elegant, hid none of the contours of her body. On her head she wore a grey silk cap and her rippling auburn hair only partly hid a sapphire and ruby clasp. But it was her eyes that were so captivating – two large enticing hypnotic pools of watery brilliant blue. But for her ill-health, Nilufer could truly have been a consort to the Sultan.

"Nilufer," said my master, a little unsteadily, "I know you must be distressed by the death of your mistress but I must ask you some important questions." Nilufer muttered her consent.

"You worked for Shireen for about a year, is that not so?" asked my pasha. Nilufer nodded in agreement. "During that time," continued Adam Pasha, "were you on good terms with your mistress?"

"Yes, Pasha. I was content. My duties were less arduous than with Khurrem Sultan. You see, I have not been well. With my former mistress, I was always exhausted trying to keep pace with her. Shireen was less demanding." The young woman's voice was so soft and gentle. There was no sign of grief – just a serene calm.

"Was there anything more to your relationship? Anything unusual or abnormal?" asked the pasha shifting uncomfortably on his cushion.

"No, Pasha, there was not," replied Nilufer firmly but with a honey-coating all her own. "There has been a lot of gossip in the Harem about Shireen. About lovers amongst the Harem girls and the eunuchs. I have heard it all. Some say she was depraved ...."

"And what do you say?" interrupted my Pasha.

"Shireen had visitors late at night, certainly, but I saw nothing unusual in it. The gossip is absurd."

"Who were the late-night visitors?"

"I have no idea, Pasha. I was always in my room. I occasionally heard voices but could not say whose. Perhaps it was only that twittering bird." That answer was unconvincing but my pasha let it pass. A beautiful woman always has the advantage (except in the company of another beautiful woman).

"On the night of Shireen's death," continued my master, "did she have any visitors then? Did you hear any voices or unusual sounds?"

"I heard nothing. But Fatima, one of the apprentices, saw someone leave late into the night. She thought it was a woman, veiled and not too tall."

"Then I must talk to Fatima."

"But that is impossible, Pasha. She has been sent away by Khurrem Sultan to the Palace at Edirne."

"I don't understand. Why send an apprentice girl so far away? And with such haste?" Bemused though he was, my pasha continued the questioning. "You were happy in the service of Shireen but ...." My master paused, uncertain how to phrase the question without causing offence. Nilufer saved him any embarrassment.

"Pasha, are you wondering why I am not heartbroken, stricken with grief, shattered with remorse? Not all women are feeble and ignorant. I liked the lady Shireen and she was good to me. But she is dead and I am alive. I rejoice that I have life. How can you understand, Pasha? You are not caged. Your only sight of the world is not an occasional trip to the bazaar or another palace or a stroll in the palace gardens. Some like life this way and others tolerate it but," Nilufer added, tearing at the jewelled clasp in her hair, "I am suffocating in these silks and jewels."

Such passion, such spirit. A bottled jinn. Here, thought Adam Pasha, was a woman with vitality. He liked Nilufer. He was drawn to Nilufer. He wanted Nilufer. He wanted to possess her. Was it passion on my pasha's part? Or was it simply a man's desire to collect objects, be it rare manuscripts or horses or whatever? It is strange that woman rarely want to possess people or objects. Except, that is, for mothers. Mothers like to possess children. (And Elizabeth, she hankers after rings, bangles and necklaces.)

Nilufer was right: my pasha had no inkling of a woman's life. Motherless from the age of six and without sisters, how could he imagine what life was like for a woman? He, of course, had heard petitions by and against women and it was natural for the woman to get the benefit of the doubt. A divorced woman would leave his court with her dowry in tact and the daughter of a wealthy father would get her rightful inheritance. But how could he have known how mind-crushing harem life would be for a gifted and intelligent woman like Nilufer? What the pasha could understand, however, was how a clever woman's energies could be diverted into the Harem's internal power struggles. Court intrigue was something he knew of well enough.

The pasha's lack of experience with women, the beguiling Gulshan notwithstanding, made him uncomfortable in Nilufer's presence. He shifted nervously throughout his conference with only his meagre beard hiding his blushes. He tried as best he could to concentrate.

"Nilufer, believe me, I'm trying hard to understand you and I do sympathise with you. Though I can do nothing to change your circumstances I can, *inshallah*, if God wills, with your help, find out what happened to your mistress.

"Tell me, is it your poor health that makes you unhappy?"

"My confinement accounts for my poor health. Mikhail Effendi cannot cure me. Nothing will cure me except leaving the Harem. Everyone is very kind and they all pander to my whims, hoping to divert my thoughts and energies. Shireen encouraged me to ride horses, and every day I practised archery in the gardens. I am," she added with a hidden smile, "really rather good with a bow. But nothing helps for more than a few hours. Riding just makes me crave for freedom even more. When you take control of a horse, you can sense how it feels to be a slave – the horse obeys but all the time wants to be free."

"Nilufer, like you I am also a slave but I don't feel as you do. But for my slavery, I would probably be a destitute peasant or, if I were lucky, a monk confined to a monastery."

"You are not a woman."

My master took the point, recognising that Nilufer was from a noble family and so naturally would feel differently from him.

"Would you like to return to Venice?"

"Of course, Pasha. Who does not want to return to the place of their birth?"

"I, for one," thought the Pasha but said nothing.

"But," continued Nilufer, "I was brought to the Harem a long time ago and time fades memories. So I am thankful that I am a pampered slave and not a Frankish whore. I thank Allah for his blessings." She began to make the sign of the cross but, thinking better of it, pretended to suppress a yawn. She had accepted Islam but the conversion was more or less nominal and as long as she kept her true convictions to herself no one cared very much.

"And," continued Adam Pasha, still enraptured by the sublime tones and soft curves of his interviewee, "do pampered slaves like halva?"

"Halva? Yes, everyone likes halva but I have a bad tooth and sweets make it ache. My mistress, though, liked halva. If she had not been so concerned about her figure, she would have nibbled halva all day long. If she had a weakness, that was it."

"There was some halva laid out in a green handkerchief in your mistress's room. Do you know where it came from and who gave it to her?"

"It came from our kitchens. Where else would it come from? Why do you ask, Pasha?"

My pasha passed over the question.

"Nilufer, I have one more question and then I regret I must leave you. Shireen had a necklace, one she was especially fond of. A pendant necklace set with a particularly fine pearl. When did she last wear it?"

Nilufer lowered her head, her fine veil growing impenetrably opaque, but she answered with no hint of surprise. "I cannot be sure, Pasha, when she last wore it. But, as you say, she was fond of it and wore it often. I assume she was wearing it when she died but, if not, then it is probably in the Harem Treasury ... or, more likely, in her jewel box."

***

Hafsa Sultan was presiding over the weekly Harem council meeting. Present were the Chief Stewardess and the new Chief Treasurer – a middle-aged woman who had retained some of the bloom of her youth but was no match in appearance for the dead Shireen. Also there were the Mistress of the Robes, the Keepers of the Baths and the Jewels, the Reader of the Koran, the Mistress of the Pantry and ... the Chief Linen Mistress.

Khurrem glanced accusingly out of the corner of her eye at the Linen Mistress before bending her head to greet the Queen Mother. The Royal Mother was seated on a low sofa, a sort of cushioned bench covered in velvet and running along most of the length of three of the room's four walls. The council members, seated cross-legged on the sofa, flanked Hafsa Sultan in order of precedence.

The Mother Sultan was dressed in a kaftan of deep red Bursa brocade over a yellow silken waistcoat with diamond buttons open half way to the waist to reveal a fine silk gauze smock. Over it all shone a light-blue silk sash. Wearing on her head a pearl-adorned cap and, with her eyes blackened sensuously with kohl and her lips painted red, the Queen Mother cut a strikingly radiant figure.

She beckoned to Khurrem. "My dear, you're looking so well. Come, sit next to me." The Lady Treasurer made space. "You will be going to Khadija's party, won't you?" purred the Queen Mother, referring to the festivities to coincide with the forthcoming circumcisions of the three boy princes being organised by the Grand Vizier's wife (and sister of our Sultan).

"Of course, Illustrious Mother. We are all looking forward to it very much."

Hafsa Sultan turned to speak to her Cabinet. "Well, that ends our business for today. You may go."

Khurrem, along with the others, stood to leave but the Queen Mother took hold of her hand. "No, my dear. Not you. Please sit a while. I need your advice about a disturbing matter." Hafsa's grip was firm and her tone polite but it hid a lingering hint of venom. "Ugly rumours are circulating in my Harem, my dear. You know that I only have your interests at heart. I don't want your name besmirched by gossip."

"Illustrious Mother," said Khurrem, wondering what was coming next, "you are the light of our lives. May you shine eternal."

"My dear, I believe you know Nilufer, poor Shireen's lady-in-waiting."

That question took Khurrem completely by surprise. She had been expecting "the old witch", as she called the Linen

Mistress, to have blabbed to the Queen Mother. She was not expecting to be questioned about Nilufer. "Illustrious Mother, she served me for about a year. Such a charming, vivacious girl with a quick intelligence."

"Just so. As, I'm sure you know, my dear, I've decided to take Nilufer into my personal service. She's not well. I fear our life in the Harem doesn't agree with her so I think it's time she got married. I've spoken to her and we've discussed a few potential candidates. I think we have the answer."

"I am very pleased, Illustrious Mother," said Khurrem bemused.

"Good. You and lady Shireen were not on good terms, were you?" asked Hafsa Sultan, again changing the subject abruptly, trying perhaps to throw Khurrem off-balance.

"Illustrious Mother, I liked her well enough," said Khurrem, making no pretence of hiding her surprise. "Her manner and tone of voice hinted that she liked me less but our relationship was always correct. We never quarrelled."

"I know, my child, but were you not shocked by her sudden death?"

"Indeed, I was."

Hafsa Sultan took a deep breath. "Your quarters are directly above Shireen's, are they not?"

"Yes. Is that significant, Illustrious Mother?" replied Khurrem, tempted to say, "So are yours," but wisely holding her tongue.

"Perhaps. And what do you think was the cause of Shireen's death?"

"Why do you ask me, Illustrious Mother? Surely you do not – cannot -believe I had anything to do with it?"

"Of course not, my child. But you agree the death was sinister? And there are so many rumours."

"I do not pay attention to rumours, Illustrious Mother."

Hafsa Sultan fell silent for a moment but she was not to be so easily beaten. "Perhaps you should, my dear. There's unpleasant talk. Some of it concerns you. I know it's not true but a consort to the Sultan must jealously guard her reputation. And," Hafsa said, turning a thunderous gaze on Khurrem, "if I discover someone in my Harem was responsible for Shireen's death, she'll answer for it to me."

Then Hafsa added, her tone turning as silky as her blue sash, "My dear, you are young and have so much to learn. I am worried by the poor girl's death. And so is your Sultan. Much as I respect Adam Pasha, I do not relish him loitering about the Harem. Your Sultan felt this step was imperative but I agonise over the decision. If there is something sinister about Shireen's death, then I intend to discover it and the quicker the better so our lives can return to normal. Is there anything you can tell me to help us get to the truth?"

"Nothing, Illustrious Mother."

"Nothing at all?"

"No, nothing at all."

"Very well. I'll say no more about it … for the moment."

***

The Pasha stroked his beard, greying faster than the stubbly hair on his head. "Selim Aga, Fatima was the only one of Shireen's jariyés to have seen someone leave her quarters late on the night of her death. Why, would Khurrem send Fatima so far away, before anyone's had a chance to question her?"

"Her mistress dead, she is surplus to requirements in this Harem," replied Selim. "It could be that, it could be one of a hundred reasons. It's not my business to speculate."

VII   THE DOCTOR'S DILEMMA

I showed Mikhail into the reception room to await Adam Pasha's return. When I left him, he was sitting lazily amid a pile of soft silken cushions and contentedly sipping a violet and honey sherbet. But, he was a man of insatiable curiosity and I was hardly out of the door before he was peering into every corner of the room. So curious was he that he was barely back in his place when my pasha entered.

"Effendi," said my master, "this is indeed a pleasure. Twice in one day. Are all your patients cured ... or dead?"

"Neither, Pasha," said Mikhail, chortling into his chest. "But I have another mystery for you."

"Not another mystery!" replied my pasha, only half ironically. "Tell me what this one's about."

"First we must go to the Chief Physician's consulting rooms. I will explain when we get there and on the way you can tell me about your visit to the Harem."

***

"Did you learn anything, Pasha ... from talking to Nilufer?" asked Mikhail, sitting hunched up on his grey mare.

"Effendi, what do you know of Selim Aga?" replied the Kadiasker evasively.

"Selim Aga?" Mikhail raised his dangling head in surprise. "A good man, so people say. Why?"

"Could someone have poisoned Shireen?"

"It is not impossible though hardly likely. Surely you do not think Selim Aga could have killed the girl?"

"Selim Aga's the chief guardian of the Harem," replied my master. "He had the opportunity and his status gives him the authority to hide or manipulate evidence. He could have done it."

"What motive would he have?"

"He could have been carrying out Khurrem's orders," said my master. "Or the orders of Hafsa Sultan, or a dozen others!" he added, throwing up his hands in exasperation. Then he screwed up his eyes and gave a disbelieving frown. "No, I don't think Selim is a murderer. But," he said, adopting a secretive whisper, "there is that little matter of the halva."

"What has halva to do with this?" asked Mikhail half-wondering if he had dozed off and missed some interesting tit-bit.

"Oh, didn't I mention it? That halva in the birdcage – it was poisoned."

"What!" exclaimed Mikhail, his furrowed brow visible as he threw back his head. "Pasha, I know I said it was not impossible but Shireen was almost certainly not poisoned. At least, I do not think she was."

"Really?" my master asked with a hint of disappointment. "Perhaps not. But it tells us that someone was trying to kill her. Let us imagine that she had fed the halva to her parrot. The parrot dies. Shireen is frightened, knowing the poison was meant for her. That explains the dagger under her pillow. And," my master added, "what about the cat?"

"What cat?" asked Mikhail, again thrown off balance by the Kadiasker's perplexing pattern of thought.

"My beautiful new pet," said my pasha, speaking of that evil spirit which had appeared out of nowhere. "It always slept at Shireen's feet but where was it when she was killed? It could have slipped out when the porters came to carry away the body but why did no one see it? Isn't that strange?"

Mikhail saw nothing strange about it but hoped that my master would elucidate.

"Nilufer says there might have been a late night visitor," continued Adam Pasha. "I think that's when the cat slipped out."

"So" concluded Mikhail in barely masked mockery, "you are convinced Shireen was murdered because no one saw a furry animal."

"I am sure she was murdered," replied my master ignoring the sarcasm. "More important, though, is to find her killer."

"You don't like my theory about a jealous lover," said Mikhail, "so what's yours?"

"The main suspect must be Khurrem Sultan. She sees Shireen as a potential rival with growing power. She knows the Sultan is devoted to herself but the Harem has dangerous temptations. So let us say she does not want to risk testing our Sultan's fidelity. She's consumed by jealousy and she fears for her son's future. Put that together with the considerable power she wields in the Harem and she would not have much trouble arranging a murder."

"Well," said Mikhail, "that is a compelling theory."

"Yes, but it is only a theory. There are other, equally likely, candidates. Take Prince Mustafa, for instance. He had motive enough. If Shireen had succeeded in displacing Khurrem there would have been another challenger to his mother, another beautiful girl of childbearing age. The last thing Prince Mustafa needs is another rival. And Mustafa had the opportunity: the stairs adjoining Shireen's rooms lead straight up to his quarters. Yet, could Mustafa have committed such a foul crime? He's still only a boy.

"But this speculation is not taking us far. We are no nearer discovering the truth than we were two days ago."

"Well," added Mikhail, "I have a theory of my own."

***

By now the pair had reached the fourth court of the New Palace. The journey through the second and third courtyards of the palace had been on foot and it was on foot that they approached the Chief Physician's Tower. Mikhail led the way up the winding stairs to the consulting rooms and pharmacy that were housed at the top.

The tower was built as part of the crenulated defence wall, giving an unimpeded view across the Estuary of Constantinople and the Sea of Marmara. It was a spectacular scene, the sun twinkling off the sparkling blue water with the Genoese tower in Galata and the little minareted mosques and domed churches prominent on the hills opposite.

Immediately below the physician's tower, blossomed the beautifully laid out garden of the fourth court, with its well-tended flower beds and shapely shrubs, its tulips in final bloom and the desert rose in its classic prickly pose. The gardens where the young princes sometimes flew their kites extended to thick inner walls. Beyond them were more terraced gardens and royal kiosks as the land sloped away to the fortress-thick walls at the water's edge.

"Very pretty, Effendi," said my pasha, enjoying a sight of the palace he had not seen before, "but I'm sure you didn't bring me here to admire the view."

"This is the Chief Physician's pharmacy," replied the doctor. "We keep our medicines here in these large jars and those small bottles over there." Mikhail pointed to bulbous earthenware and wooden jars with leather straps and copper tops and to dainty clear and coloured bottles with round ground-glass stops. "One of the assistants was taking an inventory yesterday and guess what he found: both opium and foxglove have disappeared."

"The opium's for medicinal use?" asked my master.

"Yes, of course. We make laudanum from it, absolutely invaluable in suppressing pain and curing corruption of the body." Mikhail, while speaking, picked up a blue earthenware bowl, left on a table by an unassuming servant who had flitted in and flitted out. He removed the cover. "Have some sugarcane," he said, as he held out the bowl to the Kadiasker. Adam Pasha picked out a particularly big piece and bit into it, sweet nectar trickling down his fingers and his beard.

"Are your stocks of opium large?" my master mumbled as he clumsily tried with his tongue to edge out a string of cane wedged between his teeth.

"Several kilos," replied Mikhail. "About half of one has disappeared. And it's not the first time either." He, too, was turning a piece of sugarcane in his mouth, stopping briefly to flick some bits carelessly into an empty dish.

"So," asked Adam Pasha, "there have been other thefts?"

"Yes, six months ago. About the same quantity was stolen then but only opium on that occasion – no foxglove. At the time, no one thought much about it, assuming as we did that there had been some sort of stocktaking error."

"And nobody checked again? Wasn't that rather slack?"

"Yes, Pasha. It was – very slack."

"And what about the foxglove? I can't imagine such a poisonous weed having any medicinal properties."

"It's certainly poisonous, Pasha. Most medicines are if taken incorrectly but even poisons have their uses."

"Who do you think is the thief?" asked my pasha.

"I've no idea," replied the doctor. "The last inventory was taken three months ago. We always try to keep a steady stock of opium because it's so useful for treating injuries and other ailments. And we keep the 'poisonous weed', as you call it, because it's efficacious for complaints of the heart. As we grow small quantities of it ourselves, we're not seriously concerned by its loss but, in any case, we've had little need of either recently so the missing quantities could have been taken any time in the past three months. Still, I think the theft was recent as someone would have noticed the loss sooner or later even without an inventory being taken."

"Have many people have used these consulting rooms in, say, the past month?"

"I can't be sure, but I don't think many. Only the Chief Physician uses these rooms for consultations and, in any case, most consultations take place in the Old Palace." Mikhail paused. "Pasha", he added with a sense of mystery, "I said earlier that I had another theory and I wasn't being quite truthful when I said I had no idea who might have committed the thefts. A few days ago – six days ago, to be precise – there was an unexpected visitor here, Prince Mustafa's tutor."

"Are you sure?" asked my pasha.

"There's no mistake – I myself saw him enter the tower."

"I see. And you think perhaps the tutor took the poisons?" asked my pasha. Not waiting for an answer, he continued, "Do you think the same poisons could have been mixed into the halva I found in Shireen's rooms?"

Mikhail nodded slowly, deliberately. "Perhaps, Pasha."

"Could anyone else have taken it: physicians, servants, assistants?"

"It's highly unlikely to be servants. The only servants

allowed in the pharmacy are the Chief Physician's and they have his full trust. And medical assistants are never left alone in here: there's always a doctor present. I can vouch for all the physicians." The doctor paused with a sigh, before adding, "Nothing like this has happened before."

"I thought you said that something exactly like this had happened six months ago," said my master, a little confused. There was a momentary silence before the doctor answered.

"Yes, Pasha, but what I meant was that theft hasn't been suspected before."

"Well, the tutor may be a suspect but we don't have any real evidence against him. And surely the tutor wouldn't have been left alone in here to take fistfuls of the stuff?"

"It's possible he was left long enough to help himself."

"And where did he put it? Stuff it in his turban did he?"

"Very witty, Pasha, but I'm only trying to help."

"I'm sorry, Effendi. My sarcasm was uncalled for. There is, of course, another possibility: we all know opium has a non-medicinal value. Aren't you jumping to conclusions by assuming the theft is connected with Shireen's death? And, even if there is a connection, it doesn't explain something that's been baffling me: why was Shireen so frightened?"

"But," said the doctor incredulously, "didn't you say that seeing her parrot die from eating the poisoned halva …?"

"Yes, but she'd have recognised the danger only if she'd already been threatened."

"I hadn't thought of that," said the doctor, picking up another piece of sugarcane. About to pop it into his mouth, he reflected and carefully put the piece back in the bowl. "An interesting mystery, Pasha, but, what are we to make of it?"

VIII   THE GRAND BAZAAR

It was still dark outside when I shook my master awake. He rubbed his bleary eyes and moistened his parched lips. Having barely slept three hours, his head stayed stubbornly anchored to his pillow. Eventually he lifted it, slowly, as he raised himself on his elbows.

"Murat, I feel awful. I must be sick," he said, with a mixture of a groan and a growl. "My head feels like a cow's udder in desperate need of milking – heavy and ready to burst. I didn't hear the call to prayer."

I kept quiet about how I felt. "It's a couple of hours until the dawn prayer, Pasha. The Aga of Janissaries begs your urgent attendance at the Goldsmith's Gate of the Old Bazaar."

I could tell my master no more so he dressed and, together with the cavalry officer sent to fetch us, we rode towards the Covered Bazaar, the city's main shopping complex.

"Whatever it is, it must be important to warrant both I and the commander of the Janissaries being called out in the middle of the night." My master was fishing for information but all the cavalry aga said was a polite, "Yes, Pasha."

Our horses trod carefully along the dark, deserted streets, the only light emanating from a three-quarter moon and linseed-oil lanterns carried on poles by the captain and me. Gradually we came into sight of the Bazaar. All we could see were a number of busy figures holding lanterns.

I glanced at the Venetian ambassador's residence nearby, a large, rambling two-storied building with its own stables and foundry.

"The spies of Venice are working hard tonight," I whispered as I noticed chinks of light squeezing through shutters where they were closed and the more visible flicker of candles and mysterious shadows where they were not. I also thought I heard voices but, as we looked up at the window from which the soft light was evident, its shutters were quickly pulled fast.

On approaching the southern gate, we were challenged by two very suspicious and edgy Janissaries on sentry-duty. Having satisfied them of our identities, we passed through the entrance, plotting a course beneath the colonnaded arches towards the Goldsmith's Gate. There, below the Roman imperial eagle of the Comneni, Adam Pasha was warmly greeted by the tall, elegant figure of the Aga of Janissaries. The grey-bearded general apologised profusely for being forced to disturb my pasha's dreams.

"Adam Pasha," explained the Aga, "in a few hours this market will open and I'll be facing some serious civil disturbance. You know that as a repository for scores of safe-deposit boxes, here is stored much of Istanbul's portable wealth. Well, between two and three hours ago the vaults were looted. Gold, silver, pearls, rubies, sapphires – the most precious stones, have been stripped from them."

Adam Pasha let out an astonished whistle. "Aren't these vaults used by the jewellers' guild? The thieves must have got away with millions of akches-worth of jewellery!"

"Not only the jewellers, Pasha. Wealthy merchants and townsfolk use it as a place of safekeeping. Even some members of the Divan think this is a safer place for their valuables than their own homes. Do you see why I am worried, Kadiasker? Once word of this gets out, the scenes are bound to be ugly. Half the merchants in Istanbul will be ruined. And what about those members of the Divan? They won't be all too pleased. I have heard that the Imperial Treasurer, Iskendar Chelebi, has buried some of his wealth here. The loss of it may bring a smile to Ibrahim Pasha's face but I don't relish explaining this to the Treasurer or to the guild representatives. How could this have been allowed to happen?"

The Aga tapped hard on the stone floor with his staff of office. "Fifteen years ago fire ruined scores of businessmen but at least then the members of the Divan weren't affected. Pasha, I think I might have my own head to worry about."

"I'm sure it won't come to that," said my master, "but how was the robbery committed? And," my pasha yawned with barely concealed irritation, "what possible help can I be?" It was an uncharacteristically callous remark for him to make but his eyelids were sinking fast whilst the enormity of what had happened was barely sinking in at all.

"I'm no investigator, Adam Pasha. I'm just a simple soldier. I haven't any clues as to who did it and I had hoped that you might be able to bring your experience to bear."

My master felt flattered (almost enough to forget he was sleepy). "I'll see what I can do. We had better take a look at the vaults." The Aga showed the way.

***

The Venetian emissary thumped the table indignantly. The Ambassador was losing a diplomatic battle and he was a sore loser.

"Signor Gritti," he said, turning to the smooth-talking, slippery son of the Doge, "can't you bring your influence to bear?" That considerable influence he wanted engaged in securing the release of the sea captain arrested in Galata. "It's monstrous that one of the Republic's subjects should be bundled away and detained in a stinking infidel dungeon." His voice was like a cracked war drum but the discordant tones gave way to sweeter, more persuasive ones. "You know the Republic rewards its servants well." There was a pause for effect, before he chided his visitor. "Everyone knows that you are a trusted friend of the Grand Vizier. Don't the Turks refer to you as *Beyoghlu* – 'son of the lord'?"

"It's true, Excellency, that I am not unknown in the city", replied Gritti. "It is also true that Ibrahim Pasha and I are well-acquainted and we have done business together but in this matter … what can I do? I fear I am powerless. And," he said with evident irritation, "why do we have to discuss this ridiculous trifle in the middle of the night?"

"*Beyoghlu*," replied the ambassador with barely disguised contempt, "will you help or won't you? Either way your father will know of it."

That threat meant little to Gritti, though he had no desire to upset a man as influential in Venice as the ambassador. He wanted to help but he also first wanted to know more before he got himself entangled in something he should leave well alone.

"I've heard a rumour," said Gritti, "that this Captain Marco is involved in some conspiracy. Do you know anything about it?"

"Conspiracy? What nonsense! What sort of conspiracy could a simpleton like Marco be involved in?" replied the ambassador, the sinews on his forehead tightening in a spluttering rage. He then added sarcastically, "Unless there's a conspiracy towards debauchery and drunkenness. Every sailor who pulls in to Constantinople thinks nothing of throwing the good name of his country in the gutter whilst he feels inside the petticoats of the prostitutes of Pera."

"I have heard, Excellency, that Captain Marco was caught with two bagfuls of counterfeit coins: silver akches and gold sequins. What do you say to that?"

"Are you interrogating me, Signor Gritti? You presume too much. I've not heard anything about counterfeit coins. You should pay less attention to bawdy-house gossip. As for the money, there's a simple explanation. He was on an errand – to purchase ship's provisions. Anyway, we're not here to try him but to save him from the hands of those cut-throats," the ambassador said. "And, you would do well to remember who your father is," he added with a twist of venom.

Gritti resented the ambassador's second reference to his father as much as he had resented the first. He was not used to being spoken to like this, especially not from a piss-pot, albeit an influential piss-pot, like the ambassador but he kept his thoughts to himself. "As you know, Excellency, I am always at the disposal of the Republic. I shall, of course, try my best to obtain the captain's release but I have to tread carefully. I have property and financial interests in the realms of the Great Turk. I have a lot to lose. One false step and everything disappears like halva at a wedding feast. And my sources – reliable ones which have served the Republic well in the past – my sources tell me that, for whatever reason, this is a delicate issue. The Sultan himself has shown a keen interest in the affair. Why would that be?"

***

The Covered Market itself is a stone building, its domes laced with high windows and supported on pillars. There are four exits each closed off by heavy wooden doors barred shut. Within these gates are cut smaller doors that can be used at night by the watchmen on patrol but are otherwise kept locked. Amongst the shops inside the Old Bazaar, as we know it locally, are great stone vaults: strong-rooms specially built to withstand fire. Inside the vaults, the strong-boxes are set into a wall of masonry under the floor.

My pasha descended the narrow stone stairs into the strong-room. Smoke was billowing out of the door and my master held a silk handkerchief to his mouth. The general took a deep breath and pointed to a pile of charred and burnt paper, turning over the ashes with his staff.

"This is the worst of it," the Aga said, coughing out the words with a mixture of exasperation and sympathy. "The swine didn't only steal the valuables in these vaults but set light to every document they could lay their hands on. Deeds, certificates, receipts, anything combustible which was locked-up here for safe-keeping has all gone up in smoke. They had no value to the thieves so why destroy them?"

"Not all the boxes have been broken into," remarked Adam Pasha, pointing to some that had clearly not been touched.

"No. Perhaps a third or so are unopened," said the general. "They must have run out of time. There are six night-watchmen, two of whom make a circuit of the market every hour. Afraid of being caught in the act, the robbers must have scarpered before the patrol came around again."

Climbing back out of the vaults both Divan members took deep breaths. The general choose to clear his throat, spitting out the smoke in his lungs. Adam Pasha preferred to swallow instead.

"The watchmen's station...," asked Adam Pasha, "isn't it about twenty metres from the market gates?"

"About that. They check the Old Market first and then

the Silk Market. The doors are padlocked, though occasionally the watchmen will unlock the chains and patrol inside. But usually they'll simply check that the locks haven't been tampered with."

"Well," said my pasha, thinking out aloud, "assuming it takes a maximum of twenty minutes to complete their checks of this building, that would give the thieves forty minutes. Enough time to break open the boxes and carry off the contents if there were enough of them."

It was the Aga who asked the question which was clearly baffling them both. "But how did they break in? And how did they get away with so much loot without being noticed? Do you think they could have got in and out through those windows?" asked the general, pointing his silver-topped staff up at the openings in the central dome.

"Possibly," replied my pasha, "but I doubt it. A boy, perhaps, could wriggle through those windows but not an adult – at least, not a man with the strength necessary to break open the strong-boxes. Even an army of boys let down on ropes couldn't have committed this robbery. Anyone clambering on the roof risks breaking his neck not to mention being caught by the night-watchmen. And, though the moon's bright enough to throw some light on the roof, that won't help much in the narrow pitch black alleys."

"Then, how did they get in?" pressed the bewildered Aga. "And how did they get away with their spoils?"

***

"Signor Gritti, I don't know what you're talking about. As far as I know, we're dealing with the antics of a high-spirited sailor. No more than that."

"These antics, Excellency, have caused almost half the city to be burned down not to mention a scandal of

97

considerable proportions," said Gritti as he tried to think of a way of extricating himself from something that was starting to take on the smell of rancid fat.

"These Turks are far too sensitive," was all the explanation the ambassador had to offer.

"Excellency, surely you understand the enormity of the crime? To have molested a Tatar woman is bad enough but to molest the wife of a *seyyid*, a descendant of their Prophet, that is a crime of such magnitude that this dolt of a sailor will be lucky to keep his head. It was an act of gross imbecility. If anyone wanted to stir up trouble on a city-wide scale, this was the perfect way of doing it."

"Yes, yes, yes," repeated the Signory's representative dismissively, "but what are we going to do about it? The wretch must be freed. Before he's tortured." The quick-witted Gritti, smelling a sewer full of rats, found his enthusiasm for getting involved draining away by the minute.

"My sources," said Gritti, "tell me he is unharmed. At least, they haven't put him to the rack – yet – but that's only a matter of time. In fact, I can't understand why it hasn't already happened. Perhaps your Excellency's forthright protests have made them think twice."

The ambassador, pacing up and down the room in the older, and more central, of the Signory's two official residences, had calmed himself a little. "I must have an audience with the Sultan. So far it's been nothing but delays and prevarications. Signor Gritti, can you help?"

"Excellency, I shall do my best," replied Gritti, relieved that he was not being asked to do more. He had a lot to lose and little to gain from deeper involvement. He was a man of shrewd judgement. That is how he had built his fortune of hundreds of thousands of ducats and he meant to keep it. He was a man who planned ahead, which is why he kept so much of his wealth in portable form, as jewels sewn into a belt ready to make a dash for safety if ever he needed to. In the meantime, however, he would approach his friend, the Grand Vizier, to try and get an audience for the ambassador. If he failed – well, he would have done what he could. And, if he were successful, he would receive his reward from the Signory – another bagful of golden ducats.

***

"Murat," said my pasha, turning to me, "what do you think? How did they get into the Bazaar?"

"They must have had a key," I replied.

"Exactly! They had the key to one of the doors: probably the one furthest from the watchmen's post. They got in and out in the forty minutes without being disturbed. Any faint glimmer of light visible on the far side of the market wouldn't have been seen by the watch."

"Slow down, Adam Pasha. You're running too fast for an old soldier," said the Aga, raising a hand and waving it in disbelief. "How did they get the keys?"

"Murat, tell the Aga." My master was playing games with everyone and I had played this one before.

"Simple. One of the bandits must be a custodian of the keys."

"Or somehow they got the keys from him," added my master, for sake of completeness. He was a jurist, after all. "Find out who has the keys and you'll be on your way to solving the crime."

The answer sounded simple but the experienced general was not so easily convinced.

"There are about ten people who have access to, or

custody of, the keys. There's the supervisory board, the four most important members of which will have access and there are the six guards, of course, each appointed on order of our Sultan. Are you really suggesting I question them all? That could take days and dawn – the time of reckoning – is fast approaching." Like all soldiers, the general was anxious to find a quick solution and did not care to waste time with preliminaries.

"You asked for my advice – I've given it," said my pasha, wanting to get back to bed. "But," he added, "there is one thing about this case that does bother me. Having got their loot, how did they get it away? The quantities taken would have required either a lot of people to carry it or a bullock cart, or mules or something. Whatever the case, if they were travelling any distance, they were running tremendous risks. They could have been spotted or heard, if not by the watch, then by your night patrols. You might try to find the answer to that when you interrogate your suspects."

My pasha then added a few cautionary words of advice, "I wouldn't use torture, at least not on the members of the supervisory board: if they were not involved, it could have nasty repercussions."

My pasha and I returned to the comfort of our home but, for the Aga, his problems had only just begun.

***

"A cup of sherbet for us both, Murat," said the pasha, deciding there was no point sleeping now. He threw himself onto a pile of carpets and cushions as he asked, "What do you make of all that?"

"Some stunningly rich people will be strutting about Istanbul tomorrow. And there will be some once-rich ones who now can't rub a couple of akches together. Allah gives

100

and Allah takes away.

"How do you think, Pasha, they got clean away without anyone seeing them?"

"Only Allah knows for sure. But maybe they didn't go so far," replied my master.

***

The general had commanded many an army in the field and this was a crisis that he had foreseen. He had positioned his Janissaries at strategic locations around the Bazaar and ensured that their presence was prominent and visible.

As the traders came early to the Bazaar to open their shops, they stared curiously at the soldiers standing at the gates. "What's going on?" asked an elderly man with a fine white beard. A sombre Janissary placed a hand on his heart and bowed his head politely but said nothing. The younger sentries were edgy, watching for trouble and expecting it at any moment. And it seemed trouble had arrived. Cries of anguish were heard from the jewellers and goldsmiths, but the Aga was quickly on hand to explain what had happened, promising the Sultan's help. And so calm returned.

As the day's shoppers started to fill the labyrinth of covered streets and alleys, the soldiers began to relax and the patrols sent to tour the Bazaar dawdled to pass the time of day with the shopkeepers.

Then, one of the Janissaries made some callous remark to an Armenian goldsmith.

"And where were you when we needed you?" spat the Armenian. "Buggering bastards," he added provocatively.

The soldier flew into a fury. He drew his sword and slashed at the goldsmith. His colleagues tried to restrain him but he broke free, flinging one of them to the floor. As the Janissary sprawling on the floor raised himself, he noticed a gold bracelet lying on a low table. It seemed to be beckoning to him and, thinking no one was looking, tucked it away in his tunic.

"Thief!" cried a sallow youth from among the small crowd that had gathered. A number of spectators helped themselves to what was left of the loot. The goldsmith sat on a stool at the back of his shop mopping away the blood leaking from his cheek. His world was collapsing before his very eyes. He began to wish the soldier had killed him.

It took perhaps five minutes for the thieving contagion to spread to the rest of the Bazaar. The narrow, confined, claustrophobic passageways of the Bazaar swelled the general hysteria as the looting took over. The frightened few, those who were not inclined to enrich themselves, tried to make for the exits but, amidst the chaos, innocent shoppers were pushed shoved, kicked and trampled under foot.

"Shut the gates! Shut the gates!" the well-fed market inspector kept shouting, intent on catching the culprits but taking care to deliver his orders from the safety of the doorway of his little office. The Aga, trapped in the middle of the Bazaar and cut off from his command, tried to beat his way through the crowd. The handful of inspectors usually on patrol in the market were helpless and ducked into the nearest of the tiny mosques dotted around the Bazaar. These mosques themselves were now filling so fast that it was almost as dangerous inside as it was out.

The fleeing shoppers panicked. Fights were breaking out all over the Bazaar, usually because one crook thought he was more deserving than another. The soldiers inside, responsible for sparking off the riot, were far too busy enriching themselves to be of much help in bringing about order. Those outside were confused, their officers waiting for

a spoonful of yoghurt before continuing. "Now, Effendi, no jealous lover would wait until Shireen was asleep before suffocating her. Jealous lovers kill in hot blood, seldom in cold."

"Pasha, listen to me. For your own sake, don't be so eager to reject the jealous lover theory. You tell our Sultan that it was a jealous lover and he will shower you with rewards – most likely make you a vizier of three horsetails, and everyone will walk away happy. Perhaps, even I will get something out of this, who knows? We will avoid a scandal and the whole affair will be quickly forgotten. If you can provide the name of a jealous lover, so much the better, and, if not, who cares? But suggest that Prince Mustafa or Khurrem conspired to kill Shireen ..." Mikhail drew back in mock horror, and then added, not entirely sincerely, "Well, who knows. Perhaps everything will work out for the best."

"It's very tempting, Effendi, to cover up the unpleasant truth, whatever that may be, but I can't do it. I shall, inshallah, fulfil His Highness' trust."

"Pasha," said Mikhail, "I don't think you understand court politics as well as you imagine. You've been engrossed in your books far too long. Tell me this: why do you think our Sultan asked you to carry out this investigation and not, say, Ibrahim Pasha?"

"I don't know. Perhaps the Sultan felt my judicial experience ..."

"Judicial experience, be damned. More likely, if you uncover a conspiracy by Khurrem or a prince of the royal blood there will be an unpleasant aftermath – and, mark my words, there will be repercussions and they will not be pretty – and the ugly aftermath will chase you like the moon chases the sun. Our clever Grand Vizier will walk away without a stain and, like a newborn babe, will be innocence itself. And you – you alone will be left to deliver the bad news. No one thanks the bringer of bad tidings, remember that."

"There may be something in what you say, Effendi, but I think the answer is simpler: we know Ibrahim Pasha is no friend of Khurrem. Our Sultan probably believes that Ibrahim Pasha will not be entirely impartial in the advice he gives. The brilliant Grand Vizier has a sure touch when it comes to making enemies."

"But," asked the doctor with cautious hesitation, "don't you owe your career to the Grand Vizier's patronage?"

"I'd like to think that I have some talent, Effendi," answered my master, a little offended, "but you're right. I owe a lot to Ibrahim Pasha. That, however, doesn't mean that I'm his puppet."

"Of course not, Pasha. I didn't mean to imply …"

"Why do you ask?"

"I have to be careful how I tread, Pasha."

"I thought we were friends, Effendi. I'm not going to repeat anything you say."

The doctor, hand on heart, from his seated position bowed his gratitude to my pasha. "Tell me this, Pasha: why is our Sultan so devoted to the Grand Vizier? Perhaps the bond goes much further than simple devotion …"

"Effendi," interrupted Adam Pasha, "is this the sort of scurrilous gossip that circulates amongst you physicians? Consider this: our Sultan has an enormously difficult and complex task in running our vast Empire. He's also a very private man who is ill at ease with the grandeur of court ceremonial. Ibrahim Pasha, on the other hand, basks in the reflected glory of his Sultan. He revels in that grandeur and wallows in the pomp that accompanies even an ordinary day at court. And, for all that, he's such a talented man – a courageous soldier, an efficient administrator, and a clever politician. The Sultan needs men like him."

"And he is cleverer than the Sultan," added Mikhail throwing caution to the wind.

"I don't agree. Where do you hear such nonsense? Ibrahim Pasha is certainly intelligent. Of that there's no doubt. But never underestimate His Highness. He is thoughtful and less impetuous than the Grand Vizier. That might give the impression that he's slow but don't be misled. The Sultan is no one's fool."

"But why then does the Sultan bear the arrogance of his Grand Vizier?"

"Arrogant Ibrahim Pasha certainly is. One day it may bring him down but doesn't he have a right to be arrogant? The man is brilliant. The Sultan, to be sure, has devolved a lot of power on him: the first Grand Vizier in history to hold the dual honours of the *Beylerbey* of Rhum and *Serasker* of the Army. That's enough to go to anyone's head."

"Not to mention that he's also the Sultan's brother-in-law," interjected Mikhail. "That's too much power."

"Perhaps. His meteoric rise has left a great many people envious and jealous. His marriage to Khadija may entitle him to certain favours not bestowed on lesser mortals but he has made a multitude of enemies. In using his immense influence to amass his fortune, there is a danger that one day he will lose all sense of reality. Even now, I sense his reaction to the slightest criticism is becoming increasingly unforgiving."

Mikhail nodded in agreement. "Yes, indeed. Poor Fighani is being hounded for a simple epigram. How does it go now …?" mused Mikhail.

"Ibrahim[1] has twice appeared on this temple that is Earth,
One destroyed the idols and the other gave them birth."

"You can see those idols, the spoils of Buda, from this very house, standing proudly in front of the Grand Vizier's ostentatious palace."

"Well, well!" said Adam Pasha with cheerful surprise. "I hadn't realised you felt so strongly about my patron nor that you had such a penchant for poetry. But you're right – those three bronze statues of Apollo, Minerva and Diana still stand brazenly in the sun. And there are more powerful men than that loose-tongued fool Fighani who can still cause a multitude of problems for our Grand Vizier over his precious statues."

"Why do you call him a fool? He's such a promising poet. He has a sharp wit perhaps but surely he's no fool."

"He has a sharp wit to be sure but he also possesses a sharp tongue. I call him a fool because he thinks that by expressing himself so cleverly he can insult a man who, save for the Sultan, is unequalled in power. Does he really expect to get away with it? The pen is far too powerful for it to be used irresponsibly. I doubt if Fighani realised what he was doing when he wrote that ditty but he'll be lucky if he escapes with his life."

"Given the chance, shouldn't a man speak out against injustice?" asked the doctor.

"Effendi, injustice is an abomination to my profession and my faith. Fighani's interest, though, is not in seeing justice done but simply in ridiculing the Grand Vizier.

---

[1] The 'two Ibrahims' being a reference to the biblical Abraham and the Grand Vizier.

There's no merit in that and Ibrahim Pasha will show <u>his</u> peculiar concept of justice by lopping off Fighani's head."

"Maybe so, and it will be a great loss to us all," said Mikhail. "Ibrahim Pasha is a ruthless man, ruthless enough to have had Shireen removed. If, Allah forbid, something were to happen to our Sultan, Mustafa would succeed to the throne, Ibrahim Pasha would see to that, and, with Mustafa so young, that would mean that the Grand Vizier would be our real master."

"Effendi, are you suggesting that Ibrahim Pasha is plotting against our Sultan?" asked my master. "Don't even think of it. And, if you're wise, you'll certainly not talk of it. Still, I agree with you on one matter – our Grand Vizier makes no secret of his support for Prince Mustafa so I doubt if he's shed many tears for Shireen."

Adam Pasha wiped his lips with a napkin and rinsed his hands in a bowl as a servant poured water from a copper pitcher. "One thing I do know, Effendi, is that I don't want to be our Abraham's sacrificial lamb."

***

The general had done his job well. He had recovered from his battering in the market crush and had retaken command of his troops. His Janissaries had saved the day (even if they were partly responsible for the disaster that might have been) and, instead of venting their anger indiscriminately, the merchants sent Shaykh Hajji Yusuf Ali, the President of the Old Market's supervisory council, at the head of a delegation to petition the Divan.

This was the first meeting of the Divan attended by my pasha since the murder of Shireen. And it was not one that my master had been relishing. He knew that Ibrahim Pasha would waste no opportunity to question him about his investigation into the Harem Treasurer's death.

Though seated next to the Grand Vizier, my master skilfully evaded the subtle questioning. Having been excluded from the affair at the instigation of his Sultan, Ibrahim Pasha could not be too obvious in his enquiries but my master was sure that it was only a matter of time before he would be obliged to reveal what he knew.

Yusuf Ali was a formidable figure, quite unlike the usual concept of a pious leader of the religious community. He had a grey beard, certainly, but it was neatly trimmed, giving him a distinguished air without any hint of decrepitude. He was a tall, strong, large-framed man with long powerful fingers. Despite the imposing stature, he showed the same respect to the members of the Divan as did the most humble and insignificant of the Sultan's subjects. He presented his petition – a plea for financial help for those who had lost their livelihoods – with all the grace and deferential bows that etiquette required.

"Hajji Yusuf Ali," said Ibrahim Pasha, "we thank you for your petition. You have made an eloquent plea which we will consider carefully and we will answer you shortly. We shall summon you to attend before us in due course. And, now, if the other Divan members have no questions ..."

The Grand Vizier was about to dismiss the petitioners when my master cleared his throat and said, "My Pasha, if I may be allowed to ask one or two questions ..."

The Grand Vizier, suspicious as ever and drumming his fingers on his knee in evident irritation, wondered what the Kadiasker knew that he did not. Still, he could think of no reason to deny Adam Pasha the opportunity to question Yusuf Ali. He said nothing but simply waved his hand regally in my pasha's direction.

"Hajji Yusuf Ali ...," my pasha said, pausing as he looked into the tall man's eyes, "you have custody of the keys to the gates of the Bazaar?"

"Yes, Pasha ... but ..."

"Yes, but what?"

"Only, Pasha that I do not understand the reason for the question. Other supervisory council members also have keys."

"Do you have your keys?"

" ... I think so, Pasha," replied Yusuf Ali hesitantly as he searched nervously inside the folds of his tunic. "I am sure, Pasha. Here they are!" he triumphantly exclaimed as he pulled a small bunch of long keys from a leather pouch. "I always have them with me for safety's sake."

***

After the Divan session, a confrontation with the Grand Vizier was only to be expected.

"Adam Pasha, we need to talk," he said.

The Kadiasker was saved the need to deceive his patron when the chief chamberlain brought a message from the Sultan commanding my master's immediate attendance. The Kadiasker obeyed with barely concealed relief, leaving behind him the haughty Grand Vizier with a darkening visage and a fuming breath.

***

Sultan Suleyman was looking carefully at a piece of imperial paper. "So, Adam Pasha," he said, waving the document in my master's direction, "you requested an audience."

IX THE VENETIAN AMBASSADOR

"I don't understand, Adam Pasha. What can Venice have to do with the robbery?" asked our Sultan. "You're making a grave allegation but where's your proof? Without it, I can do nothing."

"My Sultan, I do not have direct proof. But consider the circumstances. How could so much treasure have been spirited away without anyone noticing? What were our night-patrols doing not to spot anything untoward? And what about the busybodies in the houses nearby – why didn't they see or hear anything? The only conclusion I can come to is that the treasure was not taken very far.

"Now, when we were on our way to the Bazaar, I couldn't help noticing the Venetian ambassador's house was humming with activity. It's not even a hundred metres from the scene of the crime. At the time, that didn't seem strange – we all know the embassy is a den of spies. But what if they were more than just observing? What if they were actually carrying off just about the most audacious robbery we have ever seen? What if at that very moment they were hiding their spoils?"

The Sultan's face was sombre but resolute. "I am not convinced, Adam Pasha. After all, why should the Venetians take such unnecessary risks? It's a vassal state. They wouldn't dare raise a hand against us. We must do nothing rash. We can't act yet. Do you understand, Pasha? You need conclusive evidence before we move against them. Get me that evidence and you will get your wish."

***

He was about to take the greatest risk of his life. More than that, he was about to disobey the Sultan with a rash, impetuous act. Adam Pasha's calculation was so fine that if his hunch were wrong, the next day there would be a new Kadiasker and our dominions would be plunging headlong into a debilitating naval war with Venice. My master had decided to raid the Venetian embassy before the robbers could dispose of their loot.

There was a good deal of commotion outside the embassy and a loud banging on the door, each thud louder than the last.

"Open up! Open this door. Now!" cried a *yaya-bashi* of Janissaries as a company of soldiers hurried to surround the building. The door creaked open as careful servants and anxious embassy staff leaned out of windows to see what all the fuss was about. My master and the yaya-bashi were led into the stout ambassador's presence whilst soldiers filled the entrance hall, peeling away one by one to stand guard outside each door of the two-storied house. Despite the crush of soldiers and the threatening noises, the officers were careful to ensure that nothing was touched or damaged.

'Mr. Pomposity', the Venetian emissary, was his usual indignant self. "What is the meaning of this, Adam Pasha? I am always happy to see you as my guest but this is a monstrous intrusion. And one that the Illustrious Signory will not tolerate."

"I was hoping, Excellency, to avoid the need for this but we have information that this house has been used in connection with a robbery."

Judging by the look on the ambassador's face, he had just seen the Doge do cartwheels in the nude around St. Mark's Square. But my master was hardly less surprised when he saw Alvise Gritti step out from the shadows.

"Adam Pasha, you can't be serious?" said the Venetian merchant. "Emissary's of the Illustrious Signory are not given to common robbery."

"Beyoghlu, the robbery I have in mind was no common crime. But we are not accusing anyone – if this house has in some way been used by the criminals, I am sure that his Excellency did not have any part in it. It would be unthinkable to suspect the Signory of having taken to banditry. But I would welcome His Excellency's leave and assistance to search the premises."

"My leave, Adam Pasha, you do not require," snorted the ambassador. "When I have armed soldiers standing at my door, I think we can forgo the diplomatic niceties. I must protest in the strongest terms and shall do so to the Sultan. You won't find anything here. You want my assistance? Do I have an option? Search away!" He paused and then added with a sarcastic flourish, "I am always at the service of the Sultan."

We set to work. Floorboards were taken up, trunks were opened and their contents carefully sifted, dusty cupboards and large oil portraits were moved, exposing walls ringed with dirt but nothing else. It was all for nothing, just as the sniffy ambassador had predicted. Only his two private rooms were left untouched for reasons of diplomatic propriety – my master was loth to search these unless evidence elsewhere revealed sufficient reason to warrant it.

Adam Pasha was beginning to feel uncomfortable and it was not the feeling one gets from over-indulging in aubergine. He dug into his tunic to grab a handkerchief with which to mop the sweat from his brow. He was becoming ever more conscious that, if he found nothing and Venice chose to stand on her dignity, war was inevitable. His gaunt features exaggerated the strains and the stress. He knew that to end the search now would also end his career and perhaps his life too. He kept dabbing his forehead with his handkerchief, hoping, praying, that something would turn up. Nothing did. He had to admit he had been wrong. And he knew that, if he were to salvage anything from the battering he had given to Venetian-Ottoman relations, the time had come to call a halt to the search. He gave the order to call it off.

A superior smirk returned to the face of the big-nosed Italian, getting ready as he was to vent his anger.

"Pasha," I whispered in my master's ear, "there's something you should see before we go." I led him to the blacksmith's foundry at the rear of the house where two soldiers were turning over the ashes.

"Gold, Pasha! Someone has been melting gold here," I said with all the exuberance of youthful inexperience.

My master immediately noticed the small droplets of gold splattered around the furnace. "You're right. You are absolutely right. It is gold. And it's been melted down here. Look, there are traces here ... and here," he said excitedly, pointing eagerly like a little boy. "Well done, Murat!" he repeated several times, following each repetition with a deep sigh of relief. "Splashes of gold spilling over from the moulds. Murat, you're a treasure!" A warm, golden glow descended on me.

***

"How do you explain that, Excellency?" my master pressed the ambassador. "You have been melting gold. Why? You know that all the gold mined within the Sultan's realms belongs to His Highness."

115

The emissary blustered and stammered feebly before pulling himself together, "What is this nonsense about gold? I don't know anything about gold", he said. "The strain has been too much for you, Pasha. Please rest a little."

Gritti, meanwhile, having no desire to be associated with the ambassador in this adventure, sensibly remained silent.

"With your leave, Excellency, we will search these rooms now," said Adam Pasha as be signalled to the yaya-bashi to enter the private rooms. The soldiers started to move the stools and table into one corner of the room but stopped when my master pointed out two large oblong wooden chests standing against the rear wall. The tops of the chests were covered by a single faded blue cloth. They clearly did not function as furniture, the part exposed below the level of the cover being entirely without ornamentation. As my master gave the order to open them, the wily diplomat moved smartly between the soldiers and the chests.

"They are locked, Pasha", he observed.

"What's in these, Excellency?" enquired the Kadiasker. "Something weighty I'm sure."

"Nothing, Pasha. Nothing, that is, that will be of any interest to you. You may rest assured of that", was the ambassador's far from convincing reply.

"I would like to see inside, Excellency, to satisfy myself. I don't doubt your word, of course, but I cannot report that I have completed my search until both these chests have been inspected."

"Haven't you inflicted enough damage to your Sultan's relations with Venice?" said the emissary with undisguised disgust. "I will personally see to it that you don't survive this episode."

"Thank you, Excellency, for such kind consideration first

for my health and now for my career. Please open the trunks."

"Adam Pasha, accept my apologies. I did not intend to offend. Please don't misunderstand my hesitancy for reluctance to do your bidding. You will not find any gold in there but you are right to believe that I have something to hide," said the diplomat like a small boy coyly admitting to hiding some toy from his sister. "Those chests do contain contraband. To be precise, they contain bibles. They are for our own use and for the holy congregations in Istanbul – to provide only for our own spiritual needs. No harm was meant and, I am sure, no harm done. Surely, Pasha, you understand, as a Christian yourself ..."

"I may once have been of your faith," replied Adam Pasha, rolling his eyes in exasperation, "but that was when I was a boy and knew no better. That was then, and this is now and I am no longer an ignorant boy. You people of Rhum are too blind see that faith cannot be imposed by force. When will you realise that the contempt you show for our beliefs is tantamount to showing contempt for your own?"

"Pasha, who is it who uses force and shows contempt? It is we Christians who live with a plethora of petty restrictions imposed on our daily lives. It is we Christians whose lands have been invaded and wrenched from us by force. It is we Christians who bear the burden of taxes."

"Excellency, those restrictions are barely observed and, as for the taxes, you Venetians pay next to nothing! And you have the gall to talk about the taking of land by force! Throughout the Sultan's lands we have large thriving Christian and Jewish *dhimmi* communities. But where are the Muslim and Jewish quarters of Cordoba, Toledo, Valencia or Seville? All gone or going, dead or dying."

"Don't mention God-fearing Christians and God-killing Hebrews in the same breath to me!" said the ambassador with his usual sign of contempt for anyone or anything not Venetian.

But Adam Pasha, belatedly perhaps, realised that the emissary was playing a clever game, hoping to divert the Kadiasker's attention from the oblong boxes. "Excellency, enough of this. Open the trunks!"

"Pasha, forgive me. I meant no offence and, as the Illustrious Signory's emissary, I beg His Highness' pardon for any unintentional breach of his laws."

The sudden change in the Ambassador's attitude made Adam Pasha doubly suspicious. "I am sure, Excellency, that His Highness will forgive such a transgression if there is no repeat of it. However, I would still like to look inside." I fidgeted and my master paced up and down as the ambassador angrily flung off the cloth coverings. Then, he slowly, reluctantly, unhooked the key from his belt and unlocked the heavy wooden chests.

X   THE WEDDING

"Bibles, indeed!" thundered Adam Pasha triumphantly as he flung back the lid. "How so spiritually starved your congregations must be! Excellency, surely your priests don't listen to your confession with a dagger at your throat? Are they so lacking in skill that they need guns to force faith on their flock? Just how do you explain all this?" he asked as, with both hands, he scooped out and let drop guns and swords by the dozen, making an awful racket as they bounced on the wooden floor. The trunks were packed with scores of lethal weapons. It was not the treasure we had all expected but the discovery was potentially more significant. And, there was a special bounty – it saved my master a great deal of embarrassment. "Make your confession now, Excellency," he said. "And make it to me."

The ambassador's reply was slow in coming. He had reached the end of his book of diplomatic excuses. "What do you intend to do, Pasha? Are our masters to go to war over a few guns?"

"That is not for me to decide. For the time being, however, you and your servants will not leave this house. It will be under guard day and night. As for these chests, I am confiscating them as contraband." Turning to the senior Janissary officer-in-charge, he said, "Please make out a receipt for his Excellency: 'Two plain wooden chests with assorted contents of pistols, muskets, swords and daggers'."

***

"Pasha, you must get some rest now because soon the music will be playing at your wedding and it will not do for my

ALUM BATI

Kadiasker to sleep through his own nuptials." These words of our Sultan were still ringing in my master's ears when he returned from the palace. And, in the circumstances, they had a pleasant ring to them following on as they did from a stern rebuke for disobeying our Sultan's strictest orders.

On the command of Hafsa Sultan, my master was to be married and I was powerless to stop it. If that were not enough, this most unwelcome development came in the middle of a delicate murder investigation, where, as the Sultan had himself pointedly made clear, speed was of the essence. Why Hafsa should have chosen this moment for yet another party was anybody's guess but concentrating on a murder investigation was now well-nigh impossible. Added to all this, there was the little difficulty of our sly Venetian emissary, effectively under house arrest thanks to the bold, some would say reckless, actions of my master. He could not be held there indefinitely but nor was my master prepared to upset the Mother Sultan, even if that meant the ambassador would stay a prisoner a little longer than was desirable.

My pasha, uncomfortable with set-piece ceremonial at the best of times, did his utmost to keep this whole marriage saga within manageable bounds. Needless to say, he had no desire to delve into all the intricate and tedious wedding formalities. Not that the Mother Sultan's keen interest made much allowance for interference by the bridegroom. He was merely expected to pay for it, and that was that.

Hafsa's first duty was to the women of the Harem. They had to have their fun and, intent on alleviating the boredom of Harem life, the ladies fell upon every delicate detail with untrammelled vigour. If, through the best endeavours of the Sultan, my pasha had at all persuaded the Queen Mother to exercise restraint, he saw precious little evidence of it.

120

My master left the palace with barely concealed concern but it had little to do with his approaching nuptials.

"Our Sultan was not pleased," said Adam Pasha, as he dismounted from his horse on his return home. "Did I act too hastily with the ambassador? He's been begging pitifully for audiences with the Sultan, and the worthy Gritti has been busy lobbying our Grand Vizier. I have to get some solid proof linking the ambassador with the robbery or that miserable toad is going to get away with it."

"But what about the weapons, master?" I said incredulously. "Surely our Sultan can't overlook that."

"He can and he will, Murat. He's not ready for a war with Venice."

"But, Pasha, the weapons. What about the weapons?"

"What weapons, Murat? They were bibles. Didn't you see? Those chests were full of bibles."

***

"Murat," said my pasha with a chuckle, "I've a task for you."

"No more chasing dogs, Pasha, please," I implored.

"No more dogs, Murat. I think you'll enjoy this one. Look, I'm no investigator and I can't go running around town seeking clues. We have to find that link between the ambassador and the Bazaar robbery and we have to do it fast. And when I say we I mean you."

Secretly, I was delighted. Save for the raid on the Venetian embassy, the whole affair was descending into drudgery. Still, I tried not to overplay my eagerness. "Pasha, how can I help?"

"Murat, I'm convinced that Hajji Yusuf holds the key."

"The President of the supervisory council? Well, that line of enquiry didn't get us very far. He literally held the keys."

"Very droll, Murat. He has his keys and he is not a thief,

so where does that leave us?" I did not get a chance to answer. "It means someone borrowed the keys either with or without his knowledge. Let's find out who he knows, who his friends and associates are. Perhaps we'll find a clue there. I want you to watch him, without him knowing, of course."

***

The wedding was in keeping with tradition and conducted by proxy. The Treasurer, Iskendar Chelebi, that long-standing rival of Ibrahim Pasha and now actively courting my master's friendship, stood-in for the Kadiasker whilst Selim Aga represented the bride. Iskendar and Selim, therefore, sat respectively right and left of Kemal-pasha-zade, the Mufti of Istanbul.

The Mufti presided over the formalities, which were mercifully brief. The wedding consisted of little more than an exchange of acknowledgements of the desire to wed, a promise by my master, through his proxy, to provide a dower for his bride, the signing of the marriage contract and a short blessing by the Mufti.

With all this, Adam Pasha had no complaint. Indeed, complaint was useless. If the Queen Mother had got it into her head that he should marry, who was the Kadiasker to object? But when he counted the cost he began to wonder whether getting married was such a wise move. The enormous expense of it passed before his very eyes as the mules strained and the camels rocked from side to side maintaining a steady pace as they carried gifts for the judge's bride. The ships of the desert rolled like the tide and the bountiful Adam through half-shut eyes viewed with subdued inner pride the bales of Bursa silk, richly dyed and plush velvets strapped astride the camels' humps. Soft sumptuous shawls embroidered in golden thread and silver trays with sugared candy on them spread, elegant ewers and water vases, mirrored caskets and wicker baskets jostled with jewelled cabinets and inlaid dressing boxes, furs of sable and silver foxes. Simple pitchers and intricate rugs, bottles of perfumes and fragrant essences, blue bowls and bundles of bedding followed the tuneful cadences of the musicians heading the colourful wedding procession.

Horns played and the minstrels strummed as the veiled smooth-skinned beauty, enclosed within a golden baldachin supported by four turbaned black eunuchs, rode on a snow-white mare. Before the lady went a boy, holding a Koran above his head, and servants carried wedding palms, those tasselled roundels of fragrant flowers and tasty candies skewered together with a stick. Veiled female servants rode behind and then followed a parade of fire-eaters, jugglers, and performers. And both the bride's procession and presents were cast open to the envious stares and admiration of all-comers – the invited and uninvited alike.

The bridal bath took place in the Queen Mother's own *hamam*. The bride was smeared with depilatory pastes and scrubbed and cleaned with perfumed soaps. Her hair was braided in tresses of ten and laced with pearls before she returned to her friends. Late into the night, gypsy music played in flickering candle light and honeyed sherbet and sweetmeats were relayed, shift upon shift.

The bride and her Harem friends, dressed in their finery and holding lighted tapers, wound their way through the Harem gardens, weaving in and weaving out amongst the shrubs and leaf-heavy trees, as musicians played and dancing girls swirled away. They sang songs of love and songs of hope and songs of their dreams:

> It is night and the world about us is all aglimmer
> The light of a thousand candles glow with a golden shimmer.
> Little had I dreamt this would be my night,
> May the one wish of my life come true tonight.

As the girls partied, my thrifty master was obliged to hold his own lavish receptions. He was not an ungenerous man, on occasion he was even extravagant, but that was when it involved the purchase of some rare manuscript or a fine kaftan. This, he thought, was simply a waste of money.

"What shall I do, Murat?" my master asked. "Any more of this and I'll be a pauper before I've had a chance to enjoy married life!"

What could I say or do? I was no happier than my pasha – and, to set a turban on it all, I was stuck with seeing to the purchase of the myriad of expensive dower gifts. That is not the work expected of a spy.

Poverty was no real concern for my pasha, and the bride, in any case, came with a healthy dowry from the Queen Mother – delicate silks, fine Egyptian cottons and, most welcome of all, the rents from some land near Bursa – but the disruption to the Kadiasker's work was a calamity. Though even our Sultan had to bow to his mother's wishes, the wedding could not have come at a more inconvenient time. Could it not have waited a while? Surely, wondered Adam Pasha, Hafsa Sultan could have put it off for a month or two.

***

My master, though, did not have much time to dwell either on the cost of the wedding or on what the future held. His problems were more immediate and he was swiftly reminded of them at the grand reception he had organised for his male friends and relatives (the women, worst luck, held parties of their own).

Ibrahim Pasha, casting inquisitorial glances in the Kadiasker's direction, approached him determinedly, to congratulate him for sure but my master knew it would not stop at that. He had employed every device and all his cunning to avoid contact with the Grand Vizier. That could not continue much longer, especially now that the Sultan had grudgingly relented to confiding in Ibrahim Pasha. But it was to be done discreetly and no more than was absolutely necessary. It seemed to my master that the time had come.

Ibrahim Pasha, a short man with tall ambitions, took my master gently by the arm. "Not only are you blessed in gaining a beautiful wife but I hear that you have also acquired a magnificent stallion. I should like to see him."

"You shall, Ibrahim Pasha," replied my master with a nervous smile. "He's a little headstrong but your spies are well-informed as always,"

The Kadiasker led the dark, sallow-complexioned Grand Vizier across the dusty courtyard to the stables extending along the whole of one side of the quadrangle. This was the smellier side of our abode, though it was pretty well-tended compared to the feeble standards of some of our senior officials. There, in a veritably princely stall, was a noble mahogany bay, standing just fourteen hands high, nodding his head knowingly. My pasha was a competent horseman but no more. He had ridden the white-socked stallion only three times but had never quite mastered him (if truth be told, three times mounted and three times thrown).

"Isn't he a beautiful animal?" asked my master.

"A fine beast, so sleek and slender," said Ibrahim Pasha, as he stroked the horse's muzzle. "An Arab? No, indeed not! An Akhal-teke, isn't he? Definitely a stud animal, not some nag destined for the battlefield. Where did you find him?"

No doubt the Grand Vizier knew the answer to that but Adam Pasha replied all the same. "At the horse-market in Uskudar. The best place to find Sufis, slaves and stallions."

"I'll check it out next week. They have some nice horses there but I've never seen anything like him," said Ibrahim Pasha longingly.

"It belonged to Zulfiqar Effendi, an acquaintance from Damascus. He was hard-hit by the Bazaar robbery. A lot of merchants are cashing in what precious possessions they have left so they can finance their businesses."

My master was becoming concerned. And it was not, at that moment, the thought of the inevitable interrogation that was troubling him. Our Grand Vizier had a reputation for collecting beautiful objects, especially expensive ones. The story sprang to my master's mind of the fine saddle presented to his patron by the Sultan only a month earlier. But when Prince Mustafa, who also has a hankering after beautiful things (was there ever such a realm with so many collectors?), admired it a little too keenly Ibrahim Pasha was obliged to surrender it to him. Was the Grand Vizier about to try a leaf out of Prince Mustafa's book of tricks? If the first minister chose to drop a hint that a 'gift' was appropriate, the Kadiasker could neither refuse to give up the stallion nor could he complain to our Sultan as Ibrahim Pasha had done in respect of the royal heir's greed.

My master almost audibly sighed with relief when the Grand Vizier's interest shifted from the stallion. He turned slowly to face his protégé. "Now, Adam Pasha, I know a lot of what is going on but I don't know if it's everything. I would like you to enlighten me."

Whilst the Kadiasker had every intention of telling the

Grand Vizier the basic facts, he felt it was best done if he did not appear to surrender too easily: Ibrahim Pasha was a man who liked to think that his power and influence were unrivalled, perhaps even by the Sultan himself. It would give him greater satisfaction if he believed that he had bent Adam Pasha to his will and had forced the secrets out of him.

"Ibrahim Pasha, I do not understand you."

"Don't try my patience, Kadiasker! You know what I mean! Don't forget to whom you owe your position. Look me in the eye and tell me who it was that realised your potential as a scholar? It was I who arranged for you to follow a scholar's career, not as a lowly-paid hair-splitting professor of law at some dissembling theological college but as a well-paid judge of an important city. I have brought you wealth and distinction and you owe it all to me!

"Have you forgotten the difficulty I had in getting you the Magistracy of Aleppo? Then, you had no major academic achievements to your name; you had held no Chair of Law at any university or *madrasa*. Granted, <u>now</u> everyone respects your learning and intellect but <u>then</u> .... Who had heard of you then? You were untried and unproven.

"Remember this: your preferment by me fuelled the ire of so many academics that I came close to losing out to the nominee of Iskendar Chelebi, that new friend and mentor of yours. There are more theologians out there than soldiers in the empire's brothels and each of them back then had a better call on the office of *Kadi* of Aleppo than you did. What scholar can hope to come close to the appointment you held in Aleppo unless and until he has spent year upon year of study and teaching, teaching and study?" His brow was crinkling, his arms were waving wildly and his face seemed ready to explode. "And you achieved all of this at the tender age of, what, twenty-eight, twenty-nine?"

The Grand Vizier paused but the homily was not yet done. Ibrahim Pasha was merely trying to take control of his rage. "When, Muhyuddin Chelebi, that pimple on a whore's bum who sat where you sit now – when he sought to humiliate me in the Divan he paid for it. I saw to that. I had him thrown out on his poxy arse. And who gained by all this? You, Adam Pasha! I petitioned His Highness to show you favour and to make you Kadiasker in that dog's place."

There was venom in the words. The tale of Muhyuddin's downfall was meant to be a salutary one. One day he had been trying a case in the Divan. Ibrahim Pasha, claiming to have been a witness to the crime at issue, declared the defendant guilty. But Muhyuddin rejected the testimony on the basis that Ibrahim Pasha was a slave and the testimony of a slave was inadmissible. The incensed chief minister immediately went to the Sultan and sought his freedom, which was promptly given. But Muhyuddin still refused to accept the Grand Vizier's evidence until the proof of manumission was delivered in writing. The then Kadiasker's audacity astounded the Divan and stunned its members into silence. It almost sent Ibrahim Pasha into a fit of apoplexy. The question then sitting on everyone's lips was "how would the Grand Vizier wreak his revenge?" Vengeance was not long in coming. The freeborn Muslim, Muhyuddin, was replaced by the slave, Christian-born Adam, a native Greek-speaker like the Grand Vizier and not from the religious establishment so distrusted and derided by Ibrahim Pasha.

My master was so taken aback by the vehemence of the diatribe that he made no attempt to interrupt the onslaught. There was more to come.

"You have allowed your new-found power to go to your

head, Pasha, but mind that you don't lose it! Who do you think you are going behind my back, scheming and weaving plots like all your kind? Never trust a lawyer! You, too, can go the same way as Muhyuddin Chelebi. And heed this: I can raise the humblest peasant to the vizierate and I can reduce the mightiest vizier to penury! I would win a lot of friends by restoring Muhyuddin to power. Don't forget that."

Again, the pointed reference to Muhyuddin. Although dismissed from the Divan, he was a distinguished scholar nonetheless and our Sultan could not indefinitely ignore his claim to high office. The message was clear: my master was a traitor. Not a traitor to the Sultan but, which was infinitely worse, to Ibrahim Pasha himself.

The Grand Vizier despised theologians. And they loathed him. It was mutual contempt all round. He blamed them for every ill in the Empire – they, he said, were kill-joys who lacked imagination, stifled progress, meddled in every aspect of life. The clerics, for their part, condemned him, secretly of course, as a wanton, ostentatious, avaricious heretic (or as good as one) bent on power and the accumulation of wealth and having no regard for the well-being of the people or the destiny of his soul. More than anything else, the theologians viewed the Grand Vizier's close bond to the Sultan with deep jealousy and suspicion. They thought the Sultan should rightfully be theirs. After all, he was the *Ameer al-Mumineen*, the Commander of the Faithful. And who could be more 'faithful' than the clerics?

"Have you, too, succumbed, Kadiasker?" continued the haughty Grand Vizier. "Have the alchemists applied their elixirs and transformed you into one of them? Are you with me or not? Are you a smart man who knows where your loyalties lie or are you just a rosary-thumbing finger-pointer?"

The Grand Vizier had misjudged his Chief Justice. I knew him better than any man and he was no intolerant Koran-thumper. He was open to new ideas and his time with the priest in his childhood had given him an understanding of Jewish and Christian scriptures that few Muslim clerics possessed. The Empire will thrive as long as there are people like him. Without them it will inevitably vanish.

But the Grand Vizier had not yet finished. "We are natives of the same land – Greek-speakers, both of us. It is one reason why I wanted your talents to be recognised quickly. We stand together or fall together. So let me tell you this: neither of us chose this life and I, for one, am going to make the most of it. Now you tell me, Kadiasker, have you really turned into a 'finger-pointer'?"

"My Pasha," replied my master in a polite but masterful voice, "we were both born into Greek-speaking families, so much is true, but we are both Ottomans now. And I am a Muslim both out of conversion and conviction. If you do not believe in the power of Allah, I cannot help you."

"I don't know if there is a God, Kadiasker. What I do know is that on Earth, power is mine and, I will use it."

"My Pasha," said the Kadiasker, composed and courteous, "this is neither the time nor the place to engage in theological disputation. I have guests waiting. We should return to the reception. I have left my guests long enough."

The Kadiasker possessed a genuine sense of loyalty to Ibrahim Pasha. He was grateful for all that had been done for him but he was not going to allow that to corrupt his judgement. He could accept a friendly bias in favour of the Grand Vizier on lesser matters but he was no man's marionette. And he was determined to prove it.

Ibrahim Pasha was quick to realise his mistake. "Kadiasker, forgive me. I have allowed my frustration to distort my judgement. I have heard ugly rumours that you have conspired – no, that you <u>are</u> conspiring against me. Tell me they are not true. Tell me that you do not suspect me of Shireen's murder." For all his talk of power, the tone of his voice betrayed an almost pathetic, pleading quality. Adam Pasha made no reply and what followed was an uncomfortable silence broken finally by the Grand Vizier.

"Surely you understand my position, Kadiasker? Let us act now as brothers, not as enemies."

"Ibrahim Pasha," replied my master, "I beg your forgiveness. I know you think me ungrateful for all you have done for me: I am not. But in this I have strict instructions. There is neither a conspiracy against you nor have you ever been suspected of even so much as a minor misdemeanour, let alone Shireen's murder." The Kadiasker paused and lowered his eyes, knowing that this was not entirely true. "After all, if you were under suspicion, would His Highness appoint me to lead the investigation, all the time knowing that I owe my advancement to you?"

Another pause. It was a clever argument and he could see it was having its affect on the Grand Vizier, who was considerably happier now that the Kadiasker had reaffirmed his bond of loyalty and obligation.

Ibrahim Pasha broke the silence. "So, she <u>was</u> murdered. I had heard as much."

"I knew such details would come as no surprise to you, my Pasha," said my master. "Your network of spies surpasses even our Sultan's! I am sure she was murdered but I have no idea who did it. That is my task – to find the murderer. And," my pasha added hurriedly, "it is not because anyone suspects you or anything so ridiculous that has caused me to keep the details from you."

Inexplicably, these few sentences were all the comfort that Ibrahim Pasha sought. If he had pursued a rigorous interrogation, the Kadiasker would have been hard-pressed to think of a convincing reason why the Grand Vizier should not have been more intimately involved in the investigation. It was a question he had asked himself many times – indeed, was still asking himself. But the assured Chief Minister did not continue the questioning. He looked into the stallion's eyes, patted it gently on the neck and turned out of the dimly-lit stables into the fading summer sunshine.

"Come, Adam Pasha," he said warmly. "I have forced you to neglect your guests far too long." He took my master's arm and they walked slowly back to the house just like two friends taking an evening stroll.

***

My master knew that one day he would be married and that he would have little say in choosing the bride. He was not unhappy with the gift that Hafsa Sultan had made to him. But he now had obligations and responsibilities that only a few days before he did not have. He was far from convinced that he wanted to carry such a burden, especially at this difficult time. That there was lingering unease was natural and it owed nothing to the superstitious warnings against the 'evil eye' – my master dismissed as childish nonsense the shower of charms, fashioned out of blue-glazed pottery, which he received to ward off the 'eye'. But whatever the future held, life was heading in a new direction.

Still, though my master was no politician, it did no harm to be married to a moderately well-connected Harem girl. Especially, such a beautiful, well-connected Harem girl.

132

XI   THE MAN IN WHITE

The bride in question was Nilufer and with such a prize who can find fault? I admit, I had opposed the very idea of my master's marriage but I soon realised my error of judgement: the choice could have been worse, infinitely worse.

Nilufer was the tonic my master needed and a light-headedness fell on him in the weeks after the wedding. Once I had got to know Nilufer better, her lively presence barely masked by her veil, I understood that for the Kadiasker she was the perfect match – she was bold, intelligent and unconventional, and she laughed as indulgently as did I at his sarcastic quips. We soon formed a bond of friendship. It was like being part of a family again and it revived emotions I had long-since forgotten.

Nilufer, however, had a stubborn streak and in one regard she was adamant.

"My Pasha, are you happy?" she asked one morning, addressing my master with the full respect appropriate to his status.

"Exquisitely. Are you?"

"Yes, my Pasha. I've never been happier. But will you grant me one wish?" Nilufer was glad to have left the Imperial Harem but, though in law a Muslim, she needed some convincing that being married to a prominent Muslim scholar was really what she wanted.

"Anything," replied my master.

"My Pasha, I do not want to leave the Imperial Harem only to end up in confinement here."

***

133

A few weeks after the wedding, Nilufer asked if she could see the stables.

"My Pasha, I would like to ride him," she said pointing eagerly at my master's fine new stallion. My pasha was in no mood to deny her anything but felt a note of caution was needed.

"My dear, it could be dangerous."

"I'm not afraid. I know how to ride," Nilufer said confidently. "<u>Well</u>! I ride exceptionally well!" she added, to drive home the point on seeing my pasha's evident surprise.

"And what will all your friends in the Harem say? Think of the non-stop gossip."

"Gossip? About me?" Nilufer gave a dismissive but pleasing laugh. "My Pasha, would you think me brazen?"

"No. Unconventional perhaps, but not brazen."

"If you do not think me brazen, that is all that matters. If <u>you</u> don't mind the gossip, I certainly don't. My Pasha, you should treat Harem gossip like bird droppings – best cleaned away and quickly forgotten."

***

Married life, however, was far from helping my master either in his search for Shireen's murderer or his duties as Kadiasker. Night after night, he struggled to keep awake (made no easier by having a beautiful new wife) as he worked through a heap of petitions and depositions.

Excused from his more routine tasks, my master was too diligent a minister to neglect his official duties altogether. I felt helpless and we were both exhausted. Our heads would droop in unison and then jerk violently as we fought off sleep whilst the candle flickered in pools of dripping molten wax. One week passed and then two. And we made no progress in the investigation. No new evidence came to hand; no informant came forward. My master began to despair. And, the more he despaired, the more he confided in me.

Adam Pasha had many theories but little hard evidence. Minutes merged into hours and hours into days as we discussed possible scenarios. Sometimes, like the good doctor, our imaginations ran away with us and we dreamt up fanciful plots. But time was running out and my master was courting unpopularity: palace gossip was rife and the backbiting had begun. Those jealous of my master's special appointment or afraid of what he might report were working hard to get him dismissed from office. And that was before taking Ibrahim Pasha into the reckoning: still harbouring suspicions, he was not a man who could be ignored.

Still, the time eventually came when the chores and rigours of the wedding and its aftermath were behind me. Freed to take up my role as an Imperial spy, I intended to make the most of it.

My task was to discover a connection, if any, between Hajji Yusuf and the Bazaar robbery. My method was to disguise myself as a water carrier, wearing a tousled turban, loose shirt and baggy trousers and carrying a filled-to-the-brim buffalo hide with a little metal cup dangling from a rope around its neck. I set off for Hajji Yusuf's residence. It was not too far from the Bazaar, a solid building perfectly suited to a man of solid character. It was not long, though, before I started wishing I had chosen some other disguise – that buffalo hide was feeling heavier and heavier as I marched up and down the cobbled street outside Hajji Yusuf's house. I was worn down, inside and out, and my mind strayed to wondering what sort of fool becomes a spy. The only consolation was that I had managed to sell or drink most of the contents of the buffalo skin. The perks were minor and fleeting as I soon felt the urge to expel all that water I had drunk. I could not leave my post so I just suffered the agony and marched faster than before.

Then, in mid-afternoon, he finally ventured out, bearing down on me like a war galley in full cry. I started to sweat, and not just from the exertions of humping about water-filled buffalo hides. He had surely spotted me and my only thought was to run but, exhausted as I was, I could barely move, let alone run. I was, in any case, mesmerised – fixed to the spot as I stared wildly at Hajji Yusuf drawing closer and closer. I tried to look away but that, too, proved beyond my capabilities. My pasha's words, "without him knowing," swirled in my giddy head as my eyes were transfixed on his beard, bobbing up and down, up and down, as he strode towards me.

But he walked right past me, as if I did not exist. Of course, how could he have spotted me? We had never met before. "You miserable failure, Murat," I thought. "Your first outing as a spy and you almost gave yourself away. Get a grip on yourself!"

I did, and I was after him. At least it took my mind off my over-full bladder problem. Thankfully, there was not much chance of losing the Hajji as he headed straight for the Bazaar. Or so I thought but, just before reaching the north gate, he veered sharply to the right, down a smelly twisting alley. Where was he going?

He looked over his shoulder and I stepped into the shadows. That was not difficult. Finding a bright spot was difficult.

I hurried on after him, his stride lengthening and his long legs threatening to take him out of sight. I started to skip to keep up with him. I must have looked ridiculous – a water-seller skipping down some wretched back-street. But where was he going?

Who would have guessed it? Surely not? What business had he, a devout Muslim, to be in a Jewish part of town? "Patience, Murat," I thought to myself, "Patience will bring its own rewards. You'll soon find out."

What an anti-climax it all was. A girl, a Jewish girl, twenty-three or twenty-four years old, I judged, from the slim waist and plaited rich black hair visible under a small yellow hat and gauze veil. Lucky old man, I thought, as the two of them stood staring at each other in the street. There was no need to go home too early. There were still a few hours before nightfall and anything could happen. In fact, come dark, things could get really interesting.

But this was not going to be my lucky night. After barely exchanged a word with the girl, Hajji Yusuf ambled straight into a plain white-washed house as if he owned it. To make matters worse, the simple dwelling had no street-side windows at ground level. Still, it did possess a vined balcony overhanging the portal and that could prove useful. Wait till dark and then climb onto the tempting balcony, I thought. But there was not going to be any chance of that as the buxom girl suddenly appeared on the doorstep. I waited briefly in anxious anticipation of the Hajji following behind but, without any sign of him, I reckoned there was no point hanging around any longer. For one thing, the old women, gossiping on their doorsteps, had already spotted me as an outsider. They kept one baggy eye on their scruffy grandchildren playing in the well-urinated street (which, after the rigours of the afternoon, I had found more than useful) and the other on me. My only option was to follow the girl. The view from behind could have been worse, a lot worse. That girl had quite a wiggle: a tantalising ripple to relish and savour.

We wound and wiggled our way through those same backstreets I had navigated earlier that day. Now then, here was a mystery worthy of an imperial spy. The wigglesome journey ended up at the Old Palace and the girl went directly into the Harem. I, regrettably, had to stay outside, leaving me with little option but to get back to my pasha as quickly as I could for further instructions.

***

"Pasha, nobody stopped her. She wasn't even challenged. She sauntered into the Harem as if it were home. I don't understand it."

"It's certainly curious, Murat. She can't be a Harem girl. That's unthinkable. But who is she? Selim Aga must know the answer so you had better talk to him."

The next day, I set off for the Harem, armed with a letter from my master addressed to Selim Aga requesting him to give whatever assistance he could. This, Selim Aga did graciously without asking the reason.

"I can't allow you into the Harem, Murat," said Selim. "But ask me your questions and I will try to answer them."

I described what I had seen the previous afternoon. "She was Jewish. Long legs and very nice behind." My breath lingered over the "very". "And," I could not help adding, "the front wasn't all that bad either."

"That's Kira Sarah," replied Selim without hesitation. "You're right: nice figure. She sells jewels to Khurrem Sultan and the other Harem ladies of rank and does all those odd little tasks that Harem girls might want doing – writing letters for those who can't write, carrying messages to the outside world, delivering gifts and so on. She also buys embroideries from the girls – real works of art, some of them. But selling jewels – that's where the money is. That poor girl, Shireen, was a good customer. And, by the grace of Allah, I have good news for you: Sarah's in the Harem right now. Daud Aga took her to Khurrem Sultan about half an hour ago and if you wait here, you'll spot her coming out."

I plopped myself down by a conveniently sited olive tree and waited. Fortunately, not for long. About twenty minutes later, the diminutive Daud Aga, Selim's deputy, appeared at the gate accompanying a provocatively loosely veiled girl. That she was a Jewess was clear from that same flat-topped hat she had worn the previous day. And across her face was drawn a piece of white gauze. Daud Aga was impressively dressed as always, totally in white except for his ochre-yellow leather shoes. Sarah stopped briefly at the gate to exchange a few words with Daud Aga and then wiggled off. Once she was clear of the main gate I crept out from behind the tree and, nibbling on an olive, followed at a discreet distance.

It soon became apparent, though, that the distance was not discreet enough. Sarah must have realised that she was being followed. She picked up her skirts and dipped into one of those dark unwelcoming alleys with which I was so fast becoming familiar. I peered into the blackness but there was no sign of her. I hesitated briefly and then dashed into the passageway. But my quarry had disappeared and I had no idea how – witchcraft perhaps. That was it – witchcraft.

What chance had I of seeing a wiggle like that again? I was furious with myself, so furious in fact that I spat out my olive pit with such force that it caught a four-year old brat a ping just behind the left ear and reduced him to a wailing and tearful wretch. Disgusted and barely able to reflect upon my prowess with the olive pit, I started muttering curses and took myself over to some Roman ruins. I sat down in a dejected heap amongst the lumps of stone and debris to think about what to do next. One thing though was clear to me: only someone with a secret to hide would have been so wary, cautious enough to notice that she was being followed and worried enough to feel the need to take evasive action.

My luck, however, was about to take a turn for the better. Sarah, who had hidden herself in one of the dark doorways of the alley, thinking she had escaped, now emerged into the open, the sunlight bouncing off her yellow cap. Little had she expected me to be taking a peaceful break amidst the detritus of a dead empire.

This time I was more careful. I followed Sarah for fifteen minutes, winding our way through the backstreets and alleyways of the city. Eventually she arrived at that same humble two-storied house where Hajji Yusuf had met her the previous afternoon.

And now what was I to do? I had, of course, to return home and report to my master but, before doing so, I pondered if I should continue observation for a bit longer. I decided on the latter and for two long, hot, hours I sat at one end of the alley, observing the door of the suspect's house. And nothing happened.

Then, I started to think. What a complete imbecile I had been. Surely, Sarah's behaviour was no more suspicious than one might expect of someone carrying gemstones: it was the most natural thing in the world to be vigilant.

I was beginning to think that being a spy was not so much fun after all. It was dawning on me that the long spells of tedium were more the routine than the short bursts of random excitement. Then, with my head drooping, out of the corner of my eye I saw a tall, grey-bearded figure enter the house. My luck was in again. It was Shaykh Hajji Yusuf Ali.

I sat on watch for a bit but, with about an hour to dusk, I saw little point dawdling in the gloaming and, so, scampered home, running where the streets were deserted, walking briskly where they were not.

***

Adam Pasha, sitting on a cushion, listened attentively, without interruption. When I had finished, he stood up, straightened his full-length gown and thoughtfully paced the room saying nothing. After a couple of circuits, he stroked his beard and said, "Murat, have my horse saddled and be ready in the courtyard in fifteen minutes with Ibrahim and four of our best troopers."

Nilufer, however, had other ideas. "My Pasha, it's late. Where are you going?" she asked gently. "Stay with me."

"I'm going to see an old man and a young girl," my master said with a smile. He was about to turn away, when something occurred to him. "Nilufer, dear, have you ever met Kira Sarah?"

"Yes, many times. Are you going to buy me a present?" she teased. The Kadiasker kissed her on the cheek.

"Perhaps. Would you like that?"

"Who doesn't like presents?" she replied with a grin.

"I imagine Khurrem Sultan knows her well?"

"Of course. They're close confidantes, always sharing secrets. Khurrem is also one of Sarah's best customers. Shireen used to buy from her, too. I introduced them," said Nilufer proudly. "You remember that lost pearl necklace? Sarah sold it to Shireen. But why do you ask about the Kira?"

"You trust her, then?"

141

"She sells, Harem girls buy. There's no more to it than that. Her prices are extortionate but what else do we spend our money on? Are you really going to see her now? At this time of night? I want to go with you."

"Out of the question. Are you jealous? I hear she has a very nice figure."

"The harlot!" said Nilufer, with a squint and a lop-sided smile. "I'm not jealous, truly, but you need someone to look after you. Think of me as your guardian angel. Please …," Nilufer implored lovingly. "Please let me go."

"No, my angel. It's out of the question," said my pasha firmly, before taking Nilufer's head in his hands and planting a lingering kiss on her lips.

Fifteen minutes later, the men mounted and fully armed, we set out for Sarah's house, with me in the lead.

The only light there was came from lanterns carried by me and, on the tip of their lances, by each of the troopers. We made good time through the deserted streets and, nearing the alley where Sarah lived, we dismounted and covered the last fifty metres or so as stealthily as possible. That was a hard task in a narrow alley watched by busybodies.

On reaching the house, my master deployed his men. Two troopers remained with the horses at one end of the street. Two more were positioned at the opposite end whilst my pasha, Ibrahim, a strong man built like a wrestler, and I approached the house quietly and carefully. The door was unlocked and, apart from the sound of a rat scurrying for cover, there was an eerie silence.

My pasha, lantern in hand, led the way up the narrow rickety steps. A stair creaked, another groaned under Ibrahim's bulk; a sword clattered against the steps. My master gave up any attempt at surprise and burst into the single large room upstairs.

My pasha's careful precautions had all been unnecessary. There was no one in the room. At least no one alive, but lying supine in the far corner on a mattress was the half-dressed body of Yusuf Ali. The thin mattress had soaked up the blood that had gushed out of the single stiletto-dagger wound made in his heart.

My pasha threw open the closed shutters to let in some air. Yusuf Ali had been dead for two or three hours and already, in the warm stuffy atmosphere, the flies were beginning to swarm around the congealed blood on the body and the rats had started to gnaw at the flesh. My master recoiled at the revolting sight and I scrambled to hold a perfumed handkerchief to my nose in a vain attempt to fight the rising stench.

"What do you make of it, Master?" I asked, my voice muffled by the handkerchief.

"I don't know, Murat. I don't know!" he said in exasperation. "Where's the link between Yusuf Ali and Sarah? And why should she want to kill him? At least, I'm assuming she killed him. And what's a pious Muslim merchant doing flirting with a Jewish girl?"

"You didn't see that wiggle, Pasha."

"Well, the wiggle explains why he's half undressed and lying on a mattress but his clothes, his purse ... everything is here, so why kill him? I doubt if we'll find the answers in this room," he said, eager to leave,

We were about to go when a verminous rat shot from one shadow to another. Startled, I looked back and noticed something that had lain hidden by the mattress but had been dragged into the open by the rat.

"Pasha, look!" I said excitedly, pointing to the corner of

143

the mattress.

Lying by Yusuf Ali's left hand was a pearl pendant necklace. My master, not wanting to touch anything the rat had crawled over, gratefully took the handkerchief that I offered him and daintily picked up the locket. He started idly playing with it, turning it over and over again in his delicate hands. Suddenly the moulded gold surround sprang open. The Kadiasker had, quite by accident, flicked open a secret clasp, revealing a small hollow compartment beneath the pearl.

"That's strange, Murat," said my pasha pointing to the cavity. "Take a look. This little treasure bears a remarkable resemblance to the necklace Shireen was wearing – or, rather, was not wearing – on the night of her death. What's the Hajji doing with it here?"

***

That evening, our Sultan was dining together with Ibrahim Pasha in a small room in the third courtyard at the rear of the New Palace's Harem. When he heard that my pasha desired an urgent audience he took his leave of the suspicious Grand Vizier, a man quietly seething with rage.

"So, Adam Pasha, I gather you've urgent news. Good news, I trust. In recent days you've only brought me bad news and there are times when even your Sultan grows tired of that."

My pasha was left wishing he had not found the body. Nervously, he related the events of the evening, picking his words carefully, trying to put the whole incident in as good a light as he could. And there lay the problem. The harder he tried the less hopeful he sounded. With his eyes lowered in respect, he could not see the reaction on the Sultan's face and could only imagine the scowls and frowns of a man deep in thought. The more he imagined, the more halting became his narration.

"Kadiasker, you've done well," interrupted our Sultan. These were unexpected but very welcome words. "This very afternoon Ibrahim Pasha has brought me a report from the head of our intelligence network. It makes interesting reading. For some time we've suspected that it has been infiltrated by a Venetian spy. The report cites the Kira Sarah as a possible contact of the spy. In view of what you have told me, I'm ordering her immediate arrest. She won't get far.

"Poor dupe," he added, referring to Yusuf Ali.

***

Some days after the discovery of Yusuf Ali's body, a lone horseman, a member of the Sultan's elite bodyguard of *Sipahis*, rode into the courtyard of our house. My master, hearing the sound of a horse's hooves on the newly-laid cobblestones, put aside his reed pen and peered out over the balcony. He saw the sipahi lean forward in his saddle to speak to me. Though the Kadiasker could not see the cavalryman's face, he was not dressed as an officer.

I hurried across the courtyard to convey the trooper's message to my master. My pasha, straining to deduce the identity of the mysterious sipahi, could tell little from the back of his head, wearing as he was the scalloped plumed helmet common to all sipahis. Even as he turned his dappled grey gelding towards Adam Pasha, the half-hidden face made no impression on my master.

I rapped gently on the open door to gain my pasha's attention.

"Who's the soldier, Murat?"

"He won't say, Pasha, but he wants to speak to you about a matter of some importance. I told him you were very busy and he must state his business but he says you will know him when you see him."

It was that hint of mystery that aroused my master's curiosity. "Show him up. Let's see what he has to say."

My pasha watched the soldier dismount, sling his assortment of weaponry over the saddle of his horse and walk slowly across the courtyard. There was something very familiar about him: the aristocratic aquiline nose, the clean-shaven chin, and the sallow complexion. But who was he?

The soldier removed his helmet and tucked it under his arm, revealing his high cheekbones and clever eyes. My pasha made a sign of welcome. "How can I help you? My valet tells me you have something important to say to me." My master indicated a comfortable spot in the corner for his guest to sit and instructed me to bring a pitcher of lemon sherbet to refresh our visitor.

"Adam Pasha," replied the soldier, trying hard to hold back a roar of laughter, "don't you recognise your Padishah?"

"My Sultan ...?" Adam Pasha blurted out. "My Lord, forgive me!" he stammered as he hurriedly brought himself to his feet.

"Do you like my disguise?" Suleyman asked with a childlike pleasure.

"Excellent, my Sultan, but why ..."

"Why the charade? Because Adam Pasha, you and I are about to find out what the people are thinking. I want to know what's being said in the bazaars. All the gossip, every shred of tittle-tattle. You will find the bazaars a remarkable source of information. But you can't go like that. You had better change out of your fine silks into something more robust." He tapped his chainmailed chest and added, "A soldier's outfit is what you need."

Outfitted in a chainmail suit, riding boots, wrist protectors and the other accoutrements of a cavalryman, my pasha was ready. There were none of the finely crafted silver inlaid items usually worn by him when riding into battle, but the simple good quality pieces issued to his bodyguard.

And so, the two secret sipahis, Sultan and slave, rode out towards the Covered Bazaar.

As they rode to the Bazaar, my pasha's thoughts turned to the Vienna siege, less than a year ago and still fresh in the memory. He had played an important role in maintaining a semblance of order during the long march back to Istanbul, helping to prevent the army from degenerating into a rowdy rabble. He was troubled by aspects of the retreat, loathing the summary justice he was sometimes called on to dispense, but it was an essential part of military discipline.

Sultan Suleyman, who enjoyed his occasional excursions into the real world, brought my master out of his day-dreams with some practical advice.

"We had better adopt false names and identities more suited to our purpose. I shall be Bayezid and you can be Osman. What better names can there be?" The question was, of course, rhetorical, but at least these were two of the more worthy of the Sultan's ancestors. He could have done worse.

Bayezid led the way, deciding to enter the Bazaar through the slave market. The price of slaves had been falling fast as Khairadeen, decimating shipping in the western Mediterranean, sent back more and more captives to a market that could absorb no more. As prices fell, speculators sensed bargains to be had and started to buy up good quality human stock for resale when the market took an upward turn. And though only Muslims ought to own slaves, others were not unknown or unwelcome buyers.

"Look, Osman," said our Sultan pointing to a crowd on the right. "Do you see him?"

With a surprised nod of the head, my pasha acknowledged that he did. "It's Mikhail Effendi."

Indeed, it was. Our friend was examining a strong Spaniard and it was not a medical diagnosis. The shrewd doctor was an inveterate speculator, be it in goods, ideas or anything else. He was a man with a good eye for a bargain and the Spaniard was worth a look, his muscles bulging and sinuous like a fat cucumber. That was the result of years of straining at the oars as a one-time galley-slave, and now he was a miserable slave once again. Still, for one reason or another, he was not to Mikhail's taste.

"Did you see, Osman, how he passed by that big Sicilian?"

"Yes, my Sultan … forgive me, Bayezid. But why – he looks a good, strong specimen?"

"I was here a month ago, just after the robbery. Business was slack at the time. The Sicilian was up for sale then, too. No one wanted to buy him. Flat feet, you see. What a stupid, superstitious people we are! A flat-foot is a hard-sell."

"Our good doctor, so superstitious? I'd never have thought it."

"No, Osman. Our Mikhail's a pragmatist. No superstition there. He knows that he can't give the Sicilian away in a bad market. He clearly can't have any faith in a quick recovery."

"Look! I think he is about to make a purchase," said my pasha. The commercially-minded doctor had turned his attention to a rough but handsome Roman, as strong as the Spaniard, with biceps like camel-humps, but with a less arrogant mien. A check of the teeth, a rough inspection of the shape of the head, a poke in the stomach, and Mikhail nodded to the slave-dealer. The Roman was his and, having now revealed his serious intentions, a woman slaver became importunate with her claims for the quality and value of her female slaves (discreetly hidden behind a curtain). Mikhail, wisely keeping on the move, graciously declined her offers.

Amused by the spectacle, Osman and Bayezid rode on for fear of being recognised by Mikhail. Passing by the professional story-teller, sitting on his box and enthralling a goodly-sized audience with vivid images conjured up by his thin hands and gravelly voice, they reached the gate of the covered portion of the bazaar. They dismounted by a large stack of cages, each cage holding a small bird. Bayezid, in a common act of charity, stopped briefly to buy a sparrow to set it free. The sipahis, leaving their horses there in the charge of a scruffy little boy for a small payment, entered the noisy, burbling covered market.

The bazaar was perhaps quieter than it had been in times past but outwardly it seemed to have recovered remarkably well from the shocks of the robbery. The two sipahis passed by the shops of Persians, Armenians, Jews and Greeks selling silks, satins and fine cloths. They passed by the perambulating market brokers crying out the selling prices set by their principals. They dodged nimbly around the sweating, straining porters calling "Permission!" as they weaved and wobbled their way through the shoppers, bent double under their over-sized burdens.

Once they reached the part frequented by the sellers of falconry and riding paraphernalia, Adam Pasha knew that the Sultan would not walk past without a peek and a rummage. "Look!" he said to my master, grabbing his arm. "What lovely hoods for my falcons!" Some time later and a few akches lighter, we moved on. Then the Sultan came to a sudden halt, catching sight of a burly man in an untidy turban. He was a market inspector, chuckling as he meted out punishment for short measure to a middle-aged man in baggy red trousers and white shirt. Placing his head in a pillory, his hands tied behind his back, he led the shopkeeper through the streets carrying his encumbrance in disgrace. A short while later, another miscreant was thrown over the back of a Janissary and the soles of his feet lashed with a cane. Our Sultan smiled with pleasure at how his law officers were carrying out their duty and his justice.

But, the pleasure was momentary. It soon turned to rage and our Sultan could barely restrain himself from rushing forward and tidying up the inspector's turban by wrapping it around his throat. My master, too, could not believe his eyes as he saw the man in the pillory set free: the wooden block was unlocked, the hands untied, and money was passed between the inspector and the trader. Our Sultan looked away but asked his Kadiasker to remind him of this incident when they returned to the Palace.

Meandering on, the two sipahis arrived at the widow Aziza's shop, occupying a corner spot in the Silk Market. It was small but typical of the shops in the bazaar. Nestling up against the walls were wooden benches covered with soft rugs and velvet pillows. This picture of cosiness beckoned enticingly to tired shoppers to stop, take some refreshments and, more to the point, examine the merchandise.

At the rear of the shop, stood wooden boxes draped with valuable silks and other fabrics. The narrow market passages were, in normal times, filled with thrifty shoppers comparing prices and taking time and care to select their purchases. Since the robbery, however, despite the outward hurly-burly of a thriving market, business had been poor – some shops had closed and others had been forced to cut prices. Many wealthy citizens, the mainstay of the Silk Market, had suffered in the robbery and were no longer buyers. And scores of shopkeepers had lost their working capital and could no longer afford to replace their depleted stocks.

The widow Aziza, as the only woman shopkeeper in the bazaar, was a well-known and well-respected figure. She had lost a great deal in the robbery and tears were trapped in her eyes as she contemplated the ruin of her business. Her thoughts fell to selling off the remainder of her stock and acquiring a cheaper site or moving to another market altogether. Her days of selling silks seemed over. My master, compelled by compassion, bought large quantities of cloth for Nilufer. He tucked two rolls under each arm as our Sultan stood pondering what he could possibly do to help the ruined traders.

As the two soldiers were about to leave Aziza's shop, the young widow stopped them. She was throwing furtive glances beyond the Sultan towards a scene about twenty-five metres away. "Don't go yet, Sirs. Please stay and have some sherbet," she pleaded. "Business isn't good today," she added with a forced smile.

Our Sultan turned to look behind him but his view was blocked by a particularly inconvenient convergence of shoppers. He could not see what Aziza could see. Standing on the wide bench that formed the floor of her shop, her eyes were fixed on that same market inspector Bayezid and Osman had passed some twenty minutes earlier. He was engaged in his favourite pastime, doling out punishment to erring merchants. When we realised what was going on, our Sultan started to wonder why this should concern Aziza unless, of course, she herself was a transgressor. But my pasha understood better. He saw the forty-something shopkeeper pass a leather purse to a large, threatening Janissary sergeant, a deep scar prominent on his right cheek.

"What's happening?" asked the Sultan, "What is it?"

"Nothing, Sir. Nothing," replied Aziza in a voice not quite a whisper but almost so. She turned her face away.

"Is it the market inspector?" asked my pasha. "Why does he frighten you?"

"He doesn't frighten me, Sir. Karim is grasping but I can live with that. Please don't ask me any more questions."

But my pasha had to know. It was his sense of justice. He had to know if an unlawful act was being committed. He suspected as much but suspicion was not enough. He had to know. "Please, tell me. Perhaps we can help."

"How can you help me, Sir?" was the sceptical response.

"We're in the service of Adam Pasha, the Kadiasker. We'll pass any complaint straight to him," said my master.

Aziza considered these words for a moment. "Sir, no one can help us, not even the worthy Adam Pasha. Those two and their hirelings … I've had enough. They've been threatening all the shopkeepers, the honest law-abiding ones and the others. Last week two store-owners were beaten up for refusing their extortionate demands. They've been mulching money from us and, now, if we refuse to pay, it's the bastinado for any minor infringement of the law."

"Everyone should abide by the Sultan's laws!" bellowed Bayezid, more than a little indignantly. For, him there was no such thing as "a minor infringement" of his law.

"I agree, Sir, but those two are using the law for their own enrichment."

"Why don't you bring your grievance before the Divan?"

asked my pasha. "You'll get justice there."

"Justice? What has justice to do with this? It's fear, Sir. It's fear that stops any of us complaining. The Janissary's bullies have fists like anvils – and they use them. I don't think they would attack a woman, but I'm still afraid. And they can still ruin my business." Aziza, looking around her little shop, let slip an ironic laugh through her dark veil. "That's rich! What business? I'm ruined anyway. I haven't got much more to lose."

"I'm sure," said Adam Pasha, "the Kadiasker will give you a sympathetic hearing."

"Sirs, we don't need sympathy. We need help."

"Take our advice, Aziza. You could still do a lot to help your fellow traders. If you deliver a petition to Adam Pasha, I can assure you it will be considered. If you do so by Saturday, it can be heard on Monday."

"Sirs, you are very kind. Do you really think the Kadiasker can help? I will think about it," said the widow.

Adam Pasha's attention was drawn again to the Janissary sergeant. He was swaying menacingly to and fro, raising his arm as if he was about to hit one of the shopkeepers. It was only the sharp tug on his sleeve by the inspector that prevented it. Then a newcomer joined the merry little band. His face was partly obscured by the oversized sergeant and partly by the unusually loose-hanging end of his white turban which was drawn like a veil across his face. He was so small – little more than a metre-and-a-half – that even his turban failed to give him stature. He was, though, evidently a man of some means: his white outfit was high quality stuff. Diminutive, pink skinned and dressed expensively in white, that was the image which settled in my master's fertile mind. The white stranger and the market official walked away from

153

the shop and for a few minutes carried on a private conversation. The stranger passed over something wrapped in a green silk handkerchief and moved briskly away.

"Come, Bayezid, we must be going," said my master, holding tightly onto his rolls of blue and green silks.

They did not go far. Only some twenty-five metres, in fact, to Aaron's 'Sparkling Satins' store. "Aaron has just the cloth for you, Sir," the short craggy-faced shopkeeper said eagerly as he plucked from his display a length of folded grey satin threaded with silver. His breath reeked of alcohol.

"Having some trouble with your customers, Aaron?" asked my pasha jocularly.

"No, Sir. No trouble," was the curt reply.

"Oh?" uttered the Sultan, the expression lingering on his lips. "It didn't look like that to me!"

"Sir," said Aaron, grabbing hold of a wooden shutter, "I'm about to close. If you want to buy the cloth, it's a hundred akches."

"What's the hurry?" asked my master. "It's not even midday – at least twenty minutes to the *azan*."

"Sirs, I'm sorry. I didn't mean to be impolite but business isn't so good."

"Well, closing your shop when you have customers inspecting the goods isn't going to help your business, is it?" asked the Sultan. "Show us some of your sparkling satins."

"You don't sound like you really want to buy."

"That's very perceptive of you, Aaron," said Adam Pasha with a hint of sarcasm. "I think you can help us. You were talking to the market inspector, weren't you?"

"So, what's that to you?" answered the cautious Jew his reeking breath forcing the two sipahis to take a step or two backwards.

"Who was the short man with the veil?"

"I don't know, and it's none of your business!"

Adam Pasha thought for a moment.

"Aaron, you like a drink, don't you?"

"Y...es," Aaron stammered, though there was still a sharpness in his guilty voice. "So what?"

"The magistrate might like to make your acquaintance. Tell us what we want to know and the magistrate stays in the dark."

"Sirs," replied Aaron in a more compliant tone. "I'm not a Muslim so the magistrate can't touch me but I'm sure there's no need to bother anyone. What would you like to know?"

"That's better," said the Sultan. "What did the market inspector want?"

"Sir, I'll tell you but first you must tell me who you are and why you want to know?"

"You've nothing to be afraid of," replied my master. "We have a special interest in the three who were talking to you. We can't tell you any more than that but, as long as you answer our questions honestly, you'll come to no harm."

"I don't know the veiled man – I've never seen him before. And you obviously know the market inspector. The soldier was Musa, a Janissary and," added Aaron, spitting as he spoke, "he's a vicious bully."

"Let's go, Osman," said our Sultan. "We're finished here. Aaron, we thank you but, next time, choose your friends more carefully."

The two soldiers turned to leave but Aaron cried out after them. "Oh! Sirs, there is just one more thing …"

XII THE ASSASSIN

"My Pasha, tell me, tell me!" entreated Nilufer like an inquisitive little child, her sky blue eyes bursting with excitement as she admired the rolls of silk my master had brought her.

"Aaron," replied Adam Pasha, "said that the man with the veil had an effeminate, high-pitched voice. He could almost have been a girl."

"Or a boy. It could have been a boy," added Nilufer.

"Yes, I hadn't thought of that. It could have been a boy. But there's more," continued my master, "Aaron said that he – or she – gave something wrapped in a green handkerchief to the others. He thought it was money because of the jingling sound – he knew the sound of money, did our Aaron. And he said something else interesting. Apparently, the three of them didn't want their conversation overheard – the inspector was not at all pleased at being accosted by the stranger in the middle of a busy market."

"What did the other two want?" asked Nilufer.

"The same – money. It seems to be the only thing people are interested in these days. About two weeks ago, with impeccably bad timing, the inspector appeared in the company of the sergeant and demanded money. At first, they used threats of prosecution for breaches of weights-and-measures' regulations and the like but then, a few days ago, the sergeant started using his fists a little too liberally. I can't say I've heard of anything like this before."

***

It was already the month of *Dhul-Kada* and the weather had

turned hot and uncomfortable. On top of everything else, we were now caught up in the city-wide celebrations to mark the circumcision of the boy princes – Mustafa, son of Mahidevran, and Mehmet and Suleyman, sons of Khurrem. The festivities, in part organised and planned by Hafsa Sultan, were scheduled to last more than two weeks and the unplanned ones would stretch out even longer. The tiresome pageantry associated with royal circumcisions could hardly have been better designed to disrupt my master's painstaking work.

***

Page-boys ran before him, tossing out shiny newly-minted coins to the crowd. And to the rumble of drums, our Sultan rode out towards the Hippodrome to receive the gifts and felicitations of the most eminent men in his domains.

The sun was bright but not yet too hot. The Corps of Janissaries lined the way as the distinguished bore their gifts to the Sultan. Khairettin, tutor to Suleyman when a boy, was given the honour of presenting first: a finely calligraphed volume of the Sultan's own poetry. They reminisced briefly before the Grand Vizier, the grandly dressed and grandly titled pasha, bowed his head to kiss the hem of the robe of his Sultan. He stood to present his gift, a Koran of the finest quality, carried carefully in two hands by a tall page-boy. The whole polity of State, viziers, emirs, ambassadors, agas and beys of every rank and region approached and withdrew one by one.

The gifts kept coming. Damask from Syria, fine cotton from Egypt, and shimmering fabrics from India, each drawing murmurs of approval from the thousands of well-wishers jostling, leaping and straining to get a better view of events. They cheered and cheered and cried out blessings

157

until they were hoarse. And still the riches flowed: Chinese porcelain, jewelled cups for the Sultan's Treasury, slave girls and eunuchs for his Harem and horses and kaftans for him to give to his favoured retainers. Each gift, and the platitudes which accompanied them, was received by the Padishah with a dignified smile and some well-chosen words of gratitude.

Sultan Suleyman retired to Ibrahim Pasha's palatial residence to get the perfect view of the Hippodrome where the main spectacle was yet to come. He was joined on the royal balcony by ambassadors, partly for whose benefit the whole theatrical event was being played out, and members of the Imperial Divan. Two agas of the Sultan's Privy Chamber stood behind him, arms crossed at the chest with hands touching the shoulders. Adam Pasha stood to his left and only the favoured Ibrahim Pasha sat in his Sultan's presence.

"So, Pasha," asked our Sultan of the Grand Vizier, "who throws the better party: you, with the one you regaled us with when you married my sister Khadija, or I?"

"Mine was better by far my Sultan," was the stunning reply. Suddenly, the noise of the crowd seemed to dissolve and all those around the Sultan, especially the ambassadors, strained to hear the conversation. They, of course, had little understanding of the words, and their official interpreters were not about to tell them exactly what they meant, but they could see that the Sultan was offended. Oh, yes, they could see that. That alone was worth reporting and that was enough to prove their own worth.

"How so, Pasha?" said the Sultan gruffly, not a little stung by the remark.

"Because, my Lord, at my wedding, I had a great and noble Sultan as my most distinguished guest, whilst today your principal guest is only a humble peasant boy fortunate enough to serve the noble Padishah as his Grand Vizier." A smile returned to our Sultan's face. He was pleased, greatly pleased, with the reply.

The women were not to be left out of this merriment. Our Sultan's sister, wife of the Grand Vizier, had herself arranged entertainments on a grand scale for her female guests. Hafsa Sultan, Mahidevran and Khurrem had brought their own sizeable entourages, drawn in covered wagons, from the Old Palace to Ibrahim Pasha's harem. They could, if they wished, look out onto the Hippodrome from special enclosures or from behind latticed windows but the show inside was almost as thrilling as the one without.

The time for feasting had come and the royal house of Osman provided royally. Or, rather, it was the House of Ibrahim but it was no less grand for that. Indeed, only a man of Ibrahim's immense wealth could have afforded the enormous expense. His guest list included every high dignitary in Istanbul and not a few feudal lords and provincial notables. The Greek Orthodox and Armenian Patriarchs were there as was the Chief Rabbi. Perhaps, most important of all was Marco Memmo, the Venetian special envoy, for this was a rare opportunity to show off to a vassal state, should it dream of rising above its God-ordained status, the grandeur, wealth and invincibility of the Empire.

It was, nonetheless, to our Sultan's deep chagrin, that the King of France - he who had begged the Sultan for help as he languished in a Hapsburg dungeon following his drubbing at the Battle of Pavia, he of the bold words and empty gestures - that that monarch did not even bother to send a representative Having pledged his support to the Frankish king when he most needed it, which our Sultan had done in the face of strong objections from some of his ministers, this snub dug deep. Memmo smirked as he gloated.

With a click of his fingers, the Sultan's command transmuted the Hippodrome into a field of food. It seemed as if the whole city had joined in the festivities – all half-a-million of its citizens. As hundreds of sheep and goats were ritually slaughtered, the streets and alleys sloshed and swilled with blood spilling from the animals' throats. The smoky smell of charcoal hung in the air as shish-skewered kebab and shashlik lamb sprinkled with spice were grilled on spits dripping with sweet-smelling fat.

For the nobles gathered from far and wide and now seated cross-legged in large circles on carpets laid out on the open ground, soup, saffron-rice stuffed with mutton and raisins, halva and sweetmeats were laid out before them.

An unseasonable late-night drizzle scarcely dampened spirits. The shops stayed open all night and the minarets of the mosques, laced with burning lanterns with tinted water in the base, gave a multi-coloured glow to the city.

Inside Ibrahim Pasha's palace, the dull weather outside merely increased the contrast with the gaiety within. A thousand candles flickered, giving out an intense heat and causing all the shutters to be thrown open.

There were at least three parties taking place in the Grand Vizier's mansion – one for the male dignitaries, one for the women of the household and their guests, and one for the males who accompanied the first lot (people like me). Musicians played and I played along. Gypsy girls danced and I danced, at a distance of course, with the most beautiful gypsy girl in the world. The acrobatic palace dwarf told tales of love and I found myself in love. Seasoned songsters sang from books of poems and Daud Aga performed magic tricks with multicoloured handkerchiefs. Even Ibrahim Pasha showed off his skill at strumming the *tar*. The next morning, I had a sore head and an empty bed. If my master did not approve of my drinking, Ibrahim Pasha's servants were more understanding. What I could barely comprehend was where such a great number of gypsies had so suddenly appeared from or where my love had disappeared to.

On the Hippodrome, lancers tilted at swivelling dummies and mock battles were acted out. And when that was done, cavalry teams knocked about a ball with a mallet in a game of *chovkan*. Soldiers and sailors vied to climb the greasy pole to snatch the prize sitting on top. Athletes raced around the Hippodrome like gazelles in full flight, javelin throwers slung their lethal shafts like falcons, flying out of sight, and children screamed with delight as shadow puppets played out their fights.

The courageous wrestled with furry bears as the timid forgot their cares, sipping sherbet at the tents pitched on every side. Princely pavilions nestled beyond the stalls selling rosewater, incense, bread and fruit, everything from peaches and grapes to melons and dates. The oily strongmen wrestled and the acrobats tumbled about. The camels fought amongst themselves, besotted gamblers betting on every bout. The smell of charcoal roasted lamb and steamed fish wafted through the air. The populace feasted and the pickpockets prospered at this singularly festive fair.

The dervish magician danced upon the ground, with a feverish passion plucking pigeons and doves flapping from the folds of his gown. The dancing girls twisted and turned, this way and that, their simple flowing skirts billowing in the breeze. A lutenist strummed lazily upon his lute and a gypsy girl sang her song in mime as if mute. The tingle of the

161

tambourines flew upon the wind, kissing the whistle of the flute and, so enjoined, both died amidst the din.

The war drums beat and the bugles blew. The bullocks bellowed their tuneless sighs and the asses jostled and gave out cries. The horses' hooves beat the dirt and drew the carts. It seemed an earthquake had struck, as the whole city reverberated to the sound of marching feet and booming drums.

The wagons and the palanquins passed before the Sultan Suleyman – Padishah – the King of Kings. Atop the fabulous carnival floats, the city guilds displayed their skills. The stuffed birds of the Taxidermists rose above the dust. Barbers and Bakers, Goldsmiths and Candymakers all marched proudly past, showing how they earned their crust. The Tailors cut their cloth to size and the Glaziers shaped their glass in new styles devised for the occasion. And all for the Sultan's pleasure.

And, then, with a thunderous roll of kettle drums marched past the resplendent regiments of the Sultan's bodyguard. First to appear was the Household Cavalry, dressed from top to toe in mail. Their horses plumed and saddled in finery, displayed their elegance from mane to tail. And at their flanks rode the frontier scouts, with their fanciful feathered helmets, each carrying a pennanted spear.

To their rear marched the Janissaries, before whom the great cities of the World have trembled in fear. Their yaya-bashis and agas rode at their flanks, as if framing a succession of vignettes, great bulbous turbans upon their heads. Heron feathers rose like fluffy puffs of white smoke from their jewelled aigrettes, adding a dash of distinction to each man and setting off to perfection the blues, greens and reds of their finest kaftans.

The advance ranks wore battledress – white baggy trousers and shirts of yellow, blue or red. Then followed the main body in richly coloured tunics with kaftans to the ground, heads capped by pillbox hats with broad stiff white-cotton bound around to produce a swallow-tail effect from head to shoulders. And all the time the Janissary band beat out its triumphant sound.

The ringing of the bells heralded an eerie chant. The battalions of Janissaries sang, softly at first, then getting steadily louder. The band-master held up his baton and the parade stopped. Serpents sounded, cymbals clashed, cornets blew, a roll on the drums and the regiments marched on once more. As they passed the royal balcony, the Sultan rose to take the salutes of his soldiers. And then …

A shot rang out. It flew past Adam Pasha's ear. The stunned Sultan was seized by the arm and pulled back from the balcony by Ibrahim Pasha. His pages hurriedly stepped in front to form a protective shield. Our Sultan was visibly shaken.

The shot had been fired by a Janissary sergeant. Amid the noise of the pageant, few people realised what had happened. Taking advantage of the confusion, the would-be assassin broke ranks. He grabbed the sleeve of his company commander's kaftan and dragged him from his horse. Leaping onto the steed like an experienced rider, he galloped off downhill towards the sea. A shocked cavalry officer had enough wits about him to gather together a small detachment of sipahis. "After him, men! To the sea-walls! Cut him off at the walls!"

163

XIII   THE TRIAL

The festivities continued as if nothing had happened. Those whose view had been obscured or were too far away to see clearly what had occurred assumed another firecracker had exploded. Ibrahim Pasha acted quickly to ensure there was no suggestion of anything untoward. The story was quickly put about that a Janissary had accidentally discharged his musket and in panic, having disgraced his regiment, had tried to run away.

***

The sergeant rode furiously along the Roman sea walls. He turned sharply up a long narrow alley, his horse almost throwing him into the gutter as it lost its footing. Recovering, he left one dark alley only to enter another. He lost sight of his pursuers and gave a sigh of relief. He could no longer hear the clip-clop of horses' hooves behind him. The blood surging through his veins and the pounding in his head had deadened his senses.

"Got you!" cried the officer. The sergeant suddenly found three riders coming up fast at his back whilst the jubilant aga and two cavalrymen blocked his exit. The smug officer grabbed the reins of the Janissary's horse. He did not struggle. What was the point? He knew he was a dead man.

***

He cut a pathetic figure. Abdullah, the Janissary sergeant, lay sprawled on the floor of one of the dungeons of the New Palace. The guards, his former comrades, were rotated, two at a time, in four-hour shifts, day and night. There was no shortage of volunteers, each Janissary more eager than the

164

last to prove his loyalty to his Sultan and to remove this despicable blot on the good name of the Corps.

The Ninth Regiment of Janissaries, one with which our Grand Vizier was well-connected, was in such disgrace that it had come close to being disbanded. The head of its commanding officer was already rotting on one of the example stones placed near the incongruously named Gate of Peace. Abdullah had thought himself lucky not to be taken straight away to a torture chamber to have his flesh seared with hot irons and his limbs torn from him bit by bit. But at the hands of his vengeful guards he suffered little better. Each sentry took turns to inflict another cruel blow. Two in particular vied with each other to see who could make the cringing soldier cry out the loudest. He made feeble attempts to ward off the flailing fists until he lay almost senseless, groaning in pain and covered in bruises and blood. Longing for it all to end, he simply waited to die.

But first Abdullah had to be tried, for which purpose an unprecedented meeting of the Divan had been called. Ibrahim Pasha and my master were both present but neither could understand the reason for the trial. There was no doubt of the soldier's guilt, so what was the trial designed to achieve? Indeed, the Grand Vizier had already privately, but pointedly, argued against it. He, backed-up by the resolute Aga of Janissaries, pleaded that a public trial was not the place to air the Empire's woes. The Aga's worries my pasha could understand – regimental pride and all that – but what was the Grand Vizier afraid of?

In any event, speculation was pointless. The Sultan had ordered a trial and no one, not even Ibrahim Pasha, would openly question the Sultan's command.

The trial for treason and attempted regicide was the most

important there had been for a long time, bringing with it a full turnout of ministers and bureaucrats. The last to arrive, with all the colourful pomp and ceremony that the first minister could muster, was Ibrahim Pasha. He bowed in the direction of the auspicious gate, entrance to the Sultan's private domain, and strode confidently into the Divan. The ministers rose smartly to their feet, heads respectfully bowed, as the grandest of viziers took his place.

Watched by the Sultan through the iron grille above the Divan, a short prayer was read and the Grand Vizier, dominating the centre of the cushioned bench that ran along the walls, took charge of proceedings. Adam Pasha and his fellow Kadiasker sat to Ibrahim's left. The Aga of the Janissaries was present to hear the charges brought against one of his men and, if he were brave or foolhardy enough, to speak in his defence. The whole body of Ottoman officialdom waited patiently in silence for the prisoner to be brought before them. And, whilst he may not have wanted a trial, Ibrahim Pasha was not too concerned: he was, at least, in an ideal position to control the public examination and to cut off any potentially embarrassing line of enquiry.

All Istanbul waited too. There was talk of nothing else in the mosques and the bazaars. Any doubt of what had happened the previous day had gone. If the Sultan had wished the incident to go unnoticed, he had clearly changed his mind. The first courtyard of the New Palace was crammed full with Istanbulis. There was an eerie silence, as soldiers controlled the crowd by waving batons in an intimidating manner and as two rows of brightly uniformed Janissaries lined the route the dignitaries had taken to the Divan. It was a great theatrical event.

It was also a great anti-climax. Nothing happened and

the viziers in the Divan were becoming restless. Ibrahim Pasha looked suspiciously out of the corner of his eye at Adam Pasha, wondering if the Kadiasker knew more than himself about what was going on.

No prisoner arrived. There was no guard, no sombre procession. Instead a court usher, at a brisk walk, approached the entrance to the Divan. He had a message for the Grand Vizier. He spoke briefly to Ibrahim Pasha, the other members of the Divan straining to hear what was being said. For a fleeting moment, there was a look of embarrassment on Ibrahim Pasha's face. He spoke a few words to the chief steward and then closed the meeting with a curt announcement. Rising, he asked both Adam Pasha and the Aga of Janissaries to follow him.

Outside the Divan, an ill-disciplined whispering broke out amongst the serried ranks of soldiers. A stern look from their commanding officer, given with an authoritative swish of his staff, put a stop to the murmuring but not the confusion.

The Grand Vizier, Adam Pasha and the Aga were led towards the gaol where the prisoner was incarcerated. What they saw was the sergeant dangling from the ceiling, his broken neck and battered body hanging by the cord of his tunic tied around a central beam. His corpse was cut down.

When questioned, the sentries revealed that Abdullah had lain in his cell barely conscious for several hours and his last guards, taking pity on him, had left him alone. They heard nothing, except for a few groans, and they saw nothing. He had clearly committed suicide. The Aga of Janissaries was satisfied, and Ibrahim Pasha, too. He went through the motions of reprimanding the officer in charge for allowing Abdullah to cheat the executioner but, beyond that, he did not seem much concerned. He and the Aga went to make their report to the Sultan, leaving my master behind to examine the corpse.

The sergeant was not a big man. He had been clean-shaven but his bruised features hid the beginnings of stubbly new growth on his face and a mass of congealed blood covered his mouth and chin.

Except for a straw mattress, the small cell was bare and my master was standing in the middle of it when entered Mikhail.

"A sorry affair, Effendi. What do you make of it?" asked the Kadiasker.

The doctor, bending down to make a clinical examination of the body, replied: "Is there any doubt? He committed suicide. Dead maybe two hours. I imagine he killed himself with this." He held up the woollen cord, which he had carefully unwound from the Janissary's neck. "He took quite a beating – lots of bruises and I suspect not a few broken bones." Pressing on the dead man's ribcage, he added, "A couple of broken ribs … a fractured leg, a broken nose …"

"Yes," mumbled Adam Pasha, "broken bones … Well, I must leave you to deal with all the details. I have to make my report to His Highness."

***

The Sultan was in a sombre mood. "I know the details, Adam Pasha. Suicide. May Allah forgive him. Wasn't it crime enough to attempt to kill his Sultan that he had to compound the offence by a greater crime? That only Allah can forgive."

"Your Highness, if he committed suicide, he has cheated his human executioner but no one can cheat the All-Knowing and All-Powerful."

"Just so, Adam Pasha, but why do you say "if"? Is there

any doubt of it? Ibrahim Pasha has none. What do you know that he does not?"

"My Sultan, Ibrahim Pasha is not a man of doubts. I invariably am. There are few men wiser than Ibrahim Pasha and I am not one of them. But the Grand Vizier may have his own reasons for supposing it was suicide."

"Own reasons?" repeated the Sultan, "What are you implying Adam Pasha? The Grand Vizier's reasons are my reasons. If you question his motives, you are also questioning mine."

My master wanted to explain that he had no derogatory intent but thought it best to concentrate on the causes of death.

"My Sultan," he said hesitantly, "I cannot be sure that it was not suicide. He had suffered badly at the hands of his guards and may well have wanted a quick death. But he had taken such a beating. I don't see how he would have had the strength to kill himself. Not by hanging. And, even if he had the strength, I can't see how he did it? Though the beam from which he was hanging is low, he would have needed some agility to reach up and tie the knot, which would be out of the question for a man in his condition. And he would have needed to stand on something but the cell was bare – no stool or bedding for him to stand on. So, what did he jump from?"

"So, Pasha, what's your explanation?" asked the Sultan.

"I don't have one. It could be that his guards killed him as an act of mercy. But, if so, I wouldn't have chosen hanging as the method. Then, again, it might have been a zealous sentry who, out of some misplaced sense of loyalty, wanted to avenge Your Highness. Or ...," my master paused, straining to see the Sultan's expression, "there could be a much more sinister answer. He could have been murdered to prevent him from speaking. Now, we shall never know what he could have told us."

"Very well, Pasha," said Suleyman, "then we must find some answers. I don't like the crude methods we sometimes use to obtain information but the results are quick. We'll soon know the truth."

Almost as soon as the Sultan had stopped speaking, a chamberlain ushered the Grand Vizier into the Audience Room. My master stepped back to a respectful distance behind Ibrahim Pasha.

"My Sultan," said the Grand Vizier with his usual assuredness, "I am pleased to inform you that there has been no assassination attempt on Your Highness' person."

There was a stunned silence from the Sultan and a look of disbelief on my pasha's face as Ibrahim Pasha, with the hint of a gloating smile, elaborated.

"Adam Pasha was the soldier's target, not Your Highness." My pasha, mouth aghast, said nothing.

"Ibrahim Pasha," said Suleyman calmly, "I am surprised to hear this and so, I see, is the Kadiasker. Why should a simple soldier want to kill Adam Pasha?"

"It appears," replied the Grand Vizier, "the reasons were several and compelling. Following our victorious campaign last year against the King of Austria, Adam Pasha dealt firmly and quite properly, in accordance with your noble laws, with some deserters. The Kadiasker acquitted himself well and no one can criticise the actions he took. But a brother of this Janissary was one of those transgressors. Charged and convicted of cowardice, he was sentenced to death."

Adam Pasha coughed nervously but the Grand Vizier carried on.

"And there is more. The sergeant had petitioned Adam Pasha last winter and the matter was brought before the Divan. The sergeant requested his father be exempted from tax in accordance with Your Highness' noble decrees. The local governor was instructed to observe the law faithfully but not only did he continue to levy taxes from this soldier's family but he imprisoned his father and brother on a false charge of banditry.

"In anticipation of Your Highness' orders, I have seen to it that the governor will not disobey your laws again."

"Ibrahim Pasha, such wonderfully quick work. Well done!" said the Sultan. "But where did you get your information?"

"From one of the sergeant's comrades. I don't know whether he was hoping to get a reward, avoid punishment, or simply showing his loyalty. He approached me and begged me to intercede on his regiment's behalf. He told me that the sergeant harboured a grudge and on several occasions had spoken bitterly against the Kadiasker."

The Grand Vizier's reply was convincing. The shot fired at the Parade had narrowly missed my master. It was quite possible that everyone had leapt to the conclusion that it had been aimed at the Sultan but the reality could have been different.

"There, Adam Pasha, where does that leave your theory?" asked Suleyman. "This man was clearly deranged. He had foolishly taken it into his head that you were to blame for his family's travails." The Sultan gave a regal wave of his hand. "And now that the assassin is dead, I consider the matter closed."

Suleyman yawned. "Your Sultan is feeling tired."

***

171

Once outside the Audience Chamber, the Grand Vizier gave Adam Pasha a superior look and a patronising smile. "My Kadiasker, you can't be loved by everyone. You'll soon forget this unfortunate incident."

Adam Pasha had, with difficulty, come to accept the condescending manner of the Grand Vizier. He replied with a respectful bow. But he was worried: whether Abdullah had meant to kill him or the Sultan did not explain the circumstances in which he had met his own death.

As my master walked slowly through the second courtyard of the Palace, he stopped now and again to breathe in the sweet-scented air, and to marvel at the beauty of the small gazelles that hopped playfully between the tall cedars and the leafy planes. He listened to the soothing sound of the black marble fountain, the water tumbling in a steady splish, splash, plop. His mind wandered back to his childhood – he could almost hear a Greek choir chanting out its rhythmic hymns, splish, splash, plop.

Just as he approached the exit, the Chief Chamberlain summoned the Kadiasker back into the presence of the Sultan.

As he entered the Audience Chamber, he noticed the absence of pages and attendants: this was to be a very private meeting. Suleyman, sitting at the back of the room, head lowered, was far from happy. He lifted his head slowly and his almond-shaped eyes fixed on Adam Pasha's bowed head.

"Kadiasker, it's dangerous for my subjects to believe there's been an attempt on my life. The army's morale is critically low. It fought with courage at Vienna but Vienna is still in enemy hands and, however we describe the 'victories' of that campaign, you and I know that the result was a shambles. I lost hundreds of good men and whether we call it a retreat or a tactical withdrawal the result is the same. It was a bitter blow." The Sultan indignantly thumped his knee with his fist. "It was humiliating! Your Sultan's humiliation!"

"This," he continued, "was an attempt on my life. I am convinced of that. It is part of a chain of troubling events and we may not have seen an end to it. Do you understand me, Pasha? I want to snuff out any thought of conspiracy or rebellion. Rumours of trouble act like a cancer, like a hungry dog gnawing at the bones of the Empire. This is one reason why Ibrahim Pasha is not here now. If any man can restore confidence, he can. And, if he believes this plot was aimed at you and not me, he will do a more convincing job of it."

"Your Highness, I understand," said my master. "But Ibrahim Pasha, if ever he found out, he would … he would be offended."

"Kadiasker, I'll deal with that when the time comes. I've other reasons for not telling him now of my suspicions.

"You see, I think Shireen was a French spy." My master kept his head lowered but his eyebrows were definitely up.

"She was a cousin to the French king, as you know," continued the Sultan. "Captured on a galley that barely put up a fight, she entered my harem soon after her cousin's defeat at Pavia. I offered her freedom, she chose to stay. We offered her a new faith, she accepted. And I became fond of her. But now I wonder all the more whether she was a French spy, sent to win my affection and, through that, my support for her cousin. If that's the case, she was wasting her time. I was happy to support the King of France: no monarch should be locked up like a dog after being humbled in defeat.

"You see, Adam Pasha, I, too, have a theory about Shireen's murder. You know of Signor Alvise Gritti? Yes, of course you do. He's been lobbying me on behalf of the

Venetian ambassador who in turn wants me to release that sailor who sparked off the conflagration in Galata. I've come to believe that Venice is at the centre of it all. Could it have been a Venetian spy who killed Shireen? I'm sure now it was not Khurrem Sultan, fool though I was to suspect her."

"Then," said my master, "we must at once turn over the murder investigation to our intelligence services."

"No, Pasha, we must not. The Grand Vizier and I are convinced that our network of spies has been infiltrated by the Venetians. That is a matter we are dealing with but in the meantime I cannot trust them with these sensitive matters. In any case, investigating this affair involves access to my harem and I have no intention of letting those cut-throats anywhere near it."

"My Lord, may I know the nature of the evidence pointing to Shireen as a spy?"

"Shireen," replied the Sultan, "was never backward in promoting French interests but that was only natural and I've no hard evidence beyond that. Still, thinking back on it now, isn't it odd that a galley carrying a royal passenger should make such feeble attempts to stave off capture? But I don't know how she got word to her French masters and nor do I know who killed her or how. Those are questions for you. Continue your investigation as you see fit."

"And," asked my master, "sergeant Abdullah, should I also investigate the circumstances of his death?"

"I have sent for the two guards who last saw him alive. That should conclude the matter," said Suleyman.

"My Sultan," asked Adam Pasha, "may I continue to enlist the help of Mikhail Effendi? He knows the Harem and some of the girls have been his patients. His knowledge of Court relationships and the Venetians will be invaluable."

Sultan Suleyman gave a disapproving frown that faded into a thin smile. "I realise you can't do this alone. Choose whomever you have faith in to help you, only take care in your choice."

My master had one last question. "Am I to understand that members of your noble household are no longer under suspicion?"

"Adam Pasha, we both have theories. Theories need to be tested and proved. Don't close any line of enquiry unless you are satisfied."

Just then, one of the Sultan's messengers begged permission to approach.

"My Sultan," he said in a faltering voice with a fair sense of the dramatic, "the two sentries summoned by Your Highness ... They have been found – dead."

Suleyman was not pleased with the news. "How?" he asked.

"Mikhail Effendi is making his examination. Poison, he thinks."

"Have him come at once to make his report."

***

"I last saw the two sentries standing outside the assassin's cell," explained Mikhail. "I left them guarding the body. About twenty minutes later, I was called back to the gaol, where I found them lying in an adjoining cell. They had been drinking from a flask of wine laced with poison – foxglove judging by the contorted corpses dripping with vomit."

"So, Adam Pasha," said our Sultan, "where does that leave us?"

"My Lord, those two were silenced for a reason. It confirms that sergeant Abdullah was murdered."

The Sultan stroked his new beard. "Yes, it does seem to

do that."

***

"Are you convinced now?" asked Mikhail as he and my master left the Audience Chamber. "It's all the work of someone both very clever and very close to the Sultan. It," he said, counting off on his fingers, "must be one of Prince Mustafa, Khurrem or Ibrahim Pasha. I'm convinced that the prince's tutor lifted the poison from the pharmacy and mixed it into the wine drunk by the guards. Mustafa can gain access to the cells and so can his main supporter at Court, Ibrahim Pasha. Where was he when you were making your report to the Sultan? He was rather quick, wasn't he, to jump to the conclusion that the sergeant committed suicide? And who gains the most if the Sultan is assassinated? You don't believe that cock-and-bull story about an attempt on your life, do you? Our Grand Vizier has close links to the Ninth. Behold, a soldier of the Ninth comes to him begging forgiveness and lays the blame at your door. And, surprise, surprise, Ibrahim Pasha deals with the problem in the ruthless way he knows best, before anyone can challenge the story.

"Look here, Adam Pasha, the princes are too young to take over the reins of power. Ibrahim Pasha is respected by the troops. And we've both heard rumours that his mind has been turned by his massive fortune and almost limitless power. People say he's getting ready to seize the throne."

This conjecture was too much for my pasha. "'People say', 'rumours'! Repeat it often enough and it will become fact. Our Sultan doesn't believe Ibrahim Pasha is involved." He could have added that Mikhail, too, was pretty quick to label Abdullah's death as 'suicide' but chose not to.

"His Highness' judgement is clouded by his love for the Grand Vizier," Mikhail ploughed on. They've grown up together and the Sultan relies heavily on his Chief Minister. So heavily that he won't even consider the possibility that he is plotting against him."

"Maybe so," said my master, eyes raised skywards in disbelief, "but what about Khurrem? Where do you think she fits into your reasoning? Surely," he added with a hint of sarcasm, "you're not suggesting she approached the guards and offered to quench their thirst with poisoned wine?"

"Scoff if you like, Adam Pasha. She didn't have to kill them personally. One of her eunuchs could have done it. Together with Ibrahim Pasha, she's closest to the Sultan. Can we be sure that she hasn't charmed from His Highness details of every scrap of evidence you've discovered. She can wind our Sultan round her little finger and bend his will in any direction she wishes."

"Of course," replied Adam Pasha, "we can't be sure of anything. But Khurrem couldn't have learned of the assassin's death – at least not from the Sultan. And why should she have wanted to kill the one person who can free her from the Harem's silky chains?"

"Rumour has it Ibrahim Pasha's the real father of Khurrem's first born," said Mikhail. "Wasn't she in his harem first?"

"Enough, Effendi! That's enough of this scandalous twaddle! Your conjectures are becoming more extravagant by the minute. Soon you won't be able to tell the difference between myth and reality."

Adam Pasha's exasperation had finally bludgeoned Mikhail into silence but the seed of suspicion had been planted in the Kadiasker's troubled mind.

XIV   MUTINY

The noble ministers of the Imperial Divan, absent the Grand
Vizier, joined together for morning prayers in the mosque of
Aya Sophia. Beneath the majestic glory of its dome, having
asked Allah's forgiveness for their sins, the great officials of
the Ottoman State, dressed in greeny silks, and satins of
mustard yellow, prepared to ride to the Imperial Gate.
Bobbing turbans and feathered plumes were carried forth on
a tide of clashing colour along a route lined with smartly
turned out troops. As each vizier neared the massive gate,
the Janissary Aga encouraged his horse a few paces forward
in respectful greeting. A prayer recited, the iron gates were
thrown wide-open and Janissaries, armourers and troopers
filed through in the order prescribed. The members of the
Divan stopped by the Gate of Peace and were served there
with sweet fruit juices cooled by mountain ice. They waited
for the heralds, striking the ground with their ceremonial
gavels, to announce the approach of the Grand Vizier riding
in resplendent procession to open the Divan session. And
how Ibrahim Pasha relished it all: every bow and every
scrape, such wide-eyed looks and mouth-drooping gapes.

The Divan's caseload was, as always, varied in subject,
regional origin and importance. From Salonika came an
appeal from a rabbinical court which had held, upon the
opinion of a young but influential rabbi, Samuel de Medina,
that a Jewish merchant was not required to repay debts owed
to a Muslim creditor. That was not the only matter involving
the Sultan's Jewish subjects. There was also a petition from
Miriam, the daughter of a Jewish tax collector, asking for a

178

share of her father's inheritance in accordance with Muslim law, something denied to her under her own law. But, important issues as these cases raised, my pasha was anxious to hear one petition in particular.

Murmurs of surprise and concern swept around the cushioned courtroom as the veiled widow Aziza revealed her sorry tale of corruption and extortion. Ibrahim Pasha referred the matter to my master for a decision, he having already alerted the Grand Vizier of his special interest in the case. Adam Pasha was, however, intent on giving Karim, the market inspector, and his Janissary accomplice the fullest possible opportunity to answer the grave charges laid against them. Their immediate presence was demanded before the Divan and the case was adjourned until they were found and brought before it.

My pasha had hoped, and expected, that it would be no more than an hour or so before the examination could begin. But neither Musa, the Janissary thug, nor Karim, the greedy inspector, had been seen for two days. Musa, it turned out, had been killed in a drunken brawl, so it was said, in a Christian quarter of Galata; and Karim had suffered a seizure from which he did not recover. "Your luck's not good today," said Ibrahim Pasha, with the hint of a supercilious smirk.

Musa had belonged to the Ninth, that same regiment of Janissaries to which Abdullah, the attempted regicide, had been attached. The ignoble Ninth had not yet recovered from that scandal and now there were fresh rumblings of discontent.

The new regimental commander expected trouble at the quarterly pay-day review and made his views known to his Commander-in-Chief. He suspected, he said, that the whole regiment, excepting its officers, had shared in the spoils of Musa's extortions and, now that the truth was out, anxiety was giving way to boldness. Certain veterans, the ring-leaders, knew all too well that attack was the best means of defence. Trouble could be expected. The Aga of Janissaries immediately sought, and was granted, a special audience with Suleyman.

***

As pay-day approached, the rumble of discontent grew louder. Six regiments of Janissaries, over five thousand men, were lined up in disciplined and orderly ranks along one side of the second courtyard of the New Palace. Before them, at the door of the Divan, were heaped piles of leather purses. Ibrahim Pasha stood to receive the imperial rescript authorising payment and raised it to his lips before removing the silk binding. He broke the royal seal and, after reading the command out aloud, sat down and signalled to the company representatives to approach.

The subalterns stepped forward to collect the pay for each of their companies and began distributing it. Dissent was already visible in the serried ranks of the Ninth. It was a show of unseemly indiscipline but it might have been worse. It was not until the traditional meal that always follows the distribution of pay that more began to stir than just the giant cauldrons of chick-pea soup. The dissent was audible.

"Our Sultan is a cheat," cried out one gawky Janissary. A lanky colleague reprimanded him but another concurred. A fourth said, "Na, it's not our Sultan who's the cheat. It's that Iskender Chelebi – he's the Treasurer! It's his responsibility. He must be the one who's trying to palm us off with fake coins!" The powerfully-built soldier took a silver coin and, holding it out in front of him between the index finger and thumb, he spat on it. Several others jumped up and, tossing handfuls of silver coins onto the ground, stamped on them as a sign of dishonour and disgust.

The experienced Aga of Janissaries had expected trouble but not for this. What did the soldier mean by 'fake coins'? He grabbed an unopened bag of silver akches and broke the seal of the Imperial Mint. Taking out a few shiny coins, he fingered them, tried to bend them, turning them over and over in his hand. He weighed them up and down, first in one hand and then the other. The coins were good, he was convinced of it. He took another bag, this time sealed with the Treasurer's seal, signifying that they were not new coins but had come from the Imperial Treasury. These coins were a little worn and not as shiny but were also good. The grey-bearded veteran was mystified.

And all the time signs of irritation and agitation were growing amongst the troops. Whether or not they had been paid in false coinage, the Aga knew that his soldiers had not seen serious military action that year and the shocking events of the previous few months, following as they did upon the harsh realities of retreat from Vienna, were contributing to a serious breakdown in morale and discipline.

The greatest sign of unrest was, surprise, surprise, in the ranks of the disgraced Ninth. Everywhere and at every opportunity, they were promoting dissent. It was the soldiers of sergeant Abdullah's company which first signalled revolt by overturning their giant soup cauldrons. Great trays of pilaf rice spun in the air as the agitation spread. The officers of the Ninth tried to impose their authority on the ringleaders but the yaya-bashi was wrestled to the ground and the subalterns were hemmed in by a circle of Janissaries, waving their swords wildly above their heads and drawing daggers across their throats in mock imitation of an execution.

Ibrahim Pasha, seemingly in a state of shock, had to be helped away, seeking protection in his offices beside the Divan. The famous general appeared incapable of taking command to quell the rebellion, content to leave everything in the hands of the Aga of Janissaries.

"We want our Sultan! We want our Sultan!" went up the cry from the ringleaders, now inciting the soldiers to open rebellion. "If he won't come to us, we'll fetch him out! Bring out the Sultan! There's no place to hide. Bring out the Sultan!"

XV DEATH OF A SPY

Ibrahim Pasha was rumoured to be incapacitated by some sudden mysterious ailment. All too convenient – for the Grand Vizier, that is. But the Aga, the old campaigner, was prepared. He was sure of the loyalty of the First and Second regiments and, with a show of force, could probably win over the others too, barring, of course, the shambolic Ninth. The officers of the First and Second had already received their orders: at the first hint of trouble, they were to take up their positions together with their men along the perimeter of the courtyard and at the gates. They did so, efficiently and quietly, fanning out behind the Ninth and the other three regiments of the corps that were present. The soldiers of the Ninth, a rowdy bunch at the best of times, barely realised what was happening before it was too late. It was foolhardy to continue their ill-conceived mutiny without the support of the other regiments or their own officers. The excitement fizzled out and the soldiers of the Ninth stood around looking confused, dejected and shame-faced. Some of the ring-leaders, trying to slip out, were quickly rounded up for questioning. They should have been executed but escaped with a dose of the bastinado. The rest of the regiment was docked a month's pay but no sterner action was taken. That was as inexplicable as Ibrahim Pasha's all too sudden disability.

***

"What do you make of it, Pasha?" I asked.

"I'm as puzzled as anyone," was my master's reply. "We've launched an investigation but no counterfeit coins

183

have turned up in the batch distributed on the day of the mutiny. We've questioned the Director of the Imperial Mint and the Paymaster General. Neither can throw any light on the origins of the debased coins. But we do know that bad coins are circulating."

"No theories, Pasha?"

"Oh, I didn't say that," my master replied with a smile. "I'm pretty certain that there's been no impropriety at either the Imperial Mint or the Paymaster General's office. So the bad coins have come from somewhere else, somewhere that is not an official source. What we do know for certain is that the complaints are emanating from the Ninth. Now, Murat," he said looking at me quizzically, "what does that mean to you?"

"That the Ninth were looking for trouble, and they got it but not what they bargained for. They've always been a rough bunch. And having the Grand Vizier's patronage doesn't help with discipline."

"Yes, but there's more to it than that. The Ninth as we know, or some part of it, has been extorting money in the Covered Bazaar. And now it's the Ninth that's complaining about debased coins. Well, the coins didn't come from the Mint or the Treasury, so they must have come from somewhere else. They're forgeries – good forgeries to be sure – not cleanly struck but they have a good weight and in all other ways are pretty deceptive. The vital link, I believe, is between the Bazaar and the Ninth. Each day a lot of money changes hands in the Bazaar. It's a perfect venue for someone to swap good money for bad. There's a nice fat profit in it for someone but the real question is, who? Who's behind it all? That's what I want to know."

"Any clues, Pasha?"

"Yes, Murat, I think I have. Note how our leads have a strange way of ending up in some blind alley. Our best lead, Musa, the Janissary bully who was accused by the widow Aziza, should have been at the ceremony to collect his pay or better still in a dungeon for his dishonesty but he wasn't in either place. They say he was killed in a brawl. A little too convenient, don't you think?"

***

My master had just walked into another of those blind alleys. He could not look at the body anymore. He closed the dead girl's pretty brown eyes and turned his back in sorrow and disgust. He walked away, breathing in deeply as he did so. Behind him, he left Mikhail Effendi examining the corpse.

A few hours earlier the imperfectly weighted sack containing Kira Sarah's bloated body had been dragged out of the Bosphorus at Galata by a startled fisherman who had spotted it wedged amongst some rocks.

"Nowadays, I seem to spend all my time looking at corpses," said the doctor in a matter-of-fact sort of way.

"Was she drowned?" I asked.

Mikhail nodded. "Although she was probably drugged before she was tossed into the bag,"

"When ... when did it happen?" asked my master, sitting on a low ragged stone wall behind us.

"About a day ago – no more," replied Mikhail.

"She was killed in the last twenty-four hours?"

"Yes, why?" asked Mikhail. "Is it important?"

"Such sloppy work, Effendi – failing to send this sack to the bottom of the Bosphorus. If there is a master-spy behind all this, this could be his first big mistake."

"Or, hers," interjected Mikhail. "It might be a woman. Working in the palace teaches you one thing if nothing else.

185

You can't trust them – women are the more cunning of the two sexes. Take Khurrem for instance. She…"

This was a line of enquiry Adam Pasha was compelled to head off: discussing the doctor's outrageous speculations in private was one thing but it was quite another matter to do it in public. "Yes, Effendi. Quite. Now let us return to the matter in hand. If Sarah was murdered within the last twenty-four hours someone could have spotted the murderer – man or woman – and may remember seeing someone heave a heavy sack into the water."

"But, Pasha, surely, it would have been done at night," reasoned Mikhail.

"I doubt it, Effendi. The spot where the body was found is a treacherous place. At night it would be lethal. And a boat taken out at night runs the risk of being seen from the watch-tower or by the night-watch, even if it carries no lanterns. Don't forget, last night we only had a quarter-moon so the light would have been very poor."

"But, even at night there are dozens of fishing boats on the water," countered the doctor. "How can you be sure?"

"I can't. But my suspicion is that our man is too careful and too clever to tempt fate in that way. And, whoever is our man, he would have needed help. The body was taken out to sea and dumped. It was then washed up on the rocks. They would have needed to hire a fishing boat and I guess they joined the fishermen on the water during the day. The body, cast overboard in full view of hundreds of people, would have attracted less attention than a noisy splash at night upsetting all those patient fishermen.

"I mean to get our murderer, Effendi, and I <u>will</u> get him. Now we have a new avenue of investigation. And the real fishermen will have recognised strangers in their midst.

186

Someone would have noticed them. And it didn't happen so long ago for that someone to have forgotten."

"Murat," my master called out to me, "we have to find Sarah's murderer – and quickly. Mix amongst the fishermen. Ask them if they saw anything unusual or out of the ordinary yesterday, or this morning. Someone must have seen this sack being tossed into the water."

"But, Pasha, there are hundreds of fisherman all along the Bosphorus, on both shores. Where do I start?"

"The currents of the Bosphorus," replied my master, "are one of Allah's great mysteries but they have a directional certainty that is bound to help us. I suggest starting here and working northwards along this shore."

I bowed and obeyed. I was in the hunt once again but I could not help feeling remorse, even responsibility, for the death of Sarah. After all, I was the one who had followed her to her house and I was the one who had led the my pasha to her.

***

"Kadiasker, who's behind it?" The Grand Vizier's voice was quivering with anger, like a confused parent who had just lost a child.

"My Pasha, perhaps I was wrong. I know I cautioned against mistreating that Venetian captain arrested in Galata. As always, your judgement was better than mine. I have deliberated long and hard and still I hesitate to say this but I think the time has come for us to see where his tongue takes us."

"Oh, Adam Pasha, do my ears deceive me?" mocked the Grand Vizier, sick of my master's imagined disloyalty to himself and tired of my master's liberal-minded lawyer's ethics which he held responsible for endangering the State.

187

"Are you suggesting that we use extreme measures?" he asked with a barely disguised sneer.

"Yes, my Pasha. Let the torture masters have him."

"This is, indeed, a new Kadiasker! No more concerns for the law? Aren't we a little forgetful about civilised behaviour?"

Adam Pasha bit his lip. He was tormented by guilt for countenancing torture but he was also blaming himself for Kira Sarah's death. He was forced to compromise his principles and he did not like it. Not one bit.

***

"So, Effendi," said my master, tossing a dossier onto the cushion beside Mikhail. "That's what our Grand Vizier has managed to dig up from our intelligence services. It doesn't tell us much and even so Ibrahim Pasha urges caution in relying too heavily on it – we know there's a double agent at large."

The doctor picked up the sheaf of papers and thumbed through them carefully. "Our intelligence service is just a hangout for wastrels – most would sell their mothers for a couple of ducats. I wouldn't trust their reports even if the service had not been infiltrated."

"What do you think … about the report?" asked Adam Pasha.

"She was a jewel-broker," said Mikhail as he read through the report. "Well, nothing startling about that. But here's something new." He raised his head, and his eyebrows, in surprise. "It says she was a prostitute. That's a little hard to believe. But, then, dervishes in a trance usually make more sense than those donkeys in intelligence."

"Effendi, for a Jewess in Istanbul I agree prostitution is an unlikely occupation, though not unheard of," said Adam

ing on a tit-bit of information he had picked up
But she was from Salonika ..."

"...at, your home town?" interjected Mikhail.

"Not far," replied my master. "And I know it well. It has a large Jewish population and though Jewish prostitutes in Istanbul may be rare, they're not so rare in Salonika. With all those vigilant toothless old women arbitrating on morality, it's easier to police morals in the smaller Jewish communities of Istanbul than in Salonika. Where there's a human need, it'll always be satisfied by someone.

"Sarah came to Istanbul three years ago and was recruited by us soon after. Her records are replete with praise for her resourcefulness and devotion to duty. Resourceful, I've no doubt. And I'm sure she was devoted – but to which master?

"It's clear she was intercepting messages from Shireen to French merchants and passing on the details to our boys in intelligence. But there's more to her than that."

A royal messenger entered and handed my master a paper sealed in the Sultan's name. Adam Pasha treated it with all the respect due to anything emanating from the Sultan. He raised the paper to his lips and forehead and broke the seal. He frowned, bewildered and shocked. Ostensibly from the Sultan, the note was, in fact, from Ibrahim Pasha. Written in the regal and ostentatious language used by the ruler, it was expressed in terms usually reserved for the Sultan. My pasha disguised his reaction as best he could and read the note. The Sultan, so said the Grand Vizier, wanted to see him. My master had no idea why.

XVI   THE HAMAM

"Once more Ibrahim Pasha has found the key!" exulted an elated Suleyman. "Adam Pasha, learn what you can from him – he's brilliant, absolutely brilliant! He has discovered that the Kira was carrying messages between Shireen and the agents of France." My master wanted to interrupt, to remind the Sultan that he had come to that conclusion long ago but to say so was unthinkable, and pointless.

"My Sultan, Kira Sarah was, to be sure, a master spy of the first order. She betrayed the French to us and probably we to the French."

"The French service, Pasha, is amateurish and bumbling in comparison with the Kira's real masters," said the Sultan. "Before delivering those messages, she took a short detour to the Venetian embassy where the despatches were opened, read and resealed."

Evidently, our torture masters had won – they had extracted the confirmation we had been looking for.

***

A new day, another conference with Mikhail Effendi. He was visiting us so frequently that he might just as well have moved in with us.

"The records don't show it, Effendi, but the Yusuf Ali affair establishes the connection."

"What connection?" asked the doctor but he didn't wait for an answer. "For one reason or another, half the city seems to have been chasing after Sarah," he said, with mild surprise and what might have been a twinkle in the eye. "I suppose, then, that Yusuf Ali was a spy, too?"

190

"No, I don't think he was. A dupe, that's what he was. A poor, benighted dupe under the spell of a beautiful temptress. Our Sultan realised that before any of us."

"So, you think Sarah was selling sex to Yusuf Ali?"

"I don't know but I doubt it because it wouldn't get her what she wanted. I suspect she seduced him and, in the process, stole the deluded man's affection, honour and good name. All thrown away for the sake of a cunning and duplicitous prostitute." Now here was a novelty: my master, he who had scandalised the mullahs of Damascus, sounding a mite prudish.

"But," asked Mikhail, "if it wasn't all for money, what was she after? What else could a merchant like Yusuf Ali offer her?"

"Yusuf Ali was only the means to an end. She wanted the keys to the Old Market, Effendi. She probably stole them and had duplicates cut. The robbery executed, he had outlived his usefulness. And when he returned to her house, he sealed his own fate.

"When I questioned him before the Divan, he was troubled by something. At the time, I thought the financial disaster that had just struck him and his friends was preying on his mind. But, now I'm sure it was more than that. He must have suspected Sarah at some point. Perhaps he had missed his keys or perhaps Sarah was acting suspiciously. We shan't know for certain but I think he went to Sarah's house that one last time to discover the truth. The rest you know."

"She was spying for Venice? Is that what you're saying? But, Pasha, I still don't understand why the Venetians should go to such lengths to pull off a robbery. A daring feat to be sure, but what does it gain them? Money? What do they need stolen gold for, even so much of it?"

"Effendi, don't think I haven't asked myself that question a dozen times. Each time, the answer is the same. The robbery must be part of something bigger. The Venetians are growing fat at our expense and ruin is staring dozens of merchants in the face. I'm haunted by visions of the widow Aziza weeping as if the world had come to an end. It has to be part of something bigger, part of some sort of grand plan."

"What 'grand plan', Pasha? Do stop talking in riddles."

"Effendi, remember those fake coins turning up all over the place? Well, there's your Venetian connection. I'm sure they were minted at the Venetian Embassy. Think of the consequences – large quantities of counterfeit coins in circulation would bring trade crashing down around us. There could be a total economic collapse."

"Wow! A touch melodramatic, Pasha," was the doctor's disbelieving response.

"Not at all, Effendi. Look at the reaction of the Janissaries: a full-scale rebellion was averted only because the Aga had been forewarned. But the Venetians have got a bit too clever for their own good. Passing off counterfeit coins wasn't enough for them: they had to go one step further and finance the operation with our own gold! The Ambassador has a residence just by the Old Market. So very convenient! And he has his own iron forge at the rear of the house. Perfect! Perfect, that is, for forging gold sequins."

"Pasha, let's accept for a moment that your rather fantastical theory is true. How do you suggest the Venetians intended to get large quantities of counterfeit coins into common circulation? Small amounts wouldn't raise suspicion and might cause a certain amount of disruption and disquiet. But to cause the sort of financial collapse envisaged by you, you need bucketfuls of the stuff. How did they plan to put about such large quantities?"

"Don't you remember the fire in Galata? The ship's captain was caught with bags of counterfeit coins. The Venetian Ambassador has a second establishment over there and it wouldn't surprise me if our friend the captain had visited it."

"What do you think he intended to do with the money?" asked the doctor. "He said it was to buy ship's victuals."

"I can't be sure but it wasn't provisions for the ship. I have a theory which I need to test."

***

As my pasha sipped lemon sherbet, he looked dreamily into Nilufer's eyes. Nervous and irritable, that dazzling brilliance that had once so struck him was now only a faint glimmer of that earlier radiance.

"Pasha, what does Mikhail Effendi say? About me ... did he say anything about me?" The question was totally unexpected.

"About you? No, why should he talk about you?"

"No reason, my Pasha. Kiss me."

***

In the middle of the tiled marble hot room of a public hamam, the Kadiasker lay on his back on a circular marble slab waiting for the arrival of Mikhail. Naked, except for a towel lying across his midriff, he stared up at the vaulted ceiling. The rays of the sun twinkled through the small glazed apertures in the dome above him. Water condensing within the dome dripped slowly, irritatingly, onto his bare arm as he recalled the Sultan's parting words about Sarah.

His ruminations were interrupted by the masseur, who first soaped his body and then pressed hard, his hands sliding along the slippery surface of my master's soapy limbs. The masseur dug deep into every nerve and, with an occasional grunt, my pasha clenched his teeth and bore the pain.

The massage over, my master put on his silver-tipped clogs and trod his way cautiously over to one of the marble basins lining the walls. He sat on a stool as the muscular masseur soaped and scrubbed his back with a coarse glove and then doused him with copious bowlfuls of warm water.

There was still no sign of Mikhail.

The doctor was there, however, resting in the relaxation room (or recovery room as my master preferred to call it). It was a large enclosed grey marble courtyard divided into cubicles by low wooden partitions. Dressed in a loose flowing cotton robe, perched up on cushions against the thigh-high balustrade that separated his cubicle from its neighbours, Mikhail waited patiently, sipping a small cup of sweet herbal tea. He did not notice the hobbling approach of my master.

"Ah, there you are!" said Adam Pasha, smiling and relieved. "Peace be upon you, Effendi! I thought perhaps you hadn't got my message or had better things to do."

Mikhail, spilling some tea, returned the pasha's greeting. "Have no fear, Pasha. You couldn't have a keener student. I'm eager to hear everything. But before all that …" Mikhail clapped his hands and a pale-skinned attendant appeared almost instantly by his side. "Two cups!" was the simple but mysterious order that Mikhail gave and the attendant momentarily disappeared.

My master was curious but said nothing as he donned his white robe and sat down cross-legged facing Mikhail across a boldly designed kilim. Barely had he settled down against some cushions that the attendant returned with a steaming silver pot and two porcelain cups knocking gently together on a silver salver. He poured a dark bubbling liquid into the cups.

"I brought this with me," said Mikhail. "A treat for us both," he added, leaning forward and handing a cup to my master with a mischievous wink.

But even before my pasha had taken the cup, he had guessed at Mikhail's secret. The distinctive smell had given it away. "Coffee!" proclaimed my master as a look of mild disappointment flashed across the doctor's face.

"Yes, Pasha, it's from Yemen. You've had it before, then?"

"Yes, Effendi. You've forgotten I was Kadi of Damascus for two years and of Aleppo before that. Since returning to Istanbul, though, I've only tasted it once and that was months ago at one of Ibrahim Pasha's receptions. I do like it. It's a delightful treat. Thank you, Effendi, I really appreciate the gesture."

"You don't mind, then? I wasn't sure if it would offend the religious sensibilities of our leading canon lawyer."

"You flatter me, Effendi. But why should it offend me?"

"Coffee's forbidden in the Koran isn't it? I've heard of preachers condemning its evils from the pulpits of Al-Azhar in Cairo."

My master frowned with irritation. Why was it, he thought, that everyone assumed that if one *alim* had given an opinion on something or other, however trivial or ridiculous, the whole of the *ulema* must hold the same view? And why attribute every crackpot idea to the Koran? Unlike the Christian Pope, mullahs do not have power to lay down the law – the best they can do is to express an opinion. It is only

195

by judging the character and learning of the person giving the opinion that one can assess whether it carries any weight.

"Regrettably," my master said, "I, too, have heard the sorry tale from Al-Azhar. When I was in Syria the odd fanatical rabble-rouser would condemn this or that, including coffee. I didn't take any notice of it then and don't take any more notice of it now. They knew little of the Koran or the words of the Prophet, may peace be upon him, and they understood the *Shariah* even less.

"The Holy Law forbids the imbibing of intoxicants," continued my master. "That's because they're bad for our health, both mental and physical. I don't deny that coffee can spoil your sleep and I've heard it said it can make a man impotent. It's a mild stimulant but what's so unusual in that? Many foods are mild stimulants, which, if taken in moderation, are harmless. It's the abuse of Nature that is abhorrent to Islam, not its proper use. It's not like the wine of the Greeks or the cider of the Jews - these even in moderate quantities can seriously dull the senses. Don't you remember Atik Aga who, after two mouthfuls of wine, would slur his speech and swagger and stumble like a mad bear? I don't know of anyone so affected by a couple of cups of coffee. Of course, I don't approve of over-indulgence in coffee or anything else but coffee just doesn't have the same effect."

"But you must agree, Pasha, that a little wine makes one merry and unmasks the real person," said Mikhail mischievously.

"Nonsense. For every person made 'merry', as you put it, I've seen one fall flat on his face. And it doesn't reveal anything other than the idiocy of the imbiber. Quite the contrary, it hides his true character. That is what Allah has made visible to all and it's mere insecurity that drives a man to don the cloak of intoxication.

"But enough preaching from me. What you say about Al-Azhar's preachers worries me more than ever did the ranting of the clods in Damascus and Aleppo. Al-Azhar is one of our great centres of learning and we can't let such intolerance get a foothold there. It could threaten the very fabric of the Empire."

My pasha sat back and took a defiant sip from his frothy cup of coffee. The two companions briefly fell silent and all that could be heard was the murmur of the fountain in the centre of the court and the clip-clop of the bathers walking to and from their cubicles.

"How's your investigation progressing?" asked Mikhail. "What was that theory of yours – about the ship's captain?"

"Guns, Effendi! Guns!"

The doctor smiled and rolled his eyes, as if to say "Here we go again. More riddles."

"If I were a gambling man, I would wager that our captain was buying weapons."

"How? Why? Where would he get them?" Mikhail was almost wishing he had not asked about the investigation.

"To answer the last question first, he got them from the Ninth. Don't you see? He buys weapons – guns, swords, whatever he can get his hands on. He buys from the Ninth with counterfeit coins. That's how they get hold of the fakes."

"And Shireen … where does she come into this?" asked the doctor, still confused.

"Kira Sarah is the link."

"You're jumping too far ahead, Pasha. Let's come back to Kira Sarah later. For now, let's stay with Shireen. Why was she killed? I can't see how her death fits into your conspiracy theories."

"Effendi, let me first get your views on a few of those theories."

"I'm listening. You won't find a more attentive student or one more eager to help."

"Good. Let's consider the facts. A young woman is found dead in the Imperial Harem. There are no signs of a struggle but she seems to have died from suffocation. Did she have a late visitor on the night of her death? Apparently so but no one knows who it was. Was it Prince Mustafa perhaps?"

"Of course, we don't know if the Sultan himself paid her a visit," interposed Mikhail. He paused briefly before adding, "But that's preposterous."

"Preposterous. Quite," replied my pasha sternly. "His Highness hasn't mentioned it and why would he make a nocturnal visit to a Harem girl when he's clearly devoted to Khurrem Sultan. And, in any case, Shireen was at the Old Palace and there's no suggestion that our Sultan was anywhere near it on the night of her death. We must assume he didn't visit her."

"I apologise for interrupting, Pasha. Please continue."

"Prince Mustafa, fearful of losing the battle for the succession and with it his life, could be our murderer. Certainly he had no lack of motive – he has enough rivals for the succession without wishing for any more and, if Shireen did ever succeed in winning His Highness's favour, who knows what might have happened. Shireen was never a serious candidate for our Sultan's bed but many think she had designs in that direction and the cunning to achieve it. The mere perception may have been enough to drive Mustafa to stifle the rumour before it became fact. Still, we have no real evidence and I can't accuse a boy prince of a capital crime on such flimsy circumstantial evidence.

"Having said that, it's possible that even our Sultan suspects Mustafa: didn't he tell me not to discuss the affair with Ibrahim Pasha? Why? Could it be because my mentor favours Mustafa for the succession and the Sultan suspects the two of them of a conspiracy against him? To favour Mustafa certainly puts Ibrahim Pasha on a collision course with Khurrem. There's always been a coolness in the Grand Vizier's affections towards her – his eyebrows shade over at the very mention of her name. So, if Mustafa is in the ascendant, it will mean victory over Khurrem and will put Ibrahim Pasha beyond challenge. I'm already hearing whispers that Mustafa is to be named the governor of Sarukhan. If true, that alone would bear witness to the Grand Vizier's victory."

"How's that, Pasha?" asked Mikhail.

"Sarukhan – it's the nearest province to Istanbul, of course! If, Allah forbid, something were to happen to our Sultan, the prince nearest Istanbul is likely to get here first. The first man to Istanbul controls the treasury and he who controls the treasury, such are Allah's miracles, wins the loyalty of the Janissaries every time."

"Will miracles never cease!" tut-tutted the doctor.

"It's common gossip in Court circles that the Queen Mother favours the Mahidevran and Mustafa," continued my pasha.

"The '2Ms' or 'Double Trouble' as I'm told Khurrem refers to them," interjected Mikhail.

"That's as may be," said my pasha, not welcoming the frivolous interruption. "Common gossip says that Hafsa Sultan would dearly love to break the power and influence of Khurrem. "That would explain Shireen's appointment as the Harem's Chief Treasurer. In one fell swoop she got the power of patronage and a prominent position bringing her into frequent contact with our Sultan, a situation that could, in time, develop into a close personal relationship. Why else should such a young, relatively inexperienced woman be given such an elevated position? It's unprecedented – the post is invariably reserved as a reward for an older woman unlikely to catch the eye of His Highness."

"Pasha, now do you believe me when I say the Grand Vizier is behind all this? He's up to his neck in conspiracies," said Mikhail.

"Ibrahim Pasha will certainly win a victory if Mustafa becomes governor of Sarukhan," responded my master. "He'll be in a prime position to dispose of the Sultan and bring Mustafa to Istanbul at the head of a rebellious army. Still, I suspect any victory of the Grand Vizier's will be short-lived – Khurrem will see to that and then all Ibrahim Pasha's wealth and power will mean nothing. It all ties up so well, does it not, Effendi?"

"It certainly does," replied the doctor. "And Mustafa, backed by our chief minister, is most definitely the chief suspect. Let's not forget that his tutor also had the opportunity to steal the poison you discovered in the halva. All the evidence points straight at him."

"Effendi, you weren't listening. Where's the real evidence against Mustafa? It's all conjecture. And I don't believe any of it, at least not that Mustafa is the murderer. I have another theory but first let me rehearse the various possibilities – you may be able to see something I've missed."

"I'm listening," said Mikhail.

"Khurrem Sultan is an obvious candidate. There's no better reason for seeing off Shireen than jealousy and when you add to that the mother's instinct to protect her children, it's a powerful motive. So, we have a desperate woman who's in danger not only of seeing her children disinherited but also of losing her own grip on power. She has both motive and ample opportunity and her apartments are so near to Shireen's."

All the rumours Mikhail had heard, or thought he had heard, pointed to a royal connection with the murder and here it was, shining radiantly. "You have it, Adam Pasha! But how will you prove it? I don't envy you having to explain this to our Sultan." Mikhail, favouring this theory almost as much as my pasha's first, was brimful with confidence.

"Effendi, you're galloping too far ahead. I was merely putting forward a theory. I don't suspect Khurrem at all."

Mikhail stared at my master with a furrowed brow and with confusion brewing under his blue skull cap.

"Let me explain," Adam Pasha continued. "I accept Khurrem had reason enough to kill Shireen but would she have done so without the Sultan's permission or, at the very least, tacit consent? Without it, she would risk losing his favour, and why would she do that? No, I believe she feels herself sufficiently secure from the wiles of other women not to risk everything in such an ill-judged move. She's a consummate politician: she'd have found other ways to overcome any influence gained by Shireen. Murder's not her way."

"Then who is it, Pasha!" exclaimed an exasperated Mikhail. He slumped back against the wall, dispirited that all his theories had been tossed aside and as yet nothing half as scandalous had replaced them.

"So far," said the Kadiasker, counting off on his fingers, "we have Hafsa Sultan, Khurrem, Ibrahim Pasha, Mahidevran, and Prince Mustafa with excellent motives for murder, quite possibly two or more of them conspiring together. Indeed, half the Court and most of the royal family had good reason for wishing the poor girl's death. And, as I say, I don't believe any of them is guilty of her murder."

"So, who, Pasha? Who?" pleaded the doctor.

My master was enjoying teasing the doctor. "Patience, Effendi. Patience brings its own rewards", he said gleefully. "I haven't mentioned the most bizarre possibility yet!"

Mikhail sat up erect, rapt with attention. Here was a true seeker of gossip. He devoured tales of Court intrigue and every secret, and not-so-secret, love affair. Adam Pasha grinned broadly, pausing to draw out the doctor's agony.

"Nilufer has another theory. She believes that story about a Harem love affair and thinks Shireen was murdered by a jealous lover!" Adam Pasha paused again.

"It isn't easy for a prominent Harem girl to take a lover," said the doctor raising his eyebrows in surprise. "But it has been known. There was that incident with the black-haired Spanish girl and ... But who is she? Who's the lover?"

"There was no lover, Effendi."

"Then who was it?" asked the doctor testily.

"Let me explain," said my pasha. "Nilufer says Shireen had a number of nocturnal visitors who would call on her from time to time. She assumes women but their faces were veiled – not usual within the Harem is it?" Mikhail shook his head but did not want to interrupt the flow.

"Nilufer didn't see anyone but thinks there might have been a visitor on the night of the killing. Now, Shireen was a frightened woman. Someone had already tried to kill her". Mikhail looked aghast at my master. "Oh, yes, Effendi, an attempt had already been made on her life. She was given a bowl of poisoned halva and fed some to her parrot. That much you already know. But, what made Shireen think that the parrot had been poisoned? She must have been expecting it, which means that either an earlier attempt had been made or that she had been threatened."

"I see," said the doctor. "But any previous attempt could not have been much earlier as none of her jariyés was aware of the concealed dagger."

"Exactly, Effendi. She was frightened and it's unlikely she'd be so frightened of some scorned lover. Most crimes by lovers are not pre-meditated – they're crimes of passion committed in hot blood. If a lover had killed the wretched girl, is it likely that she would have been asleep? Surely there would have been a struggle – a cry for help? But there wasn't a whimper of a struggle. Her maids slept soundly through it all and, but for those bruises and cuts on the mouth, there were no signs of violence. Would she have submitted so meekly having taken the precaution of keeping her dagger under her pillow? No! It's all too unlikely. She knew her life was in danger. And her attacker entered unheard and uninvited."

"So who could it have been?" asked Mikhail.

"I said I had another theory, Effendi," said my pasha, pensively repeating the words "another theory". He was about to restart the game of wits with Mikhail. "Fatima, the jariyé, remembered a late-night visitor but, in the light of a single candle, can't describe the stranger. We're told the caller was veiled like a woman and as tall. That's all we know. But, Effendi, when is a woman not a woman?"

"Ah, it's time for riddles again! Very well, let me see ..." Mikhail thought for a while, muttering to himself as he turned over the possibilities in his mind. Then he raised a hand, and his voice. "I think I have it!" he exclaimed, wagging his forefinger at my pasha. "I have it! The stranger was not so tall, so we're assuming it was a woman. But it could just as easily have been a boy – Mustafa, perhaps," he said with a mischievous twinkle. "Or … yes, that's it!" he added excitedly in a rising crescendo. "It's Gedik, Khurrem's pet dwarf! That's who it is," A smug smile of satisfaction rippled across his face.

"Very good, Effendi, that was very clever", responded my master, smiling in return. Lowering his voice to a whisper and signalling to Mikhail to do the same – they were, after all, in a public place – he beckoned to the doctor to come closer to hear what he had to say.

But Mikhail was intent on proving that his powers of deduction were equal to those of the Kadiasker. "I suspected as much for a while now. He's a creature of Khurrem's and he's always poking fun at Ibrahim Pasha. His puns and satirical barbs are replete with veiled allusions to the Grand Vizier. And the insults haven't gone unnoticed by Ibrahim Pasha, either. It's only the patronage of Khurrem that prevents him lopping a few more centimetres off the dwarf. In fact, I doubt if even the royal favour can save him! Gedik the Dwarf it is, then. His quarters are near Shireen's, he can be mistaken for a boy and yet he's strong enough to suffocate the sleeping Shireen and smother any struggle she might have put up. He did so on orders from Khurrem for reasons we both know. He had the opportunity and we know the motive."

"Brilliant!" exclaimed my master. "All wrong but I admire your creativity. I really do," said my pasha with genuine sincerity. Still, any attempt at gravitas was futile and he knew he was fighting a losing battle when he glimpsed the hurt expression on Mikhail's face. The learned physician stood up in such a flurry that he trod on his robe and had to juggle with it to prevent himself falling over.

"Well," asked Mikhail gruffly as he straightened his bathrobe again, tying it snugly around his waist, "if it's not the dwarf, who is it?"

"I've teased you long enough, Effendi", replied my master. "It can't have been Gedik although I admit I once suspected him." He never had but was driven by pity and the hope of restoring a glimmer of self-esteem to Mikhail.

"We're told or conjecture that the visitor was a woman," my master continued. "You were on the right trail, thinking it might be a boy or a dwarf dressed as a woman. It was certainly a person of no great height. But there's a strong reason for excluding Gedik as a suspect. Though his quarters are a stone's throw from Shireen's, how would he have got past the guards? The maid says the visitor was veiled and dressed as a woman but, what would a lady of the Harem be doing coming from the direction of the eunuchs' billets?"

"I see that, but who do you suspect?" asked Mikhail.

"Effendi, I'll tell you. It was ...," replied my master with the flourish and timing of an entertainer, "It was Daud Aga! What do you say to that?"

Mikhail screwed up his half hidden face to resemble something quite horrible, before replying. "Daud Aga? Selim Aga's deputy? You can't be serious. That's preposterous!" The mildly scoffing tone suggested that he was still smarting from Adam Pasha's teasing. He preferred his own theory about Gedik the Dwarf and it was my master's turn to take offence at not being instantly congratulated.

"Effendi, have you ever seen Daud Aga perform his magic tricks?"

"Yes, of course I have. What of them?"

"Have you seen the one using the three green silk handkerchiefs?"

Mikhail murmured a deep guttural sound as if to say, "I think I know where the opium went."

"Well, think back to that halva – the poisoned halva – it was wrapped in a green silk handkerchief, wasn't it?" Adam Pasha looked straight at Mikhail before adding, "Just like the ones used by Daud Aga."

"So?" enquired Mikhail far from convinced. "What of it?" he asked as he pulled a length of green silk from his bathrobe. "Look, I've got one, too. There must be dozens of people in the Palace with green handkerchiefs. Isn't the Sultan, himself, partial to that colour?"

"Yes, but I've other reasons to suspect Daud. Do you remember the extortion racket in the Bazaar?"

"What has Daud to do with that? Next you'll be telling me that Daud is some common criminal."

"There's nothing common about him. He's deep in it." Mikhail was now reduced to shaking his head in agitated disbelief. But my master was in no mood to stop now. "I saw him. I witnessed an attempt at extortion by the Market Inspector and his Janissary accomplices and at one point they were joined by a veiled figure cloaked in white. I couldn't of course see the whole face but it wasn't a woman. Now, Daud Aga is strongly built but he's no giant of a man. More importantly, being a Nubian albino who burns easily in the sun, he's always veiled. And we know he always dresses in white. Nilufer could have been right about the eunuch lover, or, if not a lover, at least a eunuch visitor. It could have been Daud Aga. I'm sure he's involved but I don't know how. My fear is that he's part of something much bigger, something much more sinister and dangerous. I think we've stumbled across an enormous plot to destabilise the Empire and Shireen's murder was just part of it."

"Plots, now, is it? Well, for someone who accuses me of having a vivid imagination, I think yours has something in common with Scheherazade. I've just heard the one thousandth and second tale of the Arabian Nights. What's your evidence, Mr. Judge?"

"No real evidence but I know Daud Aga is up to his eyeballs in it. He passed a small bundle of what seemed to be coins to his confederates – money tied up in a green silk handkerchief."

Mikhail rolled his eyes in disbelief. "So, we're back to the handkerchiefs, are we? Well you might as well arrest me along with him. And don't forget to call on His Highness whilst you're at it. By the way, have you told our Sultan of your suspicions? Personally, I think you should keep this to yourself but if you really want to give our Sultan the best belly-laugh he's had for ages, you'd better do it quick because he's off hunting tomorrow."

"I think I'll have the last laugh, Effendi," answered my pasha, who was starting to doubt his own theory. "I'm intending to join our Sultan's hunt in Belgrade Forest. Murat will soon find Sarah's killer or, at least who hired the boat used to dump her body. If it turns out to have been Daud we might have to risk leaving him at large for a while. I'll have to get the Sultan's consent before I can arrest him because if my suspicions are wrong ..." Adam Pasha clenched his teeth and gave a gentle whistle.

XVII   THE CISTERN CHASE

"Fishermen, damn it! Are they blind? They must have seen something." I was muttering away to myself as I kicked some rotting meat into the sea. It seemed that everyone I asked had, on the very day Sarah was murdered, decided to take the day off. Apparently, no more than two-dozen fishing boats were on the water and even tracking down their owners seemed an impossible task. No one wanted to talk to me. Now, why would that be, I wondered? Not that I had the time to ponder why the fishing community had suddenly turned taciturn: someone was watching me. At first it was just a feeling but I was being stalked like a wounded animal. I only got a glimpse of him out of the corner of my eye – a lean, muscular, lanky man with unwashed hair, perhaps a sailor – but I did not like the look of him.

I quickened my pace. Leaving the quayside, I walked briskly up a hill into a wooded area where I crouched down behind the largest tree I could find and waited. I must have sat there for half an hour, though it seemed like considerably more. With a wet bottom, bored and tired of the company of midges, I struggled to my feet and shook the stiffness out of my limbs. I could see no sign of my pursuer. Perhaps, I had imagined it all. Perhaps not. Either way, I had to resume the search for that elusive fisherman.

Weary, with sunset not far off, I decided to make one last visit and marched up to a modest but sound mud-brick and wood house with smoke billowing from the cooking hearth and the door and windows wide open to let in the breeze. My approach observed, a fresh-faced youth called out to his father. The latter had barely uttered a greeting before I realised that they were not Greeks as I had imagined but from a village near my own in the mountains of Georgia.

"You have a Georgian accent," I said.

"That's because, thank our Lord, we are Georgian," replied the black-haired father in a hoarse, crackly voice.

"*Mashallah*, Allah be praised" I said. "So am I."

We passed a very pleasant evening together. Minced-meat kebabs, charcoal-grilled chunks of lamb and two flagons of red wine made for a very merry evening. No fish. It was a lavish feast for such simple folk. We reminisced and toasted our families back home and, when I was ready to go, the broad-shouldered father pressed me back on my stool and called for more food and sweet wine. Too late to go home, a comfortable bed was made for me and, the next day when we parted, we kissed on both cheeks and hugged each other as if we were long-lost friends.

***

"Pasha, they're wonderful people. And I'm sure they can tell us something about Sarah. They were out on the water that day but I didn't seek any details. The fishermen are frightened of something … or someone. As soon as I ask about unusual sightings, they bounce shifty glances back and forth and suddenly go mute. I'm pretty certain I was being followed and whoever it was has a nasty line in persuasion."

"But you think these Georgians know something?"

"Oh, yes, Pasha. They know something. I didn't want to press too hard. I thought I'd go back today to renew the acquaintance."

"You've done well, Murat, though watch the drinking. I'll come with you this time. This is too important to miss – I'd like to go to the Sultan with something more definite than just my suspicions."

***

"Nilufer, my sweet, we'll be back in a few hours. We're expecting Mikhail Effendi this evening for dinner. He might stay the night. Better get in some goat meat – you know how he likes it. Oh, and we might ask him to give you a check up."

"There's no need for that, my Pasha. I'm fine. I told you I'd be fine without Harem chains. I just needed some space to breath."

"Still, he might as well have a look whilst he's here."

"But, dearest…"

"No 'buts', my sweet." My pasha took Nilufer tenderly in his arms, resting his cheek against hers. They smiled lovingly at each other and he kissed her fondly on the forehead, on the eyes and on the mouth. "I must go," he said as he gently pushed her away.

It was a warm summer's day, perfect for putting everyone in a jolly mood. My new Georgian friends were certainly that and they were also over-awed when they realised I was valet to Adam Pasha, the Kadiasker. Suddenly, the youth's beautiful sisters appeared, Natella and Nino, just in case I might be looking for a bride. Natella was the taller of the two, dark-haired like Zurab, her father, with strong features and high cheekbones. Nino was blue-eyed, shorter but with rounder breasts and long blonde hair. Temptation beckoned with a glance and a wink but how could I choose between the two of them?

Chicken stuffed with walnuts, the finest steamed fish with fermented sweet pomegranate sauce, pickled cabbage - we ate until we could eat no more. Zurab left the wine off the table in deference to his new and distinguished guest and substituted some delicious pear juice that he had got in from his neighbour. Eventually, we touched upon the reason for our visit. The laughter died as suddenly as if a scorpion had been spotted in a baby's cot. Zurab said nothing but his dark eyes told me that he thought I had betrayed his hospitality. But, as a true Caucasian host, he could not deny his guests and told us what he had seen.

By the time we took our leave, the warmth had returned and we hugged and kissed, at least the men did. I would have preferred to say my farewell to Natella and Nino in like manner, rather than the tame wave that I was reduced to giving. Still, I swore I would return. My master offered help if ever the family needed it, perhaps with some position in the navy for the father. Zurab proudly declined. He agreed, however, not to see us off, for his own safety.

"Tomorrow, Murat, you must find the captain of the 'Theodora'," instructed my master as we stepped out into the fresh air. "But tonight," he added with a groan, "we must entertain the good doctor." Neither of us could face another big meal.

Stepping out into the twilight, we had no warning, no inkling of what was about to happen. As we were mounting our horses, the man with the unwashed hair, he who had followed me the previous day, sprang down from the roof of the fisherman's house. This time he had a companion, a big, even more muscular man. 'Unwashed' grabbed my master's sleeve and pulled him to the ground. I came up behind him but, kicked in the knee, I collapsed in agony and fell straight into the arms of 'Muscles'.

Unwashed had a knife in his left hand and his right was wrapped around my pasha's throat. My master was writhing on the ground, trying to break free but Unwashed's strong grip was gradually choking the life out of him. I strained to pull forward but Muscles wrenched my arm behind my back until I felt it was about to snap. On one knee and helpless, the best I could do was to stare at the pointed blade of the knife poised to plunge deep into my master's chest.

The next I knew, Unwashed was grabbing at the back of his neck. He stood up, his eyes wide-open as if about to burst from his head. As he twisted around, another arrow struck, thudding into his heart. He dropped, missing me by centimetres but showering me with droplets of blood. Muscles threw me forward and ran for it, an arrow whizzing past his left ear. He got away.

Everything had happened so quickly that it was all over by the time our Georgian friends came rushing out to help us. My master was half carried to a stool by Zurab and I limped along with the assistance of Nino and Natella. Nino raised my baggy trousers a little to look at the bruised knee, giggling as she did so. Natella caressed my brow with a damp cloth. I wondered if I could marry them both. Damn! Visions of Elizabeth wielding a broom at my head kept intruding into my fantasies. Ah well…

"What happened?" asked Zurab.

"I don't know," stammered my master, still breathless. "We had barely stepped outside when two men jumped us. I thought this was it – I was a dead man. Then, out of nowhere, we hear the twang of arrows being loosed and one of the attackers falls to the ground. The other scarpered. Who our saviour was, I have no idea. I never got as much as a glimpse of him."

"What about the attackers. Any idea who they were?"

"None whatsoever," said my pasha, "though there was something vaguely familiar about the one who got away".

"I don't know about the one who got away," I added, "but the dead one was the same man who followed me yesterday. And his hair was still unwashed."

***

My master, dressed in a cool blue kaftan, was accompanied by Mikhail, fitted out in something altogether gaudier. Luckily for me, they had not yet passed through the gates of the house as I approached, riding at a quick trot.

"Adam Pasha!" I called, exhilarated by my discovery.

"You have news, Murat?" my pasha asked.

"Yes, Pasha. I've found the boat, just as Zurab had described it. It was a rented barque. The owner's a Greek called Andreas who hires it out from time to time. It's a coastal trader but occasionally goes further out and doubles sometimes as a fishing boat if there's no trade to be had. Luckily for us, this Andreas lives only a stone's throw from here – above the great cistern by the Mosque of Aya Sophia. I also managed to get a description of the fellow who hired the barque and, guess what? It matches the description of the man with the unwashed hair."

"What do you intend to do, Pasha?" asked the doctor.

"First, find Andreas and take him into custody. I don't want to act against Daud Aga without some corroborating evidence and, inshallah, Andreas will lead us to our master-spy. If it is Daud, I'll have to inform His Highness before I can arrest him."

"You're still fixated on this Daud Aga theory of yours," said Mikhail Effendi. "If there's nothing I can say to dissuade you, you know that, with our Sultan hunting in Belgrade Forest, that could delay the arrest by several days which will give Daud Aga time to escape."

"I realise that, Effendi, but Daud Aga's too important for

me to take without the Sultan's express consent. All I can do in the meantime is to have him watched. And before we can do anything about the eunuch we must take Andreas."

"How many men shall we take?" I asked.

"Four will do. And Mehmed to look after the horses. With you, that makes six. But you must be tired. Take a rest and I'll get someone else to go in your place."

"No, Pasha, I want to come. I'll have the men ready in ten minutes."

"Take a rest all the same and be ready in two hours. I don't want to waste time but Andreas won't be expecting us so I don't see how a couple of hours can make any difference. Will you join us, Effendi?" asked my master, turning to Mikhail.

"No Pasha, I must return to my duties at the Palace but I'm looking forward to hearing of your success. May God go with you."

***

We approached Andreas's house on foot, leaving our horses at the end of the street with trooper Mehmed.

"Murat, you come with me," said Adam Pasha. "Yaqoob, take Faik and watch the back of the house. Farooq, you and Zaman watch the front. Let's go!"

We banged on the door. There was no answer. My master turned the rusty iron handle, opening the door with a jerk and a discordant scrape. The door's upper hinge was beginning to come apart from the frame and one corner of it dragged and stuttered along the stone floor. It was dark inside, and within half an hour it was going to be dark outside too. I lit a lantern that I found lying in a corner whilst Adam Pasha lit the stub-end of a candle. The room was close and damp and there was no sign of Andreas or anyone else.

My master stepped out into the glinting light of the sun's fading rays and swept away the musty smell in his nostrils, taking in a few deep breaths of fresh air. He gave orders to our men to conceal themselves discreetly outside the house whilst he and I waited inside for Andreas' return. We did not expect to wait long: Andreas would surely be back before it was dark, so we seated ourselves on stools and waited.

"What was that, Murat," asked my pasha, suddenly breaking the silence. "Did you hear it?"

"Hear what? I didn't hear anything, Pasha," I replied, rising to my feet at one with my master.

"It was the sound of water, Murat. We didn't check that door," whispered my master pointing to one of the two doors leading off the room. "Where does it go to?" I pushed open the small, narrow door and stooped to go through it. It was the entrance to the cistern, one of the biggest of the Imperial Roman reservoirs constructed to provide a constant water supply in the hot summer months.

"It's the cistern, Pasha, but there's nothing here but water."

Adam Pasha squeezed past me and, taking the lantern, walked cautiously halfway down a flight of wet and slippery steps. The air was still, warm and moist. My master peered into the darkness. The silence was broken only by the sound of droplets of water falling gently to the lake below. The rays of the lantern's light made little impact upon the blackness of the cavernous cistern but, as our eyes began to adjust to the dimness, we could see the forms of half-a-dozen columns – massively smooth masonry crowned by cushion capitals covered in green slime. They supported the bricked arches of the cistern roof. Adam Pasha swung the lantern horizontally through a semi-circle, to and fro. The shadows moved with the arc of light but all else was still.

"We're wasting our time, Pasha," I whispered, "Andreas will be back soon."

"Perhaps you're right, Murat but ...," Adam Pasha felt uneasy but could not tell why. He turned to leave and, as he did so, the light in his hand fell upon a piece of paper lying a few steps below him. He stooped to pick it up but before he had the chance to read it, he heard footsteps in the house above. He placed the lantern on the steps and held a finger to his lips, beckoning to me to stand by the door. My master approached the door as quietly as possible. He could see in the candlelight a tall, cloaked figure moving towards him with a rapier in hand.

Adam Pasha, realising that both of us could be trapped in the cistern, dug out his purse from his tunic and flung it into the stranger's face. It struck him in the eye and, as he blinked away the pain, my pasha dashed forward and grabbed the hilt of the sword. I followed quickly behind, dagger drawn, but the cloaked figure was stronger than he looked and we struggled to subdue him. With my dagger at his throat, we finally succeeded, just as Farooq and his comrade burst into the house.

"Pasha, are you alright?" Farooq asked with concern. "We heard the sound of a struggle."

"Everything's fine, Farooq," replied Adam Pasha.

"Better late than never," I felt compelled to add.

Before dealing with the stranger, the Kadiasker, a man always elegantly dressed even on campaign, straightened out the wrinkles in his clothes and reset the turban on his head. He took a handkerchief and mopped the trickle of blood running from his aquiline nose.

"Are you Andreas?" he said in Greek. There was no

reply. "I shall ask you once again and I shall expect an answer. Or else …." The forthright manner, the gruff tone, the piercing stare, must have had the desired effect for when he repeated the question the stranger answered without hesitation but not without indignation.

"Yes, I'm Andreas," he answered in a staccato Turkish with a Greek accent. "What mean to you? Who you are? What you doing in my house? What you want? No valuables, no valuables!" he kept repeating like a half-wit, concluding with, "Nothing to steal."

"A lot of questions," I said, "for someone who's just tried to kill one of the Sultan's ministers."

Adam Pasha raised his hand to command silence. "You know what we're after, Andreas, but you act your part very well," he said in Greek. "As for who I am, you're entitled to know that. I am Adam Pasha, Kadiasker of Rhum. Does that mean anything to you?"

There were signs of recognition in Andreas's face – the raised eyebrows, the furtive glance – as Farooq and Zaman held him down on a stool. He answered in perfect Greek. "But what do you want of me, Pasha? For five generations my family has cared for and maintained these cisterns – since before the days of the Conqueror. We have proved our loyalty as few others have done."

"Do you own a red and white barque called the 'Theodora'?" asked my master.

"Yes I do, Pasha." Andreas was far more respectful now but still his terse reply gave away no more than he had to.

"Have you recently hired the boat to anyone? To a slim, tall, strong, muscular man?"

"With unwashed hair," I added in Ottoman.

Andreas shook his head.

"Search him and the room!" ordered my master. Andreas was thrown against the stone wall as the stool slid from under him.

"What are you doing?" he cried. "I'll complain to the Metropolitan. You've got no right …" A slap across the face showed him who had what rights. Adam Pasha admonished the erring soldier, but not too harshly.

"You had better co-operate," advised my master. "Afterwards, you can complain all you like. I'll even help you write the petition."

The search was surprisingly productive. On Andreas we discovered a well-concealed dagger and in a secret place, behind a loose stone in the wall, Farooq plucked out a heavy purse. He emptied the contents into his hand, a mixture of gold and silver coins, and then returned them to the purse.

Adam Pasha took the leather pouch and shook it in front of the Greek's nose. "So," he said, "as you have no valuables, I imagine these can't be yours."

"Of course they're mine. I thought you were thieves. That's payment for services honestly provided."

"What sort of 'services'?"

"For the hire of the 'Theodora'. But it wasn't a tall muscular man who hired it. It was a Greek - medium height with a split lip."

"Name?"

"I can't remember. Wait … Stavros. That was it. Stavros."

My pasha turned out a few coins into the palm of his hand. It was then that he noticed some gold ducats and, taking one, held it under the dim light of the candle, weighing it carefully in his hand. "Venetian ducats and fake ones at that. It doesn't look good for you, Andreas. The fate of a spy is a thoroughly unpleasant one. It begins with beatings with a long cane on the feet. If you can still walk after that, then there's the rack. If you survive the stretching, there's the drenching. If you don't drown, there are the floggings. Are you ready for all that? You know you only have one chance now. Tell me the truth and I can still save you." The handsome, unshaven Greek stared wide-eyed but said nothing. "Now!" shouted Adam Pasha, making Andreas flinch in fear. He swallowed hard and his right eye twitched.

"Where did you get the money?" my master continued. "And why the concealed dagger?"

"I told you, Pasha," stammered Andreas. "It was Stavros – he paid me the money. As for the dagger, there's nothing sinister about that. I always carry one – pirates, it's a safeguard against pirates." Andreas could have been telling the truth – my pasha was not sure.

"I think we're done here. Take him to the Palace guardhouse," ordered my master as Andreas was pushed towards the door. He gathered up the purse he had earlier flung at Andreas and tucked it away inside his tunic. In doing so, he remembered the scrap of paper that he had picked up on the cistern steps. He took it out and read the crumpled note. "All is lost. Save yourself", were the only words that it bore and they had been scribbled in haste in Ottoman. Adam Pasha stopped and thought a moment.

"What does this mean?" he asked Andreas. He read the note aloud. "All is lost. Save yourself."

"I have no idea, Sir."

"Murat," said my master, turning to me. "What do you make of it?"

"If the note were meant for Andreas, surely it would have been in Greek, not in Ottoman. Unless, of course, it were written by an Ottoman who doesn't know Greek."

"And feel the paper," suggested my master, as he handed me the chit. Rubbing it gently between my fingers, I raised it to my nose and sniffed.

"Palace notepaper," I ventured.

"Exactly, Murat!"

I gave myself a metaphorical pat on the back.

"Andreas," said Adam Pasha, "you can prove your loyalty now. Come with me."

A lantern was handed to Andreas and he led the way down the cistern steps to a stone jetty where a small rowboat was moored.

"Murat, you wait here on the jetty with Zaman," ordered my master. "And Farooq, you keep watch in the house."

"Get in and take the oars," my pasha said to Andreas and then, taking hold of the lantern, followed him into the boat.

"Row!" ordered my pasha as I gave a helpful shove.

Andreas had rowed ten columns deep, out of sight but with the glimmer of the light still visible, when my master, trying to steer and keep a watchful eye, accidentally struck the lantern against a pillar. The lamp fell into the water with a loud splash and the light went out.

"Pasha!" I cried out in concern. "Is everything well?" There was no reply.

***

"Wait till our eyes adjust to the light," said my pasha. "Then we can feel our way back to the jetty and get a new lantern."

As the boat rocked gently like a baby's cradle, the water suddenly began to lap more strongly against it. Someone, or something, had stirred it. My master turned his head but all he saw was a pair of white hands. They gripped him by the throat and, before he had a chance to cry out, he was pulled sharply backwards in the now violently rocking boat. He grabbed at the short, strong fingers but his head was already touching the water and his turban had fallen off. The water was in his nostrils and just seconds away from his head being completely submerged beneath it. He was gasping for air. He clutched hopelessly, uselessly, at the fingers. It was too much for the rocking boat, which suddenly flipped over, throwing Adam Pasha and Andreas into the water.

Andreas had been considering his best course of action. With soldiers in the house, escape would be difficult but, perhaps, with the help of Daud Aga who was about to drown Adam Pasha, he might yet escape.

"I've got him! I've got him!" squeaked the albino. "Help me!" But Daud lost his grip on my master as the boat capsized.

Adam Pasha, a poor swimmer, was keeping himself afloat with the help of his turban whilst trying to cling to the boat, coughing out water and gulping in air. Andreas, clinging to the opposite side of the upturned vessel, scooped up an oar floating nearby and swung it wildly. It struck my pasha painfully on the shoulder just as Daud Aga again appeared behind him, his fingers once more around his neck.

My pasha was slipping lower and lower. The water had reached his mouth. One more push and his head disappeared below the waterline. Little bubbles rose to the surface and Adam Pasha gave up the struggle.

"I'll finish him off!" said Andreas but Daud whispered a sharp retort. "Don't waste time! He's dead. Get into my boat and row for the jetty. Pretend I'm your prisoner. Without a light, they won't realise the Kadiasker's not with us until we're almost there."

XVIII   TO THE FOREST OF BELGRADE

The eunuch rowed whilst Andreas hung out over the edge of
the boat, ensuring with his arms extended and fingers
outstretched that they avoided collision with the ancient
columns.

The boat was five or six metres from the jetty when I
noticed that my pasha was not in it. I had heard the
splashing and thrashing in the water but I had no idea of
what had taken place in the distant darkness.

"We've captured Daud Aga!" cried Andreas.

"Where's Adam Pasha?" I asked. It was my only concern.

"He fell from the boat in the struggle," replied Andreas.
"Without a light I couldn't see him but, God willing, he's still
alive. I'll hold the prisoner here on the jetty whilst you two
take the lantern and search for the Kadiasker." Frantic with
concern, my mind was a whirling blur. My only thought was
of my master as I visualised him sinking in the water.
Quickly, desperately, I wanted to draw in the boat.

I held out a hand to Andreas, leaning out as far as I
could. Then I felt a sharp tug on my sleeve and my master's
predicament was blown clean away into a distant world. I
fell headlong from the jetty. I was no swimmer and started to
pray, though whether aloud or not I have no memory. Being
summer, the water level was low but was deep enough for
me to drown in and I kept praying that Andreas would not
let go. He did not. He kept a firm hold with one hand on the
sleeve of my kaftan, now hanging heavy with water. But
with the other hand he was pushing my bursting head below
the waterline and all I could do was to cling desperately onto

his arm or be consigned to the bottom of the reservoir.

Zaman, standing confused on the jetty, was briefly disoriented. Finally, he drew his sword but hardly had he raised it up to slash than Daud, javelin-like, hurled an oar at him. It struck Zaman in a full facial crunch, sending him reeling back towards the wall. He dropped bruised and senseless to the floor and his sword plopped into the water. There was a cacophony of elated whoops and yells as Daud scooped up the sinking sword and did a dervish-like twirl.

Farooq, a formidable man, squeezed awkwardly through the narrow door at the top of the cistern steps and came charging down them. Daud, still whooping and yelling, thought he would try his luck again and launched the sword at our bayraktar. As it left Daud's pinky-white hand, Farooq slipped on the wet steps and the sword flew past him, clattering harmlessly on the stone. Recovering from his heavy fall, Farooq staggered to his feet, drew his own sword and slashed at Andreas. The blade cut across the Greek's cheek and he screeched so loud, so terribly, that the whole cistern quaked in fear. Blood gushing from his ear to his mouth, he let go of me and I started to sink.

Farooq scrambled to unhook his scabbard. Fumbling, he dropped it as I thrashed about wildly trying to stay afloat. Farooq threw himself flat on the jetty, grabbed the scabbard and held it out to me. "Take it, Murat! Hold on!"

I was still praying fervently and with my fingertips I hung on as Farooq hauled me onto the jetty.

As I coughed and stumbled, sprawled on the jetty, spitting out water, Andreas, one side of his face covered in blood, took the second of the two oars from Daud in the boat and he rammed it into the back of Farooq's head. His helmet cushioned part of the blow but he staggered forward, falling on top of me and pinning me to the stone jetty.

Andreas now whirled the oar wildly and slammed it down at my head. I managed to roll my head out of the way, only to see Daud climbing onto the jetty with Zaman's scimitar again in his hand. I heaved the dazed Farooq off me as Andreas, with the oar, came at me from the right and Daud, with the sword, came from the left. I struggled to my feet, with my back to the wall. The Greek jabbed at me with the oar. He caught me a sharp blow in the midriff and I doubled up in pain as Daud raise his sword to finish me off.

Zaman had barely regained consciousness but somehow managed to stumble forward and grab feebly at Daud. The eunuch easily shook off the weak attempt to hold him but both Andreas and Daud were distracted long enough for me to throw myself forward and swipe the oar out of Andreas's hand. I wielded it straight at Daud. There was a crunching, cracking sound as it met his head and he fell half-conscious into the water. He struggled hopelessly, gasping for air and clutching at the side of the boat. "Help me! Help me!" he gurgled as his head slipped below the water. I felt no remorse or any inclination to help – it was small punishment for the murder of my master.

Andreas was confused, giving Farooq just enough time to take up the sword dropped by the drowning eunuch. Farooq slashed and the blade caught Andreas over the eye. Shrieking, he tottered backwards into the water. He did not reappear. It was all over.

Zaman was groggy and unsteady but lifted himself to his feet. I sat down on the edge of the jetty, in my dripping kaftan, kicking angrily at the water. The master-spy was dead and so was my master. Farooq and Zaman each gently rested a hand on my shoulders, squeezing tenderly in a vain attempt to comfort me. But tears were welling in my eyes. What now? The empire had lost one of its true champions of decency and integrity and I had lost a dear friend, a learned teacher and mentor. For several minutes we sat silently, before Farooq broke the silence.

"Murat, did you hear something?"

"Hear what?" I replied.

"Listen ..."

A cry for help was echoing faintly around the cistern. It was Adam Pasha. It was a miracle but he was alive. A poor swimmer and weighed down by his water-soaked clothes, he had managed, nonetheless, to slip under the capsized boat. A pocket of air had saved him and bit-by-bit he had struggled to a pillar. He clung to it desperately, still dazed and concussed. But he was alive, *mashallah*, God be praised!

***

Nilufer, was clearly agitated. On hearing of Adam Pasha's impending departure for Belgrade Forest, where the Sultan was passing a few weeks in the pleasures of hunting and falconry, Nilufer could hold back no longer.

"Dearest," she pleaded, "wait for His Highness's return to Istanbul. It can only be a few days – a week or two at the most. Surely a few days won't matter?"

"I must go, my dear. You know I can't wait," replied my master. He was eager to reach the Sultan to make his report about Daud Aga's treachery. He gave his wife a loving kiss on the lips and opened the door to leave. Nilufer, realising that any attempt to prevent the mission altogether was going to be in vain, made one last plea to my master to postpone his departure for a few days at least.

"Dearest! Listen to me!" she cried out tearfully. "For God's sake, listen to me! There is danger on the road ahead. I dreamt it last night. Don't go yet – wait a day or two for a more auspicious sign."

"Nilufer, I don't believe in 'auspicious signs'," said my pasha firmly. "Don't worry, my dear, no harm will come to me," he added tenderly. "Murat's here to look after me and we'll travel incognito so no one will know who we are."

"You don't understand, my love, I ..." Nilufer broke off her sentence with a sigh of resignation. She tried another approach. "But, my Pasha," preferring to use the respectful honorific, "it's too dangerous for the two of you to travel incognito on your own. Take an escort. They can protect you and, with everyone knowing who you are, you will travel much faster and you'll be able to take the most direct route."

Adam Pasha reflected for a moment. "You may be right, dearest. Perhaps a small escort makes sense." It was not long before nine troopers were mounted and ready to leave. Nilufer, hiding her head as tears dribbled down her cheeks, waved Adam Pasha away, unable to look at him for fear that she would break down completely.

"No need for tears, my dear," begged my pasha softly. "After all, our Sultan's camp is barely thirty kilometres away. That shouldn't take us four hours. What can possibly happen to us in that time?"

And so, we marched out. Our escort consisted of Farooq, carrying the Kadiasker's insignia of two horse-tails, the Chief Equerry, Yaqoob, and seven other cavalrymen. Each man wore full battle dress and carried a lance and scimitar, with a bow slung diagonally over one shoulder and a quiver of arrows over the other. And each man had a circular shield strapped to his back. It was a magnificent sight.

Our party moved briskly past the gatehouse downhill towards the ferry crossing. My master, Farooq and I took the lead. The rear was brought up by Mehmed, a sweet-looking youth of nineteen, with green eyes and dark hair. Whether walking beside his black mare or sitting astride her, he was constantly whispering to her, patting her gently on the neck and muzzle. The horse licked her approval in return. To look at them, one would think they were in love.

It was already well past noon and Adam Pasha was not pleased with the poor time we were making. In trying to push our way through Istanbul, our journey was first delayed by an upturned bullock cart and then by a funeral cortege of some local big-wig. It was led by a mullah uttering worthy prayers and the coffin, draped with a green pall with gold bands bearing Koranic verses, followed behind carried by six turbaned bearers. Out of religious sensibility, we stood aside, lowered our heads and muttered prayers for an unknown soul. To top it all, following the laborious ferry crossing of the Golden Horn, a route that we deemed to be safest, we ran into a large flock of sheep being herded towards the city on the coast road which ran along the western shore of the Bosphorus.

Vigilant and nervous, there was not much talking done during the journey. Except by Mehmed, that is, who was constantly engaged in horse-talk with his one love. Incapable of hurting any living creature, Mehmed would have been totally useless in a fight but was wonderful with horses. Too tender to be a soldier, only his love for horses had made him willing to bear the rigours of a soldier's life.

"I don't like it, Pasha," I ventured.

"I know, Murat. Nor do I. We're going too slowly."

Even allowing for a certain optimism on my master's behalf, our journey was going to take much more than the four hours he had predicted. To be sure, the land route around the Golden Horn would have taken longer but ferrying horses across the Golden Horn was hardly less laborious and it was starting to look as if our chosen route could take almost as long.

Once on the other side, we passed the outskirts of the medieval Genoese township of Galata and pressed on towards the royal gardens at Dolmabache, gardens laid out by our Sultan's father on land reclaimed from the Bosphorus. Once through Galata and out into the open countryside, we expected progress would be better. We were wrong. The Kadiasker, no less than I, was becoming increasingly concerned about the forced halts to our journey. With every rustle of a bush, each bark of a dog, every croak of a crow, our senses were fired up during our plodding progress.

The undulating dirt road closely hugged the shores of the vital waterway that linked the Mediterranean with the Black Sea. The Bosphorus lay to the right, with a mixture of fishermen's huts and pleasure kiosks running along a goodly part of it. The road was overlooked to the left by wooded hills where the nightingales and blackbirds fluttered amongst the cypress and chestnut trees. The planes and the pines basked in the early autumnal sun but neither Adam Pasha nor I could afford to enjoy the wild beauty all around us. These same wooded hills provided perfect cover for a hidden assailant.

"Master...," I started in a concerned voice.

"I've seen him, Murat. We have to make better time. Much better time." We were being followed. It was hard to make out who it was, or, indeed, if there was more than one, but we had both glimpsed at least one soldier, helmeted and fully armed, on the hilltop above us. The Kadiasker ordered Yaqoob and two troopers to drop behind to protect our rear.

As we approached the garrisoned fortress of Rumeli Hisar, no more than ten kilometres away from Galata but more than six hours since we had set out, I suggested we accept the governor's importunate invitation to stop and rest at the castle. But Adam Pasha graciously declined, only too conscious that we were in danger of not reaching our destination before nightfall. And so we pressed on, passing through a succession of hamlets where we drew the stares of fishermen and the attention of bands of smiling children running alongside our horses.

It was at the village of Istinye, not more than three kilometres from Rumeli Hisar, that Adam Pasha admitted defeat and called a halt for the night. There was still an hour of daylight but, at the current rate of progress it was barely enough to reach the Sultan's encampment. In any case, the gentle Mehmed's horse had gone lame and my master had to decide whether to leave Mehmed behind or to rest.

The bay at Istinye was deep and there was a thriving harbour and boat repair yard. At the edge of the village was a small pious foundation containing a plain, functional mosque, some ramshackle workshops and a small hostelry with pretensions to being a caravanserai.

"We'll rest up there," said Adam Pasha, pointing to the caravanserai. "Be ready for an early start in the morning."

The troopers dismounted in the courtyard of the hostelry and, once inside, removed their pointed, plumed helmets, chainmail and weapons. Shod of their armour, they shook the stiffness out of their limbs and tucked into the bread, white-cheese and honey that were always on offer at such inns. I ordered soup for the soldiers, leaving my master and Yaqoob, his equerry, to consider the rota for the night-watch.

Meanwhile, Mehmed, always one to put the comfort of

229

his mount before his own, and the outsized Ibrahim were busy fetching fodder for the horses and rubbing them down.

The hostelry was empty, but for the innkeeper, his assistant, and a single dervish presumably making his way to or from the nearby dervish convent. That at least is all I noticed at first until I caught sight of a sleeping figure curled up in a dark corner. I guessed from his shabby appearance that he was a Turcoman, a nomadic sheep-herding peasant. He must have lost his flock or something.

The light was beginning to dim as the sun fell and the air took on a slight chill. The innkeeper stoked up the fire, as much to provide light as warmth, and closed the door and shutters. The call to prayer sounded from the mosque nearby and we all prepared for our devotions. The sleeping Turcoman, a stocky man with a drooping head, dressed in a well-worn sleeveless gown with an earring in one ear, rose from his slumbers and limped to a pitcher of water. I assumed he was going to perform his ablutions along with the rest of us but all he did was take a drink. He did not join us in the mosque, presumably preferring to pray inside the hostelry.

As we returned from the mosque, my pasha, rubbing his hands for warmth, walked towards the brazier, taking care not to disturb the again recumbent Turcoman. (I was later tempted to kick him awake to stop his wretched snoring.)

Adam Pasha, the brown-haired Yaqoob and I sat near the door, stretching out our blistered hands in the direction of a glowing brazier. I ordered some more of the indifferent soup in a vain attempt to fight off the chill from the draught blowing in from under the ill-fitting door.

It was whilst discussing how to make better time the next day that the inn-keeper approached my master.

"Pasha, a room has been prepared for you upstairs. If you will follow me, I will show you the way."

"Thank you," replied my master, "but I think I'll sleep down here tonight." Observing signs of concern in the innkeeper's face, Adam Pasha added, "I'll be perfectly comfortable." The Kadiasker leant forward and unfurled a brown blanket on the floor. He removed his grey kaftan and supple leather boots, laid aside his white turban, gave a nervous scratch to the stubbly new growth of hair on his recently shaven head and stretched out on the blanket.

We followed his example but it was too early to sleep. We chatted for a while about nothing in particular. We were thankful that the stables were at the far side of the courtyard and I for one was glad that I was not required to spend a night cuddled up with my mount.

As we talked, a second dervish entered the hostelry. He approached the first, a rough-shaven moustachioed man, and, after exchanging whispers, took out a piece of paper from a pouch and placed it carefully in a crack in the wall in one corner.

The two dervishes left together. Nothing special, I reckoned, about the ritual we had just witnessed: there being countless pieces of paper filling the equally abundant cracks and all contained some passage from the Koran which, being the word of God, no one would dare destroy.

Shortly before daybreak, the lazy Turcoman woke from his long hibernation, slowly unwound himself and, hobbling over to the wall, plucked what looked like the same piece of paper from the crack. He stoked up the embers of the dying fire, unfolded the paper, read it and carelessly tossed it into the sparking flames. Gently opening the door of the inn, he limped outside into the chilly morning air.

231

I had watched all this through half-opened eyes. At the click of the door closing behind the Turcoman, I nudged awake Adam Pasha and Yaqoob and explained what I had seen. My master was at once concerned. "Quick, after him! Follow him – and don't let him get away!"

***

The tall, broad-shouldered Ibrahim, even shod of his chainmail jacket and plumed helmet, was an imposing figure, built like a wrestler (which, if he were not soldiering, he would probably have been). He had taken some bread to his close friend Mehmed, who had spent a quiet night in the stables with his precious horses. Ibrahim now cut a mildly ridiculous figure as he ran ponderously from the stables towards the inn.

"Pasha! Pasha!" he called, clearly in a state of agitation. "Mehmed! Our Mehmed!" he kept repeating the name in a state of shock.

"Ibrahim!" cried my master sternly. "What's the matter?"

Ibrahim gained a measure of composure and stood to attention. He replied in a breathless stammer, "It's Mehmed … I left him with the horses whilst I caught some sleep by the fire of the inn. You know how deeply I sleep, Pasha. I'll never forgive myself."

"Forgive yourself for what?" asked the Kadiasker. "Take a deep breath and then tell me what all the fuss is about."

"When I took Mehmed some food a few minutes ago, he wouldn't move. I took a closer look and there was …," he gulped, "there was a knife wound in his back. He's dead. He's been murdered." A pained look of anguish lingered on his face. "Who would want to hurt such a gentle boy?"

We were stunned. Mehmed had been like our company mascot, everyone's favourite.

232

This dire news immersed the Kadiasker in a silent gloom from which he was only shaken when I myself came hurrying from the stables. "Pasha! The peasant's given us the slip. I've looked for him everywhere but there's no sign of him. He's vanished."

"The village! Scour the village!" said Adam Pasha with anger barely distinguishable from hate. "Find Mehmed's murderer!"

"Pasha," I said, a little surprised, "he didn't kill Mehmed. He didn't have time. And, what's more," I added, "Fazil has also disappeared." Fazil was a rather ordinary soldier whose early promise had waned but was an honest sort and a good fighter. "No one has seen him since last night. He was meant to be on watch this morning but where is he?"

"Poor Mehmed has been dead for some time," added Ibrahim. "And though one of our horses has gone, that peasant couldn't have ridden out of here without someone noticing."

The Kadiasker looked at me aghast. "What, in the name of Allah is happening?" he said. "Why would anyone take only one horse and not the whole lot? Surely, Fazil is not Mehmed's murderer? And, if not, what's happened to him?"

"What about that soldier who's been following us?" I suggested. "It could have been him."

"You must be right, Murat," answered my master. "We must be more cautious. Who's guarding the exits?"

"Adil's guarding one. Yaqoob's at the other."

The innkeeper, roused by the commotion and the sight of shadowy figures flitting back and forth in the dim light of daybreak, now appeared hurriedly at Adam Pasha's side.

"Sir, is anything wrong?" he asked, rubbing his eyes. "Can I be of service?"

"No, there's nothing you can do," replied Adam Pasha. He reflected for a moment. "Why hasn't the mullah given the call to prayer?" he asked the startled innkeeper. "He's late, very late."

"Sir...?"

"Murat," said Adam Pasha before the innkeeper could stammer out a coherent reply, "Take two men and search the mosque."

The little whitewashed mosque stood in one corner of the courtyard. The door was slightly ajar but an obstacle of some kind blocked the tight, narrow, stairs to the single minaret. As my eyes adjusted to the darkness of the unlit interior I began to realise what the obstacle was. It was the body of the mullah, his gown still warm and wet with his blood. There was, at the rear of the mosque, a small door occasionally used by the simple cleric but normally kept locked. He must have been killed by the Turcoman after refusing to give up the keys to the door. From there led a path down to the waters of the Bosphorus. The mullah's killer had escaped.

On hearing the news, Adam Pasha paced back and forth across a dusty patch of ground, deep in thought.

"But, Pasha," I enquired, "what sort of animal kills a mullah?"

"Ah! Murat, there was something peculiar about this 'animal'. Don't you think it strange that he didn't join the rest of us in the mosque? He could be one of those damned heretics, perhaps a follower of the Persian, Kabiz. The Divan saw to him three years ago but his supporters still persist."

Kabiz's trial and execution had caused quite a stir and considerable unrest. It was a time I had not forgotten. "Didn't Ibrahim Pasha release Kabiz at one point?" I asked.

"Yes, Murat. The kadiaskers of the day were not learned

enough to debate with Kabiz, a clever and adept orator. And
Ibrahim Pasha, no lover of theologians at the best of times,
doubtless took pleasure in humiliating them. It was only the
skill of the Mufti, Kemalpashazade, who finally defeated
Kabiz in the disputation.

"But," continued my master, "there was something else
about that Turcoman that wasn't quite right ...," he said
deep in thought.

"My Pasha, with that limp," I said, "I don't understand
how the peasant made off so quickly. But it's not likely he
was alone. For one thing, there's Mehmed's murderer – that
soldier who's been tracking us. We had better get to the
Sultan's camp as fast as we can before another disaster hits
us."

Adam Pasha muttered what sounded like a curse, turned
sharply in the dust and gave the order. "Mount up!"

The Kadiasker handed a pouch of silver akches to the
innkeeper to ensure that Mehmed and the mullah were
buried with dignity and within minutes our dwindling troop
passed out of the northern gate at a quick trot.

Adam Pasha dug in his heels to quicken the pace. We
rode briskly for an hour or more to within a few kilometres
of the Sultan's camp. We had entered the Forest of Belgrade,
inhabited by Slavs transported from hundreds of kilometres
to the west. Both sides of the road were wooded. If there
were to be an attempt on the Kadiasker's life, it would be
now. But, as the crisping autumn leaves crackled under our
horses' hooves, the Judas trees betrayed no assassins.

Our pace slowed to a walk and we each watched, fiddled
and fidgeted anxiously, straining to pick up any unusual
sound. The flutter of the wings of a startled bird brought a
moment of concern. Then Adil, who together with Ibrahim

235

was riding about thirty metres ahead of the main party, signalled the column to halt. He had sighted a riderless horse and Farooq galloped up to assess the situation. The horse stood some sixty metres away, tethered to a tree by a coppice. Lying at the feet of the animal was the motionless body of a soldier.

The rest of us cautiously moved forward to join our comrades.

"Now we know what happened to Fazil and the horse," said Adam Pasha. It must be a trap: we are meant to stop to investigate. So we won't stop. Put your faith in Allah and ride on. Ride on! As fast as you can!"

Adil and Ibrahim, as the vanguard, whipped up their horses with their reins and sped away. Yaqoob dropped back in case Mehmed's killer should suddenly turn up.

Then, there was an explosion of noise, a whiff of smoke. It was the crack of musket fire aimed at my pasha. A musket ball lodged in his turban. An arrow struck his saddle. His chestnut mare reared up and he lost control. The horse started to circle, exposing my master to more accurate fire.

With Adam Pasha unable to command as he struggled to control his mount, his safety was my only concern. They were not going to get my pasha. Not whilst there was blood in my veins. "Attack!" I cried. "Attack! Protect our pasha!"

Ululating like Bedouin warriors, Adil and Ibrahim charged into the thicket where the attackers were hiding. Two muskets were discharged; more arrows were sent flying. There was a moment of confusion as the musket smoke dissipated and the horses leapt into a clearing beyond the coppice. By now Ferhad and Kamran had also joined the fray – only to see Adil hit in the throat by a musket ball. Then, Kamran's horse was brought down, throwing him to the ground – his neck cracked as both rider and mount rolled forward in a tangled heap.

Ibrahim tilted at one dark-faced attacker and the point of his lance dug into his assailant's heart. Just then, that same dervish who had sojourned at the inn leapt on Ibrahim from behind, trying to stab him in the chest. Simultaneously, two arrows bounced off the burly soldier's chainmail protection. Ibrahim managed to shake the dervish loose as Zaman charged in to the rescue. But two Turcomans grabbed Ibrahim from behind and pulled him off his horse. He tried to break free, kicking away one of his attackers and wrestling the other to the grass. Zaman's lance was embedded in a third. But the enemy was everywhere. A tall, hairy man brought a cudgel down on Ibrahim's head with such force that his eyes seemed to pop. Again and again, the cudgel smashed down on his head and back. Ibrahim was past help and Ferhad and Zaman fell back to the woods on the far side of the clearing, giving Farooq and I as much time as possible to get Adam Pasha to safety.

We both grabbed hold of the reins of the pasha's horse. It was only now that the full horror of the situation became apparent to us: the Kadiasker had been wounded in the shoulder and was bleeding profusely. He was in a daze, barely staying in his saddle. Farooq slapped the horse from behind, knowing that, as the mare sped away along the road, I would be obliged to accompany my master. Yaqoob, seeing the danger, came up from the rear to join Farooq. With bloodcurdling yells, Farooq and Yaqoob launched themselves into the fight.

The two dervishes we had seen at the inn were clearly in charge of the dozen or so Turcomans who had laid the ambush. Nine attackers were left. They had hemmed in

Ferhad and Zaman so the sight of Yaqoob slashing with his scimitar brought a brief moment of joy. Yaqoob, cut into the cheekbone of one attacker and a sense of excitement raced through his body as his victim dropped to the ground.

But what none of our escort had realised was that in the woods behind them hid upward of fifteen more of the enemy. A flurry of arrows came from the direction of the woods and Zaman slumped forward as three shafts lodged firmly in his back. His horse was next to go down, pinning him underneath.

One dervish dislodged Yaqoob from his horse with a stave. Struggling to hold on to his sword, he felt an awful burning pain from a musket ball striking him in the face. The other dervish decapitated him with a single swing of his axe.

Ferhad slashed with his sword, left and right, holding up his shield to fend off the arrows loosed at him. He killed one, he killed two but the enemy were everywhere. A spear was violently rammed upwards into his neck, lifting him clean off his horse.

Farooq, alone, now faced five attackers, two armed with muskets. One discharged his weapon but missed. Farooq charged forward. As he passed one of the dervishes he felt the pain of a sword being buried in his leg. He felt faint but knew that his only chance, however remote, was to strike again and again. He took one attacker on the horns of the crescent which capped our pasha's standard and blood dribbled down the dangling horsetails. He drew his sword and slashed at another. He cut again and again with his sword, right and left but someone clutched at the reins of his horse and two others pulled him off. His helmet fell as he hit the ground. Cudgels bore down on him, smashing his exposed head, staining his fine yellow hair a bloody scarlet.

"Allah forgive me!" I kept repeating, speeding away from the site of the slaughter and tightly holding onto the reins of my pasha's horse. We were riding towards the village of Belgrade but cannot have gone more than a hundred metres before I was forced to pull up. Adam Pasha was slipping from his horse. I leant across over the neck of his mount and pulled tight on the reins. The mare kicked out her back legs and swung wildly to a stop. Adam Pasha's head swooned, his mouth was dry. He wanted to drink and he wanted to sleep. The dust swirled as the excited mare tossed her head and it was all I could do to stop her flinging my master to the ground. I clung onto his tunic, using my left shoulder to prop him up. But, as I lent across with my right arm to bring the mare under control, I was filled with an over-powering sense of fear.

I vaguely glimpsed two figures charging towards us. As they got closer I could see the bloodied face and dark eyes of one. For a moment, my mind emptied of all impressions but for the sight of those wild, threatening eyes.

A dervish was carrying a rough-hewn spear in one hand. But it was what the other man was carrying that made me curse. He held a Janissary's bow and, as he dropped to his knees, he plucked an arrow from the quiver on his back. He was preparing to shoot and we were like upturned cockroaches, not going anywhere fast.

Riding on was not an option – my master would not stay in the saddle. I eased myself down from mine, taking care that the pasha stayed in his. I then slid him gently off his saddle and laid him on the ground. Just in time. There was a twang as an arrow slammed into the ground in front of me. The dervish with the spear was barely thirty metres away and closing fast. I had to protect my master at all costs. That was my duty. My hand dropped to my scabbard searching for my sword. The scabbard was empty. I had dropped the sword back along the road. I knelt down in a vain attempt to ease my master's sword from under him but I could not risk moving him. Not that a sword would have been much good against the arrow which flew past my head.

The dervish wielding the spear was now just ten metres away. He obscured his comrade's view and the third arrow flew well wide of the mark. The bowman stood up and raced forward. He was taking no chances. Either that or he was intending to club me over the head with the bow.

I stood up, took off my kaftan and drew my damascene dagger. Only five metres now stood between the dervish and me. He lunged with his spear. I threw my kaftan at it but he deflected it with the tip of the lance. He lunged again, piercing the sleeve of my shirt and I dropped the dagger. Now what was I to do? I threw myself on the ground, making a wild grab for the dagger. I did not reach it. Instead, my eyes were fixed on a danger much greater than anything presented by the dervish. I glimpsed, from beneath the horses, a sipahi galloping at full speed towards us. It could only have been the soldier who had tracked us from Istanbul, Mehmed's murderer. And he was levelling his bow and pointing it straight at my master.

The dervish, too, saw my master unprotected. He raised his spear. I felt a knot tightening in my stomach and a sense of total uselessness. "Forgive me, Master!" I cried. "O, Allah, have mercy!" Then, there was an awful thud. An arrow hit its mark, embedding itself deep. Blood, more blood. Everywhere thick, rich, red, blood.

XIX   THE ROYAL HUNT

I raised myself to my knees as the dervish was thrown
violently forward. I looked beyond him to see his comrade
drop his bow and turn to run. Another arrow slammed into
his back. Both were dead, instantly.

The sipahi leapt from his horse and rushed towards my
pasha. Friend or foe, I did not know. I hesitated. Finally, I
went for my dagger lying in the dust but not before the
sipahi had grabbed my master's blood-soaked tunic and
taken Adam Pasha's head in his hands. He threw off his
helmet and kissed my master softly on the forehead. "I told
you, my Pasha. I am your guardian angel." Nilufer!

***

The Sultan's tents stood like blossom on the trees in spring,
nestling amongst the falling autumnal leaves. The princely
pavilions rose proudly in a blaze of purples, crimsons, blues
and greens – colours of every hue set in a scene freely
sprinkled with the sparkling morning dew. The crisp sun-
yellowed oak leaves dropped gently to the floor of Sultan
Suleyman's hunting fief. Three imperial tents stood centred
in a camp set floating upon richly embroidered cloth. The
Grand Vizier's tent was pegged out nearest of all, excepting
those of the army of servants and kitchen staff, and Ibrahim
Pasha sat with Suleyman idly chatting in a silken kiosk, three
sides of which were lifted up and fastened by loops to
wooden buttons.

The sun shone brightly, cutting through the early
morning chill. And as the Caliph, Sultan, Padishah,
Commander of the Faithful, Master of the World and master

of all of us sipped his tea, even in this wild corner of his realms he was careful not to neglect his duty. A petitioner approached, escorted by the Sultan's chamberlains, and was exhorted to make his plea. He came, he said, from Belgrade village where he had been transported after the fall of Belgrade city. He and others had been charged to look after the aqueducts and waterworks that provided water for Istanbul. But not all their relatives had been settled in the forest. He begged his Padishah to reunite him and his friends with their families and to have them brought to the forest.

"Let it be done!" the Sultan said, "And we shall punish those responsible for dividing the families of my loyal subjects." His words were instantly obeyed and a rider was despatched with the petitioner to the village, about three kilometres from the encampment, to discover the names and descriptions of the kinfolk and officials involved. The royal audience was ended. Pushing aside his velvet cushions, the Sultan rose to prepare for the hunt.

The organisation of a military campaign was required for a royal hunt. Indeed, the whole event served as a practice drill. Quite apart from the cooks and porters, there were the falconers, dog handlers, members of the royal bodyguard, chamberlains – all part of Suleyman's retinue. And then there were the similar entourages accompanying Ibrahim Pasha, the other viziers and courtiers.

So, gathered in the forest of trees was a forest of banners, the Sultan's standard high, horsetails swinging gently in the breeze. The mounted courtiers paraded their martial arms as if to meet an enemy in battle. Everything was set.

But the alarms which sounded out were not to war but signalled the beginning of the hunt. The falcons and hawks were anxious to meet their prey, and the hounds strained and tugged at their leashes eager to lead the chase.

A roaming doe bounced, idly playing, until the scent and sounds of Suleyman's hunting hounds came to her. She darted between the trees, from thicket to thicket, thinking only to avoid the terror striking her with every bay of the ferocious hounds unleashed her way. The panic-stricken creature made for some marshy water but the barking dogs, gaining with every stride, had very nearly caught her when she stumbled. One sharp-toothed beast sank his teeth into her hindquarters. An aga of the inner palace galloped by and completed the bloody slaughter, cutting through her neck with his scimitar.

At a distance, a wild boar, its hairy hide prickling with angry bristle, met no fairer destiny. The ferocious beast, its flesh forbidden to the Semite and the Turk, turned to face the attacking dogs. With one tusk he skewered a hound yelping in pain and tossed it aside. But another, disdainfully yapping took his place and, opening his mouth wide, leapt upon the snarling pig. This dog fared no better than his impetuous mate but a mounted noble skilfully sealed its fate by shooting an arrow that found its mark. Yet another and another struck the boar on back and neck and head until, gushing blood, it dropped down dead.

But Sultan Suleyman himself preferred to marvel at the wonder of his elegant free-flying falcons and sought out more open ground. As he praised his Chief Falconer for his efforts and skill in training the birds, two riders approached at a canter. One was the chamberlain sent earlier to Belgrade village. I was the other. We dismounted but I stopped short of the circle of courtiers and soldiers who surrounded the Sultan as the chamberlain continued on and spoke to the Sultan out of earshot. A few seconds later, I was called forward into the Sultan's presence.

"My chamberlain tells me you have grave news," said Suleyman.

"Yes, my Sultan ..." I broke off for a few seconds as I wiped a tear from my eye. "My master, Adam Pasha, lies close to death in Belgrade village. We were making our way expressly to meet Your Highness with urgent news of dire developments. We were attacked by a band of some twenty Turcomans on the far side of the village. I fear that our entire escort has been massacred."

I recounted the day's traumas and our struggles in the cistern two days before. The furrowing of the Sultan's brow was the only outward sign of his concern but concerned he most certainly was. He knew that only desperate men, and dangerous men, would perform such desperate deeds.

"Ibrahim Pasha," he ordered, "you must return at once to Istanbul but avoid the coast road. It's too dangerous. Before that, despatch a rider to fetch Mikhail Effendi as quickly as possible to do whatever he can for the Kadiasker. On your return to the city, you are to start an immediate and thorough investigation into Daud Aga's crimes and the attack upon Adam Pasha. You will be responsible for administration in the capital until I return. You will deal with anyone attempting to stir dissent or disorder in a swift and exemplary way. Arrest anyone spreading sedition. You have the full authority of your Sultan to take whatever measures are necessary to preserve order."

The Grand Vizier left immediately, almost too eagerly. He was master of the empire at last. He swept briskly away, colourful entourage in tow, elated that he had fully regained the Sultan's confidence. Henceforth, he was to assume his rightful position as the Sultan's chief adviser, which, in the matter of the Harem Affair, had been temporarily usurped by my master.

Suleyman himself proceeded to Belgrade village with a small retinue – a bodyguard of fifty sipahis of his Household Cavalry, together with the senior pages of his privy chamber, about a hundred halberdiers and bowmen, and some assorted servants.

***

Adam Pasha lay semi-conscious in a hut at the southern edge of the village where a work party had taken him. Suleyman decided to pitch his tent about thirty metres from the hut and pickets were posted at ten metre intervals all around the village.

Suleyman was anxious to see his Kadiasker. He was genuinely concerned for my master's welfare but he also wanted to hear the sequence of events from my pasha's own lips. But my master was in no condition to relate anything other than a few incoherent ramblings. He had lost a great deal of blood. The bleeding had been stemmed but he had been greatly weakened. He could yet succumb. Nilufer had done what she could for my master but she worried that Adam Pasha might, when he emerged from his semi-conscious state, be disturbed by her presence. She was also mindful, for the pasha's sake, that the Sultan and the villagers might not approve of the Kadiasker's wife posing as a sipahi. She had, therefore, reluctantly returned to Istanbul, having ensured that the wife of the owner of the hut was capable of providing the nursing care necessary. The owner had himself stood watch outside whilst I had ridden to the Sultan's camp and it was clear that the couple had proved their loyalty and competence.

Suleyman now dismissed them both, expressing his

gratitude for their help. He saw to it that fine bedcovers and cushions were provided and selected two servants to sit by my master's bedside taking turns with me. The Sultan himself sat with Adam Pasha for some hours, occasionally drawing a green-silk handkerchief from his grey-silk kaftan and mopping my master's sweating brow.

We waited anxiously for the arrival of Mikhail but the doctor sent word that he was too ill to travel. In his place came one Jacob, another of the Court's highly regarded physicians, a Spanish Jew whose father had thought it wiser to leave Spain before the Inquisition made alternative arrangements for him and his family.

Fortunately for my pasha, although the shot had penetrated his shoulder it had not caused irreparable damage. The skilful surgeon removed the imbedded musket ball and dressed the wound, rubbing in some herbal ointments to help it heal.

"Your Highness, there is no more I can do," said Jacob, five days after arriving at the village. "But the Pasha needs rest, a lot of rest – and good nursing. He will need someone to change the dressing and to recognise any signs of a relapse. That may yet happen if the wound becomes septic. I am afraid I must return to the Old Palace where a fever has taken hold of many of the women of the Harem as well as a number of our physicians. I am needed there."

Suleyman stroked his chin as if deep in thought. "Very well. Only his wife can provide the nursing care that he requires. We must send for her. You are to wait here until she arrives and are to instruct her fully in the requirements of a good nurse. I, too, must return to Istanbul. I shall leave a detachment of troopers to stand guard and a body of servants to provide whatever is necessary."

In the evening of the next day but one there arrived at the village a mounted escort of four soldiers riding before a covered wagon pulled by a pair of plodding ponderous oxen. The wagon carried Nilufer and three of her handmaidens. Behind the wagon struggled six fully laden mules. Clearly, Nilufer had come prepared for a long sojourn at the village though, this time, without her chainmail and weaponry. She swore me to secrecy about her erstwhile guise as guardian angel.

Jacob returned to his official duties, leaving the veiled Nilufer in charge of my master's care. She settled in quickly and, with the help of her maids and the Sultan's generosity, turned the Serb's hut into an abode of almost palatial comfort.

The chill winter winds had started to blow unseasonably early in autumn and an occasional fall of sleet made Nilufer concerned that Adam Pasha would suffer that much feared relapse. But, even without the advice of Jacob, Nilufer was well-versed in the medicinal remedies of folklore. She had brought with her a collection of herbs and applied to the wound an assortment of concoctions, some smelling sweeter than others. No doubt these had their healing effect but it was Nilufer's nursing day and night and her hot broth, especially her broth, which worked its charm on my pasha.

The fever broke after about a week and after two my master was taking more than Nilufer's nourishing broth, soup which she had prepared with her own hands and on which alone the pasha had survived for several days.

Nilufer had nursed Adam Pasha back to health, washing his wound and wiping his brow. All the same, the Kadiasker had lost a considerable amount of weight – his naturally thin and sallow face now took on the look of a barely living

247

skeleton. His large brown eyes bulged from their sockets. His large ears and nose protruded even more prominently on a skeletal face.

Slowly, the emaciated features began to flesh out. A week later Adam Pasha was taking some light exercise, walking into the village to thank the villagers for their help. He sought out the family in whose home he was resting and pressed on them a gift of fifteen hundred akches as reward for their services. It was time, once again, for Nilufer to return to Istanbul, on this occasion to prepare for her husband's homecoming.

Every couple of days a rider would arrive from the New Palace to enquire after the pasha's health. His shoulder was still a little stiff but otherwise he was almost fully recovered when he received a message from the Sultan commanding his presence at a review of the royal fleet which was due to take place on the Bosphorus. The review was ostensibly in honour of the Austrian embassy from Ferdinand, the King of Vienna, which had arrived to negotiate a truce following upon Suleyman's Rhum campaign the previous year. The real purpose of the review, however, came as no surprise to anyone – to impress the embassy with the rejuvenation and blossoming of Ottoman power and to reveal to the ambassadors the futility of their king's struggle. The previous year's campaign may not have been such a great success but, if Suleyman succeeded in gaining a truce on favourable terms, that in itself would be a considerable diplomatic triumph.

The situation also presented my master with an ideal opportunity to relate his fears and suspicions to the Sultan. He wasted no time in preparing to leave. The imperial messenger returned to Suleyman with news that Adam

Pasha should be expected soon. Nilufer and her party had already returned home and, two days later, the Kadiasker rode out of the village to cheers and rejoicing.

As we rode along the coast road at a comfortable, gentle pace, my master suddenly reined in his horse and stopped. "Murat, are you thinking what I'm thinking?"

"About the ambush, Pasha? So many good friends lost. I blame myself, Pasha. I ordered the attack but I can't help thinking that if we had ridden on they might all be alive today."

"You're not to blame, Murat. You did what you thought best. May Allah bless them all. But there's something else. The Turcoman at the inn. He still bothers me. There was something decidedly odd about him."

"You can say that again! He didn't smell too good. And his diabolical snoring ..."

"That's not what I mean. When was the last time you saw a Turcoman peasant who could read?"

XX THE NAVAL REVIEW

"Well, Adam Pasha, you're certainly looking much better than when last I saw you. Allah be praised." Our Sultan smiled with pleasure and relief at the sight of my master returned to good health.

Adam Pasha bowed to kiss his Sultan's outstretched hand but Suleyman gently took hold of the Kadiasker's hand and guided him to a window seat in the alcove of the royal kiosk. "The whole Court has prayed for you and the Koran has been read day and night for your speedy recovery," said Suleyman. "Do you feel well enough to talk?"

"My Sultan, thanks to your prayers and your attention, I am fully recovered. My life is not important but I am pleased to have lived to tell what I know. More than ever, I am convinced my earlier suspicions were right and that we have uncovered a foul plot."

Suleyman leant forward on one elbow but said nothing.

"I have struggled, my Sultan, and at times I despaired. By day I reasoned, by night I dreamed fantastic dreams. Searching for explanations for Shireen's murder, I have stumbled over motives aplenty and more suspects than gulls in the sky. My problem has been to determine the most likely of them.

"But the more I throw into the stew, the thicker it gets and with each lap of the ladle, every stir of the spoon, the mixture becomes less recognisable. And then the whole stew boiled over with that one shot fired at the circumcision parade. Was it attempted regicide or was it an attempt to kill me? We never had a chance to discover which as the culprit ended up dangling from a beam. But I always thought his death suspicious and I'm sure he was murdered but by whom I'm none the wiser. We don't even know who physically held him and who tied the cord around his neck: presumably, the two dead guards but we don't know that for sure. The stew had congealed into a sticky mess.

"All the time, I've been searching desperately for the common thread. Only now do I feel I've collected the strands together and, with each stitch of the embroidery, the picture is finally taking shape. To my mind, the embroidery spells one word and one word only: "Venice". The link with the Bazaar robbery, the cache of arms found at the Venetian ambassador's residence, Venetian gold found on the cistern keeper, a bagful of gold sequins in the possession of a Venetian sailor, Kira Sarah … The list is almost endless."

"Now do you understand, Adam Pasha, why I didn't want Ibrahim Pasha involved?" said Suleyman. "At least not until we could avoid it no longer." My master did not understand and his faced showed it. "Did you imagine that I suspected my loyal and trusted friend of a conspiracy? No," the Sultan chuckled, "that was not the reason. Ibrahim Pasha retains my utmost confidence. However, that clever sweet-tongued parasite Gritti is so often in the company of the Grand Vizier that he might inadvertently and quite innocently have divulged details of the investigation. Ibrahim Pasha has become too good a friend of Venice.

"Kadiasker, I have the power to break Venice like a dry twig," continued the Sultan, snapping his fingers. "Her wealth is built on trade with our noble lands and yet she occupies islands within spitting distance of Istanbul. My ancestors have fought countless wars against them but for myself I prefer an honest peace and a prospering trade just as

Ibrahim Pasha advises. The Grand Vizier knows how to play the Frankish princes and so, when the King of France, no friend of the Venetians, asked for my help and I wished to offer it, again Ibrahim Pasha counselled me wisely. And yet, the Grand Vizier does not want war with Venice and may be a little too accommodating. I want war no more than he but I want to be prepared if hostilities ever break out.

"We have won victory after victory against the Franks on the plains of Rhum and against those heretical Persians in the mountains to the East. But on the water … on the water we have nothing." Suleyman's face filled with passion; his fingers clenching into fists. "Our fleet has been moribund from neglect.

"Adam Pasha, for a decade we have had no significant force on the water. At least, not until now." The Sultan spoke slowly, softly, pointedly. "For months the naval dockyards have been working day and night to build me a modern fleet of warships," he added with a glow of pride. "Tomorrow you and the Christian emissaries of Vienna will see my beautiful new galleys.

"Already, my Governor in Algiers has used his flotilla of galleots to inflict misery on the infidel Charles of Spain and his Pope. And now we have built a fleet which will rival any which Spain or the Pope, or Genoa or Venice can muster.

"Do you see what I am saying, Kadiasker? With my fleet at one end of the Mediterranean and the French at the other, we will together command the sea. And what will happen to Venetian trade then? Ibrahim Pasha supports a French alliance but does not want to upset the Venetians. Why should I care about the Venetians, whose spies are crawling all over the city? No, for once the Grand Vizier is not seeing things clearly. He's spending too much time in the company of Signor Gritti."

"But," observed Adam Pasha, "Signor Gritti performs valuable services for Your Highness, both as our chief interpreter and as our ambassador."

"Yes, you're right, Adam Pasha. As the son of the Doge of Venice, he has his uses and your Sultan has made good use of him, for all of which he has been handsomely paid. But it's the smell of gold and jewels that attracts Signor Gritti. Oh, he's a very careful and calculating man who won't want to jeopardise his position in our territories but, should our Venetian vassals pay him more than we are inclined to do, who can say whom he will serve? No doubt he would like to serve both the Ottoman and the Venetian but one day he may have to pick one or the other and then which side will he choose – the land of his father which had no place for a bastard or the land which has made him rich and famous? I don't know the answer to that question but I am not taking any chances."

"Your Highness clearly saw the truth so long before your stupid slave," said my master.

"No, Adam Pasha, mine was a mere suspicion. Suspicion is not enough: I must have proof. The Lady Shireen pressed me for a French alliance. I told her that it was not the business of the Treasurer of the Harem to advise the Sultan on foreign policy. But she was of noble French birth and I made allowances for that – and, for all that, she was not unpleasing. But I am not so dull as to fail to realise the potential danger to the wealth of Venice of granting trading concessions to the French. That is the background.

"But, Adam Pasha, now it is time for you to tell me about the traitor, Daud Aga?"

And so, the Kadiasker supplied the details of the

eunuch's betrayal.

***

"And those are the facts and deductions which your humble slave has been able to glean from the surrounding circumstances," concluded my master.

"Kadiasker, as you lay ill, the Grand Vizier's agents were busy digging up Daud Aga's past. He was bought in the slave market. But before he fell into slavery, he was himself a slave master on a Venetian galley. We don't know how that came about or how our security services overlooked his Venetian connections. But he was no image of a pagan god so ending up as a eunuch should have come as no surprise. I assume he submitted freely to castration, reckoning that it would at least bring him wealth and influence."

"My Sultan", my master mumbled cautiously, "I have also heard it said that the eunuch has seduced some of the women in Your Highness's Harem. I don't know if there is any truth in it but being a gelding doesn't necessarily take away a man's natural desires." Adam Pasha, careful not to mention his wife as the source of this piece of sordid gossip, found the Sultan unexpectedly mild in his response.

"He has paid with his life for his treachery and that's an end to it. But, what you say may also explain why he was working for the enemy. In reality he had little choice whether or not to be a eunuch and perhaps he always resented the loss of his manhood. If that drove him further into the arms of the Venetians, then we're in part to blame. May Allah have mercy on him." After a brief moment of introspection, a smile broke upon our Sultan's face.

"Adam Pasha, well done! Very well done! You must be exhausted and we must let you rest. Tomorrow you will take the salute by my side at the review of my new fleet."

254

"My Sultan, have the agents of the Grand Vizier discovered anything more?" asked my master. "About the man behind it all?"

"What do you mean, Pasha? Daud Aga was our man, was he not?"

"No, my Sultan, he was not alone. There is someone else but I have no idea who he is. The only clue is a note that was scribbled to Daud Aga warning him of his imminent arrest. I assume our man, our master-spy, never expected me to find it. I have even wondered if Daud was being sent into a trap. The note was scrawled on paper available only in the palace, so our spy must himself be in the palace or have easy access to someone in it. And he is literate. He must be someone with authority. Daud Aga, a senior official, was clearly under his instructions so I imagine our master-spy to be highly placed. And that almost certainly means he has relatively free access to the palaces. Still, we now have an example of his writing and, if the Grand Vizier's agents can follow up this clue, I am convinced we shall have our man very soon."

"'Our man', Kadiasker, you said 'our man'. Does that mean you don't suspect Khurrem Sultan?"

"Of being a master spy, I cannot imagine such a thing. But just one question: is Khurrem Sultan capable of writing?"

"Of course, Pasha. I would have it no other way."

"It would have been better if she had been illiterate. Then her innocence would have been beyond doubt."

***

Adam Pasha took his leave. He was tired but felt as if a great burden had been lifted from his shoulders. He slept well that night and awoke to cannon fire as the captains of fifty galleys, each with blue beads hanging from the prow to ward off the Evil Eye, practised their gunnery by sounding the

255

time for the dawn prayer.

The call to prayer answered the thunder of the guns. The sky was overcast and the visibility poor but Ibrahim Pasha was hardly going to allow that to interfere with such an opportunity as this to overawe the King of Vienna's emissaries.

The flotilla of freshly painted galleys were assembled in the middle of the Golden Horn, just in front of the naval dockyards, a collection of shipbuilding and repair yards with almost a hundred vaulted slipways. Those very yards had worked day and night for months to turn out the new galleys and the time had come for that determined effort to be recognised.

Sultan Suleyman and Adam Pasha were carried to their vantage point in the royal pleasure barge. Sitting beneath the yellow-fringed canopy at the stern of the extravagantly curved craft, painted white with gold mouldings, the row-upon-row of strong oarsmen carefully pulled and dipped their oars.

Meanwhile, Ibrahim Pasha lavishly entertained Niklas Juristic, the Croatian noble heading the Austrian embassy, as well as the resident Venetian ambassador. Meanwhile, their respective delegations boarded their own flotilla of handsome barges shuffling gently out into the channel for a close-up view.

As each of the galleys passed by the Sultan's barge and fired its single bow-mounted cannon in salute, they divided into two groups at the mouth of the Golden Horn. One group was to play the part of a Christian fleet and the other the Ottoman. There was to be a mock battle – the first to be staged using real imperial galleys. It was a spectacle for the Austrian ambassadors to take note of and to report to

Ferdinand, their king. The 'Great Turk' was once again a power to be reckoned with not only on the plains of Europe but also on the open seas.

The rehearsed melodrama began as the flagship of the "Christian" fleet fired upon an Ottoman galley. The "Muslim" ships manoeuvred to outflank the Christian ones, fanning out on either side of the enemy galleys stretched out in the middle of the water. Clumsy muskets fired and small cannon blazed. Grey puffs of smoke wafted across the city to the hopeful rattle of the chains of the slaves. The shrill cries of battle from the zealous warriors resounded as the battle was performed with frightening reality. The Ottoman flagship drew alongside the Christian commander's galley and with shrieks and battle-cries a horde of our soldiers swept across the enemy's decks. The spectacle was capped with a blinding flash of light and a loud explosion from the Christian flagship as the Christian admiral begged for mercy and surrendered his fleet. More raucous shouting, shooting and smoke followed as our sailors expressed their joy at our glorious victory.

The Austrian representatives applauded politely but looked distinctly uncomfortable. Of course, the Venetian ambassador was too experienced a diplomat and too familiar with such displays of power that, if he had taken offence, he hid his feelings well: he was more interested in watching the new Ottoman fleet carry out its manoeuvres. He doubted the inexperienced captains and crews could ever rival the sailing prowess of the Venetians or the Spanish. It was clear to him from the clumsy handling of the galleys that we were no match for Christian ships. A whimsical smile crossed his face but it disappeared when he reflected how dangerous this fleet could be if it were to combine with the ships of France.

Late that night the Venetian ambassador wrote a secret report of what he had seen.

After the sunset prayer, Ibrahim Pasha gave a stupendous feast in honour of our foreign guests. The clouds had gone, the sky was clear, the waters calm. In the dazzling light of the sinking sun, the fleet was silhouetted against the hills. The moon was rising bright, the galleys still, the flotilla lit by lighted lanterns hanging from the sterns and masts. Slaves slept beneath the awnings raised on oars, and smoke rose idly from the chimneys erected on the galley floors. Nothing in the harbour stirred save the sailors' watch on board the decks of our Sultan's pride – his new floating engines of war.

And then a spark, a flash, a thundering explosion – timbers were sent rising to the sky and tumbling to the sea. The fleet was aflame. The ships burned. The blazing sails turned and toppled to the decks. The Ottoman insignia, green crescent on white, chameleon-like, changed to an ochre-red. A breeze struck up to fan the flames. Fire passed from oar to oar, from bow to stern, from sail to sail, from ship to ship. Mastheads crashed to the decks as blazing canvas was consumed by fire. The charred, tarred timbers burst open, spilling their gravel ballast and sleeping slaves into the channel.

Sailors and slaves desperately passed pails of water to douse the devouring flames. Splinters flew and sailors shrieked with pain as they were tossed into the sea like coins to a fountain. Disfigured bodies floated on the water as the red hulls of the galleys were rent asunder, shattering like nuts under a hammer. Human torches jumped into their watery graves whilst our admiral fought desperately to save his precious ships. Those not yet endangered, he ordered to be cut adrift.

But new explosions shook the air. The dock, too, was now ablaze, flames leaping into the night sky to light the turmoil and destruction.

There was a real danger that, if the flames were not checked, and checked very quickly, the blaze would spread to the city. The mud and wood houses of the Istambulis would merely feed the fire but that was the lesser of the dangers faced: the naval arsenal stood nearby. If the flames reached that, the admiral knew that the entire navy dockyard and part of the city would cease to exist. He gave the order to abandon efforts to save his precious ships and instead to concentrate on preserving the docks and the residential districts surrounding them.

Cannon were rushed to the scene by their gunners and, as with the cannon of the watchtower on the Golden Horn, the muzzles of their guns were trained on the burning ships, many of which had snapped from their moorings and were drifting dangerously loose. The vessels were blown into oblivion, the acrid smell of gunpowder mixing with the heady whiff of charred timber.

Next, the experienced gunnery officers turned their artillery pieces in the direction of the houses and workshops on the edge of the scene of devastation. Once instructions had been received that the houses had been cleared of their occupants, the guns opened fire. The wooden structures collapsed into heaps of useless timber.

Meanwhile, one company after another of Janissaries filed out of their barracks in orderly fashion, marching at the double down towards the docks. They set about clearing the district around the naval arsenal and hacking down the houses too near the arsenal to risk blowing up. By luck or design, behind the arsenal was a densely-wooded uninhabited area and it was only along the shore to the north that houses had to be cleared.

The town's populace, in less orderly procession than the professionals, also flocked to the water's edge, some as ghoulish spectators but most only with a desire to help.

Fortunately, there was no shortage of water at the docks. The smouldering jetties were torn up. Any container that came to hand was used to scoop the water and douse the fire-fighters as well as the flames as the intense heat charred the flesh of those in the forefront of the battle.

The blaze was fought all night and slowly it was brought under control. By dawn the next day the battle had been won. But at what cost? Fifteen galleys lay wrecked; a further eight had been badly damaged; thirty-two seamen, ninety-seven galley slaves – caught asleep on their ships – and twenty-three others had lost their lives.

Sultan Suleyman was visibly shaken. He had seen the whole episode from his wooden pavilion on the water's edge. Tears welled up in his eyes as he looked aghast at almost half his new fleet shattered. He could not bring himself to believe that his new weapon – a navy to match that of any Christian power – which had taken months of hard work and a prodigious proportion of the imperial treasury to put together, had disintegrated in fire and smoke in a matter of a few hellish hours. And the treacherous sabotage was masterminded by one man. Or woman. But who?

XXI   HOMECOMING

We cantered briskly into the courtyard of the pasha's mansion. The shock of seeing leaping flames engulf the Sultan's new battle fleet still lingered in Adam Pasha's mind but, as the rays of the sun struck him on the back of his neck, he felt reinvigorated. Physically, he was fully recovered from his wounds and that made him feel good, very good. He felt as if Allah had granted him a new life. And in gratitude for his services and in recognition of the ordeal that he had undergone, the Sultan had not detained him despite the disaster at the dockyards.

Above all, my master was eager to see his beloved Nilufer. Neither had married for love but she had taken to him and he to her. They were devoted to one another. Nilufer, in her way, had fought against it but love had crept up on her like a tiger stalking its prey and now she had no desire to escape it.

Still, the bright-eyed Nilufer did not come to meet her joy-filled husband in the courtyard. His elation, though, was only temporarily subdued. Leaping from his horse with an agility I had not seen before, he left behind him a gathering of happy but startled well-wishing grooms. He sprang up the stairs, two at a time and hurried towards the harem reception room. It was there that he saw Ferghana, Nilufer's pretty chief jariyé. She was crouched in a corner and sobbing into her woollen shawl. Adam Pasha was mystified but mustered up a sympathetic voice to mask his impatience to see Nilufer.

"Ferghana, what's the matter?" he said sensitively. Tears merely rolled faster down the cheeks of the dark-haired girl, and she pulled her cream-coloured shawl tighter over her head and across her face. My master knelt down beside her and softly repeated his question.

"My mistress, the Lady Nilufer," she stammered. "May Allah protect her!"

The Kadiasker grew alarmed and gripped Ferghana tightly. "What do you mean? What has happened?"

"The Lady Nilufer …" Sniffling and gulping, she started crying again.

"Ferghana!" The sharpness in the pasha's voice succeeded in shaking the wretched girl out of her state of shock.

"When Nilufer returned from Belgrade village, she went straight to the New Palace where she said she wanted to consult Mikhail Effendi. She said she was not feeling well. She hasn't returned home since. Pasha, I have prayed for her day and night."

Adam Pasha, in a stunned shuffle, wandered out onto the balcony. He drew a deep breath. After a few minutes reflection, he hurried into the front section of the house.

"Murat, saddle my horse. I'm going to the New Palace."

Before departing, my master returned to Ferghana, still squatting and sobbing in the corner of the room.

"Ferghana", the pasha asked, "What was wrong with your mistress?"

Ferghana looked up and wiped the tears from her eyes. "I don't know, Pasha. I think she had another attack."

**

"I'm sure Nilufer is fine, Pasha," I said, daring not to believe anything else.

"I hope so, Murat. I do dearly hope so. But to have been gone for three days … And you know that the city has been in the grips of a raging fever."

We galloped into the first courtyard of the New Palace, to the astonishment of the guards at the gatehouse. My master proceeded to the fourth courtyard, to the tower of the chief physician. The door was bolted and padlocked on the outside but still the pasha instinctively, but pointlessly, banged away on the heavy oak door. The only result was to draw the attention of two of the palace's army of pages.

"Pasha, there's no one there. Most of the doctors are ill. The few who aren't are busy trying to cure the ones who are."

Adam Pasha, desperate for news of Nilufer, moved on to the Harem of the New Palace. It was unlikely that Mikhail Effendi would be there but the Kadiasker had to be sure. Much to his surprise, he was met at the entrance by the Old Palace's chief of Harem security.

"Selim Aga, you are here?"

"Yes, Pasha. Khurrem Sultan has been here for the last two weeks to escape the fever. The air is better here. She returned to the Old Palace this morning and I am following. I will be back at the Old Palace in half an hour if you need me."

"Have you seen Mikhail Effendi?"

"No, Pasha. He hasn't been here today. He's probably in the Old Palace Harem. Most of the ladies are sick. Half the pages in the palace have been taken ill."

"I have to find him. Nilufer fell ill and came here three days ago to see the doctor. She hasn't been seen since."

"I don't know how I can help you, Pasha. There is so much sickness in the city that I have no men to spare to help you. I don't recall seeing Nilufer pass through here but that doesn't mean she didn't come. And I haven't been in the Old

Palace since Khurrem Sultan moved here. I will ask around. I wouldn't worry too much, though. The sickness is virulent but it's nothing like the plague. A few children and old people have sadly died but Nilufer is young and strong. She'll pull through."

"I do hope so, Selim Aga. But Nilufer has something else ailing her and she is very secretive about it. I'm afraid she may be suffering more than most."

"I'm sure everything will be fine, Pasha. I have to go now. If I hear anything, I'll send word to you."

"Thank you, Selim Aga."

"One thing, Pasha. Have you tried Mikhail Effendi's home?"

"No, Selim Aga. Surely Nilufer would not have gone there?"

"I have no idea, Pasha, but the Harem is not a safe place to be. So much sickness. At least, the doctor may be able to tell you where she is and you might find him at home if he is not at the Old Palace. It strikes me that a lot of people are leaving town and he may have advised Nilufer to do likewise."

"I had not thought about that. I'll send Murat at once to the doctor's house whilst I try to see if there is more I can learn here."

***

"Pasha, the doctor wasn't at home. He hasn't been home for two days. Did you try the chief physician's tower?"

"Of course, Murat. It was the first place I looked. The door was locked and this epidemic is keeping everyone too busy to have noticed anything. Murat, I'm ... I don't know what to do. Where can they be? Where is Nilufer? Where is the doctor? No one has seen Nilufer for three days or Mikhail for two. I pray she is well. Let's try the Old Palace. The physicians have offices there, too. Or he could be in the Harem. Wherever he is, we're wasting time here. Let's go!"

***

My pasha arrived at the physician's tower in the Old Palace, virtually identical in construction to the one in the New. The eunuch on duty approached and asked us our business.

"I'm looking for Mikhail Effendi. Have you seen him?"

"Yes, he left here about half an hour ago." At long last. My master sighed with relief.

"Where did he go?"

"I have no idea, Pasha. Why don't you ask his servant?"

"Servant?" said my master.

"Yes, Pasha. I saw him on his way out just minutes ago. You must have passed him. If you hurry you might catch him."

"Show me!"

***

I was standing in the second courtyard, near a cracked marble fountain, when I saw the Kadiasker and the eunuch running in. The eunuch was pointing at a handsome, but big-nosed, dark-haired man leaving the courtyard. The next I knew, my master was gesticulating wildly to me as he ran, followed by the eunuch a few strides behind. We converged on the exit, much to the surprise of Mikhail's servant as the three of us descending on him like hungry hunting hounds.

"Where's Mikhail Effendi?" said my half-breathless master.

"I don't know, Sir."

No one could explain what happened next.

XXII   HAREM SECRETS

The Kadiasker raised his fists and started pummelling the servant with a fury that I had never seen in him before. He was striking like a wild man. The eunuch was as dumbfounded as I and neither of us had much notion of what to do.

"Pasha, what are you doing?" I cried incredulously.

"I'll kill you! I'll kill you!" is all he kept repeating as he drummed away with his fists.

The slave had taken quite a beating but he was much stronger and bigger than the Adam Pasha and, once the initial surprise had worn off, he turned on my master. Now, I knew what to do, and so did the eunuch. We both leapt on the slave, each of us grabbing an arm. He continued to struggle but it was not long before a body of Janissaries, not to mention a group of spectators, arrived on the scene and restrained the slave.

"Pasha," asked an ojak-bashi, "what is this all about? You know that brawling in the palace is a serious offence."

"Arrest this man," was all my master said, wiping a trickle of blood from his nose.

"On what grounds, Pasha?"

"Because I said so!" was my master's sharp reply. I did not understand. No one understood.

***

"Master," I said, barely disguising my disbelief, "you can't be certain."

"No, I can't. I don't know anything anymore. I'm frantic with concern about my Nilufer and I can't think straight, but it all fits. Everything I learned, he learned. Every conclusion I drew, he knew. I discussed everything with him. I told him everything. That's why every time we came close to our master spy something or someone thwarted our efforts. The assassin, the gaolers, the market inspector, Kira Sarah, all murdered shortly before we caught them or had the chance to question them. And Daud Aga … Do you remember that message 'Save yourself. All is lost'? He led Daud into a trap."

"But Pasha if we had caught Daud, he would surely have revealed our super-spy's identity."

"But our man is no novice. He must have gambled on Daud not allowing himself to be taken alive. After all, even if he had told everything at the outset he'd almost certainly have been tortured. He knew that as well as any man. And he was a devoted servant of the Venetians so he was hardly likely to give away the identity of their chief instrument in the city, assuming he knew it." The Kadiasker was pacing up and down. Up and down. Cursing quietly to himself. "If Mikhail is our man, he must have been very certain that Daud would take his secret to his grave. Mikhail. It has to be Mikhail. He knew we were about to arrest Andreas. He didn't want Daud to escape at all. Instead he sent him straight to us.

"And, then," added my master, "there's the Turcoman."

"What Turcoman?"

"The one at the little hostelry in Istinye. That was Mikhail."

"Mikhail? Now that's stretching things a bit far isn't it, Pasha?"

"I don't think so. Do you remember, you remarked on the speed with which the Turcoman made his escape, considering that he had a limp? What if that limp was just a bit of play-acting?

"And," he continued, "what about his slave? Didn't you recognise him? He was the one who got away outside the fisherman's house. As soon as I clapped eyes on him in the palace I knew it was him. You remember the day our Sultan paid us a visit dressed as a sipahi? On our way through the Bazaar of the Conqueror we saw Mikhail buying a slave. That Roman slave. But the slave is more brawn than brain and could not have plotted this whole sordid affair. No, that was done by someone higher up. Who, other than his master? He was taking instructions from someone and that someone was Mikhail Effendi."

"But, Pasha," I said incredulously, "Mikhail Effendi … It's so hard to believe. In the name of Allah, he's your friend! Have you ever seen a more innocuous-looking man? Can that same good-humoured doctor who has dined on our hospitality and belched in our dining room really have been responsible for the destruction of our fleet, for stirring rebellion, for the attempt on our Sultan's life, for the murder of so many of our friends? Could all of it truly have been organised by that avuncular, lop-headed physician? He just doesn't look or sound like an evil genius."

"Isn't that the mark of a super-spy?"

"But why, Pasha? Why should Mikhail Effendi do it all? He has position, status and wealth. He is greatly respected in his profession – one day he will rival Moses Hamon. He may even become the leading physician at court. He has everything. What more can he want?"

"Murat, I know it's hard to believe. I can hardly believe it myself. Don't you think I want to believe something else? I want to be wrong. I hope I am. I pray that I am wrong. But greed drives people to desperate deeds and perhaps it drives the doctor. Whatever the motivating force, we're wasting time. I have to find Nilufer and I think if we can find Mikhail we'll find Nilufer too."

"But, Pasha, if Mikhail is what you say, what does he want with Nilufer?"

"He wants me, Murat. He's tried to kill me once already. He knows I'll be looking for Nilufer. He wants me. But enough of this speculation – we'll know the truth when we've found Mikhail."

"Surely, if you're right he would already have fled?"

"I don't think so, Murat. If Mikhail is what I suspect, he is playing a clever game with us. He's outwitted me at every turn. But he's like a master craftsman who needs people to admire his finest works. And, more importantly, he needs the world to recognise the craftsmanship. If my suspicions are right, he'll have left us some clue where to find him."

"What about the slave?" I asked. "We could beat it out of him." I was tempted to add "again" but judged it wiser not to.

"Much as I would like to, there's no time. I think the clue lies in the palace."

***

The Old Palace, what the Italians call the Palace of Women, by the Conqueror's Bazaar, was laid out in standard fashion, its Roman features somewhat clumsily adapted to the Ottoman style. The chief physician's tower was in a similar location to that in the New Palace. A certain lack of imagination, perhaps, but useful when you are in a hurry. Adam Pasha rushed up to the door of the tower and banged loudly on it. No less pointlessly than on the last occasion for, like it's twin in the New Palace, it was bolted and padlocked from the outside. A white eunuch approached at the double, wondering what all the fuss was about.

"Pasha, there's no one there."

"I know. But perhaps there's some clue inside."

"A clue to what, Pasha?"

"Where my wife might be. And Mikhail Effendi."

"I can help you with the latter, at least, Pasha. Mikhail Effendi left here half-an-hour ago."

"Was he alone?"

"Alone, Pasha."

"Do you know where he was going?"

"I think, Pasha, he went to the Harem but I have no idea if he's still there."

"Please present my compliments to the Aga of Janissaries and ask him to join me here with a detachment of his best soldiers. But, before you do that, get someone to break down this door."

"But, Pasha…"

"Just do as I say!"

The eunuch acted immediately. He returned within minutes with two broad-shouldered colleagues carrying a hammer and a chisel. The padlock was hacked off. The Kadiasker bounded up the narrow twisting stairs. He was convinced that here, amongst those jars and bottles that Mikhail was so proud of, there would be some essential clue to the doctor's true identity.

"Oh, Allah, no! Forgive me!" cried my master. "Out!" he yelled. "Everyone out!"

What we found drove my master to tears. It was worse, much worse, than we had expected.

***

"Murat, inshallah, he's still in the Harem," said the Kadiasker, breathless but once again fully in control. "But

just in case he isn't, I want you to take a detachment of the
Aga's men to his house and wait there for his return. If he
comes there, send word to me. I'm going to the Harem." The
tears had dried on his cheeks. Dried by the fire of anger and
hate burning inside. Any man would have forgiven him that.
The fire raged inside him: the devil was in his eyes and one
look from them would have stopped a Mongol cavalry
charge in its tracks. "We mustn't let him slip through our
fingers now. But I want that bastard alive."

I obeyed instantly but my head was in a whirl, as if I had
been spun around a dozen times after a night of drinking
with my Georgian friends.

Adam Pasha hurried to the Harem with four Janissaries.
Before doing so, however, he ensured the sentries at the main
gate were instructed to detain Mikhail if he should pass that
way.

"Yes, Pasha, but why?" asked the officer in charge.

"I haven't time to explain. Not now. It's vital he doesn't
leave the Palace!"

At the Harem's main entrance, a tall white eunuch with a
twisted ear barred the pasha's way.

"Mikhail Effendi! Have you seen Mikhail Effendi?"
barked Adam Pasha at the eunuch.

"In the Harem, Pasha. The Effendi is in the Harem. Is
something wrong?"

My master had no time for chit-chat. He tried to push
past the guard but the eunuch raised his staff and blocked his
path. Not even the Kadiasker could gain access to the Harem
without special authority, and a body of halberdiers, looking
mildly ridiculous with false tresses dangling from under
their conical hats, came dashing to the eunuch's aid.

"Pasha! I cannot allow you to enter," protested Haneef,

271

the slender eunuch. "You must not come any further." Fortunately, Selim Aga, now back at the main Harem, had heard the commotion and hurried over to the gate to see what was happening.

"Selim Aga," asked Adam Pasha excitedly, "is Mikhail Effendi here?"

"Yes, Pasha. He's on his way to see Khurrem Sultan. On her return, she complained of sharp stomach pains and Mikhail Effendi was sent for. But why the excitement? Is something wrong?"

"Selim Aga, we must stop Mikhail Effendi! He's our man!" cried my master, with increasing concern and a rising crescendo in his voice. "He's the murderer. Mikhail's a master spy!"

The eunuch stood mouth aghast staring at the Kadiasker in disbelief.

"Selim Aga, I have no time to explain. We must act. Now! Inside the Harem, he can't be touched by anyone other than your own sentries. He's almost free to do as he pleases. Khurrem Sultan herself could be in danger! Only your eunuchs can stop him!"

***

The horror of what we had seen in the chief physician's tower was beginning to take shape. Nilufer had been lying on a simple wooden bench, half-naked. She was alive, barely, and in a listless, opiatic trance. She had been beaten repeatedly and raped, probably by the Roman slave. Some would count her lucky to be alive. But when she recovered from her drug-induced hallucinations, she was an even more pitiable sight. She hid from everyone, not letting Adam Pasha see her, let alone touch her or comfort her. From Ferghana I learned that Nilufer was unrecognisable, no longer the Nilufer that my pasha had known. That Nilufer had, indeed, died. She had now to be carefully watched. Her state of mind had become suicidal. Only the thought of Mikhail's torment in Hell brought back the smile to her eyes.

***

The head of Harem Security shouted orders in his high-pitched voice and three eunuchs converged on the gate from inside the Harem. "Follow me, Adam Pasha!" he said and led the group briskly through the courtyard and into a long tiled passageway.

The women of the Harem scurried for shelter from the eyes of the stranger, and the one or two who were slow to do so were struck on the legs by the staffs of the eunuchs running in advance of Selim Aga and my master.

Any hope of catching Mikhail by surprise was quickly dashed. The doctor's eunuch escort, distracted by the commotion, suddenly found an arm around his neck. There was a snap, followed by a hollow splash, as he went head-first down a well. The doctor lost no time mounting the stairs to the upper storey, near Khurrem Sultan's quarters.

Mikhail had always been prepared to make his escape in case of emergency. Now that the moment of destiny had arrived, he intended to take his leave, like a conjurer performing a magic trick, in full view of the man he had so successfully deceived for six months and more.

Entering some unoccupied rooms, he removed his bulbous Ottoman-style turban and started to unwind it, twisting the fabric until it was like a length of rope. Slinging the twined muslin over his shoulder, he had now only to cover some forty metres across the rooftops of the Harem to the point where he would tie the material and lower himself to safety into the royal gardens. Mikhail clambered out onto the top of the weathered, grey-leaded roof that overhung the walkways around the perimeter of the courtyard below. Watching his footing carefully along the gentle slope, he edged along the roof, closely hugging it to avoid detection.

The sky was growing overcast and the sun was setting. The tall, thin, cone-topped chimneys took the form of sentries standing motionless in the failing light. The small, square, skylights, reflecting the gloom, peered at Mikhail like spies nestling within the undulating greyness of the domed and rounded roofs. Pausing briefly, Mikhail looked around him. He took one final glance. There was twinkle in his eye, a wry smile crinkling around his lips as he surveyed all he was about to leave behind. He could hear the raised soprano voices of eunuchs. Commands were being cried out. Feet were hurrying across the cobblestones below. He had been spotted. A eunuch, a small man dressed in a blue kaftan, was pointing excitedly in his direction.

Mikhail had no time to waste. He took a few paces forward but slipped sideways on a loose tile. In trying to break his fall, he cut his hand on the slate. He cursed. No time to worry about that. He could see Selim Aga and Adam Pasha running through the courtyard below. The eunuchs standing directly below him were waving their staffs and their fists at him, gesticulating wildly. Mikhail smiled again. "Poor fools," he muttered quietly to himself. The eunuchs seemed confused. Each carried a staff but no weapon, so what could they do? Very little, and Mikhail knew it.

The arrival of Selim Aga, however, stirred the eunuchs, and Mikhail, into action.

The doctor now ran across the rooftops as fast as his stocky legs could carry him without causing him to stumble. He jumped or climbed from one rooftop to another. He was no athlete but the rooftops were close enough together not to pose a serious obstacle even for him. He had thought of everything. He was heading for one corner in particular, where the outer walls of the Harem ran down to the royal gardens.

Mikhail could hear voices and footsteps behind him. He turned his head to glance at the silhouette of the Kadiasker's determined face. To his right, the doctor saw two fast-approaching eunuchs pointing at him in the dim light with their staffs. They were some ten metres from him and Adam Pasha was twenty-five metres or so behind.

Mikhail darted forward to only a few metres short of the point where he intended to secure his makeshift rope. He had just managed to loop the cloth over the chimney-stack when he felt a sharp tug at his sleeve. One of the eunuchs was pulling at it and the stitches snapped apart at the seam. Mikhail turned and stamped ferociously down the eunuch's shin.

"Help!" cried the sentry, losing his balance and teetering on the edge of the roof.

"Allow me," said Mikhail as he gave a shove and waved with a friendly, "Goodbye!" There followed a haunting shriek, to which Mikhail added a mocking grimace.

The second eunuch, seeing the fate of his comrade, was much more timid.

"Salaam!" said Mikhail with a smile, cocking his head gently in the direction of the dead Harem guard. The eunuch prodded at Mikhail with his staff but the doctor seized the end and pushed back.

"Over you go. And one plus one makes two," chuckled Mikhail. "That's the problem with eunuchs – no balls."

Mikhail worked quickly to secure the muslin rope to the

chimney. Just in time. Adam Pasha, followed closely by Selim Aga and another eunuch, was now only a few metres away. They stared at one another. Mikhail drew a hidden dagger from his boot, determined to fight.

"Don't be a fool, Mikhail!" cried Adam Pasha. "What's the point of fighting on? You've lost. Give up!" The Kadiasker's voice mingled hate with pity. His treacherous erstwhile friend had no means of escape.

Mikhail gave a sardonic laugh, loud and bellicose. "You call me a fool, Kadiasker! Who is the fool, me or you? You are a poor pupil, indeed. But, if nothing else, at least you will have learned never to trust a woman!"

What did he mean? The ravings of a madman, thought my master.

"You still don't understand, do you, Pasha? You're still blinded by the beauty of one woman to see her for the treacherous harlot that she was. First, she betrayed you. She lied to you to put you off the scent. And then she intended to betray me. She paid for her treachery. Kadiasker, you're the judge so judge for yourself. Has not justice been done?"

My pasha's head was spinning, his senses dulled and dimmed. Mikhail was accusing Nilufer? My master's face filled with rage. Slander, that was all it was. It was all it could be. But he was rooted firmly to the spot.

"What are you saying?" he spluttered hardly knowing what he himself was saying. "You're Satan himself. You're crazy!"

"You guessed almost everything, Kadiasker, except Nilufer's part in all this. Who do you think it was who tried to poison Shireen? It was Nilufer. Ni-lu-fer", he added in a haunting whisper uttered with malicious delight. "The story of Shireen's love affairs was her invention. And why?

Because, we're both Venetians and she hadn't forgotten her own people or her faith, at least not until she had the misfortune to meet you.

"Her greatest reward was marrying you. She got a wealthy and powerful husband. Good for her! Not that a miserable relic like you deserved her. And then she had the temerity to turn against her paymaster and her people. She told me that she intended to tell you everything when you returned from your little sojourn in the forest. She waited to give me the chance to make my escape. See! Even then she couldn't be true to either of us."

The Kadiasker was overcome by a multitude of emotions. He wanted to kill Mikhail with his bare hands but stood transfixed wanting to hear more. He had been betrayed by his friend and by his wife. He was consumed by hate. Perhaps some was reserved for Nilufer but most was for Mikhail.

"You liar! You liar!" he cried but he knew Mikhail spoke the truth. "You're a Greek, not a Venetian. Everyone knows that," cried Adam Pasha picking at the one part of Mikhail's statement that seemed to him to be an obvious lie.

"You're so easily deceived," said the doctor, tut-tutting, as he did so. "I said I was Greek and for you that was enough. I came into the Sultan's service from Coron. Greek-speaking certainly, but not so long ago a Venetian possession. And one day soon it will again be free from the hands of the Infidel!"

My master still did not believe Mikhail. He dared not believe him. How could a man who had served the Sultan seemingly so faithfully and had been rewarded so liberally have stayed inwardly so aloof from those he outwardly called 'friend'?

Mikhail was intent on wreaking a Venetian's revenge on an Ottoman and maximising the pain. "But," he gloated, "at least the treacherous harlot is dead."

It was this which finally broke Adam Pasha free of the force which had so firmly gripped him. "Oh, but she isn't. Another sloppy job." The Kadiasker gave a victorious smile and lunged forward at Mikhail who responded by cutting at Adam Pasha with his dagger. It caught his forearm as he raised it to fend off the blow. The two collided and Mikhail teetered backwards. He struggled to regain his balance, just avoiding falling off the roof by throwing his weight sideways. Adam Pasha stumbled and, as he fell, cracked his elbow. He grimaced with the jolt whilst Mikhail struggled to his feet in time to tackle Selim Aga and his fellow eunuch. Mikhail's dagger was thrust deep into the chest of the subordinate and, grabbing the dying eunuch's ivory tipped staff, he swung at Selim Aga. The Circassian caught the blow on his own staff and, swinging one end, struck Mikhail on the knee. The doctor crumpled to the floor. As Selim advanced, Mikhail snatched at the makeshift rope. The eunuch tripped over the tautly-held twisted turban cloth and, as he fell forwards, was kicked off the edge of the roof. Selim was still alive but lay helplessly groaning in pain.

Meanwhile, Adam Pasha, left arm broken and a deep and bloody gash on his right, got to his feet. He grabbed Mikhail's kaftan by the neck with his right hand but, lacking power in his grip, Mikhail easily broke free. The traitor threw a swinging punch catching my master full in the face. He staggered backwards in a daze, weakened and in pain. Mikhail thought about disposing of the troublesome judge but decided against it. He could not understand why no more eunuchs had come to the aid of the Kadiasker but he was not going to wait around for the answer.

Mikhail took hold of the makeshift rope and began his descent. He had lowered himself about half the required distance when he felt a tug on the muslin twine. It started to sway and he with it. He clawed at the wall but only caused the rope to twist forcing him to turn his back to the stone. He looked up to see, reflected in the dim light, three faces peering down at him. One was Adam Pasha's, the others belonged to eunuchs struggling to haul in the rope.

Mikhail allowed the cotton to slip quickly through his hands, burning the flesh as he slid down. To steady his fall, he gripped the rope again but could not hold it and fell the last four or five metres. By chance, he landed on some soft undergrowth, suffering only a few bruises and scratches.

Mikhail wrapped one of his green squares of silk around his left hand using his mouth and his right hand to tie a knot as best he could. He had only a short distance to run through the formal gardens that bordered many hectares of land given over to the pleasures of the royal hunt. Then he would be at the Palace walls. The flying buttresses supporting the stone walls formed a perfect ramp for Mikhail to mount and to make his unsteady leap to freedom.

And still luck ran with him. The sun was setting and the call to prayer was sounding over the city. Crowds of faithful, old and young and largely male, were making their way to the mosques for prayer. The situation provided perfect cover for the doctor.

He considered his position carefully. Several regiments of Janissaries would be out on the streets looking for him. They would expect him to try to get as far away from the palace environs as he could. So, he decided to stay as close to the palace as possible. And the one place that the soldiers were not likely to search was a mosque. As long as he could pass himself off as a worshipper, Mikhail was safe. Mingling with the worshippers, he entered the nearest mosque he could find.

Mikhail had lived amongst Muslims long enough to have learned something of our beliefs. Although he had already removed his turban, he had kept his skull cap, which was sufficient covering for his head to satisfy religious proprieties. He cut an odd figure but it would do. He removed the handkerchief from his hand to perform the ritual ablutions required of Muslims and took the opportunity to carefully wash away the blood. The next phase of the deception was to stand in line with the faithful, all facing in the direction of Mecca. He copied every motion they made. He bowed when they bowed. He knelt when they knelt. He prostrated when they did. He stood when they stood.

Mikhail had guessed right. The Janissaries were scouring the streets for him, lantern lights flitting to and fro like fireflies in the dimming light. But no one thought to search the mosques, and the streets and alleys near the palace were almost devoid of soldiers.

Mikhail waited in the mosque for an hour, maybe two. He had no idea how long it was. He passed the time in mimicking the reading of verses from the Koran, seated cross-legged on the ground and swaying gently as he muttered inaudibly to himself. Tiring of that, he pretended to read off the ninety-nine attributes of God on his rosary. He waited until he heard the muezzins sound the call to the late evening prayer from the tops of the minarets.

As the neighbourhood emptied once more into the mosques, Mikhail thought it time to take his leave. He pulled on his boots on the steps of the mosque and grabbed hold of a lantern that a worshipper had carelessly left there whilst performing his ablutions. Mikhail set off into the night.

There was a chill in the air. Mikhail knew he had to move quickly. His first thought was to try the Venetian embassy nearby. But, as he expected, it was already encircled by soldiers, letting no one in or out. No more help, then, would be forthcoming from the ambassador but he and the Venetian emissary had long planned for this eventuality: having learned of the pasha's return, he had ensured that the ambassador had been fully apprised of his intentions. Mikhail knew that waiting at the docks was a swift barque ready to carry him to safety. But he also knew that he was now left to his own devices: if he were caught, the ambassador would deny all association with him, as would he with the ambassador.

Mikhail walked cautiously in the direction of the docks. He was fortunate: the last prayer of the day was the longest and people were still generally about on the streets returning from the mosques. He had to dodge into the precincts of one mosque in order to avoid a military patrol but he guessed rightly that if he could get to the docks before the streets were deserted, the chances of him being sighted were remote.

Mikhail moved warily but quickly. He kept to the major thoroughfares as much as he could. Luck was still with him. The serene of sunset had been followed by a thickening mist rolling gently over the Bosphorus. Squads of Janissaries would almost certainly be patrolling the docks' area but the mist made for perfect cover.

The physician, always careful, always clever, waited patiently for his opportunity and crept up to the moored barque, resting where he had expected it.

The crew, well-wrapped but still quietly shivering in the chill sea air, was lying unobtrusively below deck awaiting orders to sail.

"You made it, then," whispered the captain. "We thought you'd been taken."

"Never mind that," replied Mikhail tetchily. "Let's get out of here!"

"To your oars!" commanded the captain to his crew as quietly as he could.

Without a wind, sails would be pointless and the effort of putting them up would, in any case, draw unwanted attention. The nervous crew sat at their oars, ready to pull gently away as soon as the mooring ropes were loosed.

But the oars were quickly drawn in as the voices of two sentries, aroused by the faint sounds of activity, were heard coming towards the barque. Mikhail thought quickly. As he saw their silhouettes contoured in the mist, he sent the captain ashore to divert their attention.

"Halt!" cried the sentries as the captain leapt onto the jetty. They hurried after the shadowy figure into the mist. And Mikhail was close behind. With all the stealth and swiftness of one of the Sultan's cheetahs, drawing his sharp knife, he slit the throat of one of the Janissaries from behind. Before the other soldier could fully turn round, Mikhail had plunged his dagger into his heart.

"Quickly!" whispered Mikhail to the captain. It was all he said but, as he started to drag one of the bodies towards the quayside, the captain knew what to do.

Both bodies were tipped into the water. Mikhail and the captain released the mooring lines and re-boarded the boat. Within minutes, they were clear of the quayside. The mist rolling slowly along the waterway soon hid the shore from their sight and, more importantly, hid them from the sight of the watchtowers and parapets that hug the coastline nearby. Rounding Saray Point, where the New Palace was located, the barque headed into the Sea of Marmara.

The captain knew the waterway well and he needed to if they were to avoid running aground. At least there was no likelihood of many boats being on the water. The sleek barque, with its crew of strong oarsmen, moved smoothly further and further from the point of danger helped along by the natural currents.

Mikhail was safe, his escape secure. The barque was underway at a good speed.

The fugitive's ultimate destination now was one of the Aegean Islands still in Venetian hands although his original plan had been to pull into a small bay along the Sea of Marmara. There horses were waiting for him to enable him to ride south to pick up another boat nearer his safe haven. But the mist made it impossible for the barque to find the landing point safely, so the doctor had to abandon the first plan. Nonetheless, the new plan was just as good, if not better. The mist would provide sufficient cover for him to make his dash to the open sea without even having to disembark.

Soon Mikhail had fully regained his famed self-assurance and good humour. He looked forward to the welcome of his long-time paymasters: the Venetian secret service into whose employ he had been drafted when studying at Padua University. The air was still, the water calm. Nothing stirred to raise excitement or alarm.

But as the physician glanced back, his composure was suddenly jolted. He could see nothing but as he turned his head he thought he heard a whistle, the whistle of a galley-master.

Mikhail was right. About three kilometres behind the barque were two Imperial galleys being rowed recklessly at full speed and closing fast.

Their lantern lights shone bright like eyes giving the galleys sight. The oars dipped and pulled then rose and dipped again, like wings, propelling the galleys into flight. A slight breeze picked up and the sails opened wide. The long, pointed battering ram, beak-like, stood proud at the galley's prow, the sharpness of its mouth cutting through the tide. And with the breeze, the mist began to lift.

The instinct that had impelled Mikhail to cast an anxious glance behind now caused him urgently to alert the captain to the danger. His face was draining of colour.

"Faster! Faster!" he cried, "or they'll be on us!" He grabbed an oar and pulled hard with the others, his muscles tense, his mouth dry.

But the barque was no match for a ship of the Imperial fleet and its small crew could now clearly hear the beat of the master on the galley deck.

The crew of the barque began to panic. "Surrender, Effendi, or we shall all be killed. It's you they want!"

"You fools! You snivelling cowards! Do you think those barbarians will spare your lives? Row! Row for your worthless lives!"

The mist was dispersing and the twinkle of the galley lights was clearly visible. But Mikhail had no intention of being taken alive and ordered the barque's lanterns, only recently lit, to be extinguished. His resolution remained unshaken. Just then, the single cannon mounted in the bow of each Imperial galley opened fire. One shot fell short another some way to the right. The bow chasers fired again – one shot whizzed overhead and splashed about twenty metres in front. Another crashed wide on the left. The master gunners were getting their range: even in the dark they were closing to a distance where they stood a good chance of hitting their mark.

Mikhail stood at the stern of the boat and cried out, as loud as he could, "Adam Pasha, mind that your master doesn't strike off your head for your bungling! You shall never take me alive!" He did not know if my pasha stood on the bow of the leading galley but guessed as much. And with these defiant words, he jumped overboard.

The Illustrious Signory had demanded and received total loyalty from their servant for little more expense than a few bagfuls of gold. And, what of his supposed friends and colleagues in the Sultan's service? They were left to reflect on the deceit and betrayal.

The rowers of the barque drew in their oars and searched frantically in the water for Mikhail, calling out his name repeatedly but to no avail. Mikhail was nowhere to be seen. Tears welled up in the Kadiasker's eyes, perhaps for an erstwhile friend or perhaps because of the cold air. He looked carefully over the water's surface for any sign of life. The body was never found.

***

For Adam Pasha, his time as Kadiasker had been a painful and exhausting one. His physical wounds healed well enough, although he never quite regained the full flexibility of his left arm. But the mental strain had been too much for him and his strength had been sapped. He had not expected the role of Kadiasker to be like this. The grey hairs on his head had multiplied and now he wanted some time for

285

reflection: some time that he could devote to writing poetry or studying classical Arab, Greek and Persian texts.

My pasha asked his grateful Sultan for permission to resign his office and, temporarily at least, to go into retirement. Suleyman, full of praise for his Chief Justice, reluctantly gave his consent and, to sweeten a restful break, he provided the Kadiasker with a handsome pension.

Now, thought my master, was perhaps the time to make the pilgrimage to Mecca, to give thanks for his safe-keeping and to pray for Nilufer's recovery. Yes, he was decided. He would take the Caravan to Paradise.

ISBN 142515750-5

9 781425 157500